The Truth of Vengeance: Vampire Formula #2

P.A. Ross

http://www.thornsneedles.com/

Copyright © 2015 By P.A. Ross

Scarlett-Thorn Publishing

2nd Edition

This is a work of fiction. Names, characters, businesses, places, events, locales, and incidents are either the products of the author's imagination or used in a fictitious manner. Any resemblance to actual persons, living or dead, or actual events is purely coincidental

All rights reserved.
ISBN-13: 9781514251003

TABLE OF CONTENTS

CHAPTER ONE 1
CHAPTER TWO 9
CHAPTER THREE 22
CHAPTER FOUR 28
CHAPTER FIVE 38
CHAPTER SIX 44
CHAPTER SEVEN 49
CHAPTER EIGHT 56
CHAPTER NINE 62
CHAPTER TEN 67
CHAPTER ELEVEN 81
CHAPTER TWELVE 87
CHAPTER THIRTEEN 99
CHAPTER FOURTEEN 108
CHAPTER FIFTEEN 118
CHAPTER SIXTEEN 123
CHAPTER SEVENTEEN 134
CHAPTER EIGHTEEN 141
CHAPTER NINETEEN 156
CHAPTER TWENTY 162
CHAPTER TWENTY-ONE 174
CHAPTER TWENTY-TWO 183
CHAPTER TWENTY-THREE 189

Chapter One

"Christopher, Chris, come over... Chris!"

I sat in the red leather booth at the rear of the bar, sipping a cold beer and ignoring the shouting. On the walls were wooden panels that gave the bar a mock hunting lodge style, with old black and white pictures of the first settlers in stiffened poses. Nailed to the walls were old wooden skis, ski poles, and an old sledge, giving an insight into times past.

Sat at the tables in front, two couples crowded around enjoying drinks and a plate of nachos as they re-told tales of their day's skiing: the crashes, arguments, speeds and fears. A dark haired man in a thick red fleece retold the tale of his crash, and how his girlfriend, the blonde haired woman next to him, had helped him up. She reattached his skis, then gathered his hat and poles, lying scattered in the snow further up the mountain. He looked adoringly into her eyes while gently stroking her arm, and she leant in to share a tender kiss. They continued laughing at the tales, poured back the cold beer and crunched on the nachos as they enjoyed the après ski debriefing.

I sat alone in the bar sipping my beer, surrounded by the occupants of the booths either side discussing their own tales of the day. In the next booth, with ski shoes hanging off the wall, I heard them discussing plans for tomorrow. After a ride with the Huskies, a short ski and a meal at the Chinese. To the side, a TV flashed with images of the ice hockey. The Calgary Flames centre slipped past a defender, then flashed in the puck to the side of the keeper to make it 4-2 against Vancouver. A couple of the locals clapped in celebration.

I drank more beer and continued playing with my phone, checking the news and the weather forecasts in an attempt to block out the normal happy couples surrounding me.

"Chris, come over!"

I wished Christopher, whoever he was, would get a move on as the noise was disturbing my thoughts.

It had been a strange day for my eighteenth birthday. I had spent it on the slopes at Lake Louise in Canada. I had plenty of stories to tell of my day's skiing as well; carving down the slopes, cutting up snowboarders and doing my first mini jump. During my month in Canada, I had gone from complete novice to a good skier.

My newly strengthened body through the vampire formula and from time training with Thorn had meant I learnt quickly. My instincts and senses had radically improved through the three vampire formula needles I had injected. The formula gave me the power of a vampire for the night. However, after the effects had worn off, I had grown more powerful in my human form. I had grown taller, more muscular, and my senses improved each time. It was as if the vampire formula had stretched my limits and I could never return to my original body. The psychic powers came along last as a vampire, but some of it remained in human form. Just the odd snapshot or detection of emotions. Not major mind-reading like Thorn, or my vampire self, but I wasn't your typical eighteen year old either.

During this time, Thorn had insisted I kept up my vampire training, even with the additional exercise of skiing nearly every day. We still sparred a few nights a week, and she sent me down to the hotel gym to use the weights and the cycle or treadmill. On top of the physical training, I continued to enhance my computer skills by trying to hack into the databases of the Hunters and the military research centre that had held Thorn prisoner. I hadn't breached it yet, but the practice had improved my skills; allowing me to create false identities and records to cover our tracks.

'V, get over here. I have been calling you,' Thorn's psychic voice interrupted my thoughts.

I looked across the bar at Thorn. She had toned down her dress sense after fleeing England. She wore faded blue jeans, black calf boots, and a grey sweater. Her raven tousled hair was swept back and tied in a knot. A time and place for everything and trying to fit in, she had said, but she still stood out with her sky blue eyes and flawless skin like white silk. She could wear a sack and still be the most attractive woman in the room. I was a lucky man.

She waved me over from where she stood engaged in conversation with a smartly groomed couple in their early thirties, who wore expensive designer après-ski wear.

"Chris! Come over!" Thorn shouted across the bar once again.

Oh, I forgot that Christopher Lee was my new alias. Thorn had chosen it as my new public name, but the meaning had been lost on me. She had to explain that Christopher Lee was well known for playing Dracula in horror films. She likes to mix the fact with the fiction.

I couldn't go by my vampire name of Vengeance, or V, as Thorn called me. It wasn't a name for public consumption. My real name, Jonathan Harper, couldn't be used either as I was a wanted man by the police in the

UK for eight killings - seven killings as a vampire and one as a human when I killed Barry McGown.

I didn't know how much longer I would keep count. When Barry died, I imagined and believed Jonathan Harper also died that day, and that I, Vengeance, had been born instead of Jonathan. Only after fleeing England did the remnants of my true identity come seeping back into my conscience. I remembered my real name and my past life. Flashbacks disturbed my sleep. Dreams of stabbing Barry in the stomach and defeating the hideous monster he turned into. I woke up many times thinking it was just a dream, only to open my eyes and see Thorn, my vampire lover and remembered the truth.

I took a few large mouthfuls of beer and sauntered over to Thorn and the smartly groomed couple. Thorn opened a welcoming arm and shepherded me into her side.

"Here he is at last. You were lost in a dream world," she said.

The man stood six feet tall with floppy blond hair and grey-blue eyes. He wore a smart red fleece with jeans and brown shoes. The man looked smug and arrogant, delighting in his position of being my elder, and he believed himself to be considerably better than me. But he didn't know what I could do and what I had done.

The woman was dressed in the same red fleece, accompanied with white leggings and black boots. Her blonde hair was in a long bob and face covered in makeup. She raised her overly plucked eyebrows and offered a surprised smile as she looked back and forth between Thorn and me. The normal reaction. Thorn's stunning beauty turned the heads of both the sexes. Back in London, the amazed looks had been more pronounced, but my own changes and appearance now turned a few heads, especially with young women. My eyes were turning an icy blue, and I had developed a strong jawline, defined muscles and broad shoulders.

"Sorry, Tracey, I think my mind was still on the slopes," I replied to Thorn.

Thorn, like me, had an alias for everyday life. Her alias was Tracey Horn, T. Horn, Thorn. A little play on words that amused her and allowed for mistakes.

"You should have seen him fly down those slopes. Only been doing it a few weeks as well," Thorn said, entwining her arm into mine and smiling.

Thorn had been good to her word and after eliminating the last gang member, Barry McGown, we had left London to travel. She asked what I wanted to do first. Skiing, I had answered. I had visited a snow dome in Leeds but had always wanted to do it properly on actual snow. So, first stop was Canada, Banff, and then Lake Louise.

Thorn had been there before, and the Canadian Winter suited her delicate skin condition - strong UV light could make her burst into flames. The ice-cold temperature meant everyone wrapped head to foot in ski gear, hats, goggles, masks and anything else to block out the cold, and for Thorn, it also blocked out the UV. That, combined with a hefty slap of sunblock and a dose of cloud cover, meant Thorn could venture out and take to the slopes on the occasional days, or late afternoons.

Unfortunately, that day, my birthday, it had been too sunny, and I had spent my birthday mostly by myself. I wasn't allowed to make friends with any of the other skiers or snowboarders because of my wanted status. Also, Thorn didn't know it was my birthday either. I hadn't told her. I couldn't see the point of celebrating my birthday with someone who had over seven hundred of them.

"What runs did you do?" the man asked.

"Started off on the blues and threw in a few black runs at the end of the day," I said.

"Really! Already?" the man replied, eyebrows raised as he stifled the shock in his voice.

"Yeah, he did. He's a quick learner. Plus, he had an excellent teacher," Thorn said, laughing.

"Yes. She is good," I said, and put my arm around her waist and squeezed her gently towards me.

Thorn giggled and knocked back her vodka and tonic.

"I haven't introduced you yet. Chris, this is Markus and Janine," Thorn said.

"Please to meet you," I said, and stretched out my hand.

I gently shook Janine's hand as she weakly offered it. Then Markus tried to exert himself by placing a firm handshake, but I replied with a stronger grip than he expected. He retracted his hand, his face flinching at the unexpected pressure.

"Markus is a banker," Thorn said.

"Oh," I replied, and I instantly knew the plan with no psychic communication between us.

Thorn had received some bad news on some investments following the bank crashes and had spent an evening cursing. She then got herself involved in several bar fights in the nearest town to relieve the pent up rage. I guessed Markus offered revenge by proxy.

"Yes. I know what people think, but not my fault. We have all suffered.

They slashed my bonus in half this year, and I only got £100k. As a result, we had to come here for our annual ski trip instead of Cloisters," he said, sipping his red wine.

I shook my head and tensed my jaw to control an outburst. I would enjoy tonight.

"So what do you do?" Markus asked, with a smug look on his face.

"Oh, Chris is a multi-million-pound business owner through phone and tablet games development," Thorn answered for me.

'I am?' I thought.

'Yes, you are,' Thorn thought back.

Markus' whole body deflated; I had outgunned financially as well.

Markus had that arrogant air bound to him. He had an attitude that said I was born into a better class than you. I bet he never went to an inner-city school and suffered constant bullying. He probably went to a private school. His Daddy got him the job in the city through his connections at the gentlemen's club. Life was so easy for people like him. Yet, he still complained about his bonus while the country dived into recession and people lost their jobs and homes.

His blond hair flopped across his face, as he barely contained a small snarl as he glared at me.

'He thinks he is better than you. Are you going to take it?' Thorn's words psychically spoke to me.

'You do it if you want his blood,' I replied.

'It's part of your training.'

'You're being lazy.'

'Just do it,' she snapped back into my thoughts. *'I want to watch. Everyone thinks vampires suck the life out of people. We have nothing on bankers.'*

Why not? He was annoying me anyway.

"Problem with that?" I asked, returning the glare.

"err.. No," he said.

"Seemed like you got a bit annoyed by the fact I was better than you."

His forehead frowned, and lips straighten for a split second, then he returned to his smug grin.

"You are not better than me," he replied, flicking back his floppy blond hair.

Janine's nose wrinkled in disgust and her arm wrapped around his for backup.

"Oh. Is that a challenge?" I asked.

"What? Oh grow up boy," he said.

"Put your toy-boy on a leash," Janine said to Thorn.

"He does as he likes," Thorn snapped back and faced up to her.

"I saw the way you were looking at my girlfriend. You thought you could pick her up for a threesome," I added.

"No, we did not," Markus said, looking aghast.

"Why? What is wrong with her? She's much better looking than that horsey bitch you are with," I said, delighting in the game.

'Nice one,' Thorn thought to me.

"How dare you speak to us like you jumped up, little nerd," Markus shouted and threw his drink into my face.

I wiped it off, and Thorn held me back. Markus had showed his true colours.

"Not in here. Outside," Thorn said.

"It will be a pleasure to show you how a real man conducts himself," Markus said.

We had attracted some attention. The waitresses had paused with hot snacks and cold drinks balanced on trays. The customers had stopped with cutlery halfway to their mouth's and glasses half raised, only the sound of the ice hockey game on the TV filled the void of sudden silence.

Markus and Janine stood to one side and gestured us through with ironic good manners. As Thorn and I marched outside, I sensed him sweeping up a bottle and following us quickly from behind. As we approached the door, I focused my senses, expecting the bottle to be swiped at the back of my head any second.

We went through the door into the cold, and the bottle came. I span out the way and then stepped inside his blow and judo threw him out onto the snow. Janine launched herself onto my back, scratching at my face and howling like a banshee. I threw her over my shoulder, dumped her hard into the ground and stepped over her. Thorn would take care of her as she doesn't like me hurting women, but had no problems doing it herself. Thorn twisted the handle on the door to the bar and shoved a bench against it to prevent any interference.

Markus rolled over in the snow, smashing the bottle and stood back up to face me. I had no vampire formula in my blood, just normal human blood.

He sliced the air with the broken bottle just inches away. His face seethed red and spit snarled through gritted teeth. He lurched forward, swinging the bottle back and forth in front of my face.

I flashed back to that dark night with Barry when I confronted him for the last time. I pictured him slashing the air with a knife, and our struggle on the muddy ground until I won through my rage. Defeated, he revealed the truth about his involvement and Scarlett's betrayal. I had then repeatedly stabbed the knife into his stomach until the blood slicked onto my hands.

I lost my concentration as I relived the final moments of Barry's life. Markus slashed across my front. The jagged bottle sliced open my left hand as I instinctively shoved it out to defend. I jumped back, watching the blood dripping out, staining the snow red. The cold air bit into the wound, and I gritted my teeth. It should have slowed me down and made me cautious, but the memories of killing Barry triggered an urge to fight.

Markus smiled, encouraged by drawing first blood, expecting the young boy to run off scared. He cut the air between us, jumped and swiped again. I kicked snow up into his face, pirouetted around his side with my arm spinning in a back fist connecting clean onto his jaw. He dropped into the snow like a dead man. I turned to Thorn, who held Janine around the neck, forcing her to watch.

"Is that it?" Thorn said.

"Yes, it's what you wanted."

"I wanted you to take your time and make him bleed and beg. I wanted him to apologise for ruining all those people's lives."

"Well, say so next time. Let's go."

Thorn flung Janine into the wall, knocking her out cold, and then scooped up her meal and ran into the woods behind the bar. I left her to it and walked down the side streets, weaving my way back through dark alleys and ice covered paths. I heard the sirens getting closer as I moved through the streets, and then saw a flash of blue down the main road as they raced to the bar.

I headed to the car, which had been parked at the back of a supermarket about a mile away from the bar. Thorn would feed and catch me up, and then we would drive off. Everything had been packed into the boot, but she hadn't let on to our next destination.

I sat in the car staring at the lights glowing out from the supermarket, illuminating the late-night shoppers, who were wheeling full trolleys of goods out to their cars. The car had been parked in a dark corner away from the security cameras and other passersby's.

It was a strange way to celebrate an eighteenth birthday. If my life hadn't changed, because of the encounter with Thorn and the vampire needles, I had planned to be out for a special meal with Scarlett. Maybe the next day a small celebration with my Dad. Hopefully, lots of cards and presents from my relatives. The truth was, I spent most of my birthday alone, and I couldn't let on it was my birthday as it would have raised too many questions.

A few minutes later, Thorn arrived at the car. She opened the driver's door and climbed in.

"Feeling better?" I asked.

"Much, thank you," she replied. Her cheeks and lips shone red with a post-meal glow.

"So where next?" I asked, hoping she would finally reveal the details of our next location.

"As it's your birthday, I have a surprise."

"You knew? So where are we going?"

"Of course I knew it was your birthday. We are going to Vegas and a vampire convention."

"Cool. Real vampires?"

"Not normally, it's for fans of the genre. However, we are meeting a real vampire there, a man called Cassius. He will give you the answers you crave about the history of the vampires. He will help us take our vengeance against the Hunters and discover the truth behind the formula."

"Excellent, let's go. I can't wait to meet other vampires," I said.

At last, the answers were coming.

Chapter Two

"So when did you organise the meeting with Cassius?" I asked as she drove us to the airport.

She smiled and turned the music down for us to talk.

"While you were busy skiing or down the gym. I don't just sit around pining for you. I have many fake lives to keep running and vampires to find."

"Okay, but how, where and when?"

"About a week ago, I finally had some luck on one of the web forums we use. I found his name, and we exchanged messages until we were happy we had the right persons. Then we arranged the meeting place and time."

"Web forums?"

"Yeah, fantasy role-playing internet forums. Vampire role-playing."

I looked at her wide-eyed and laughed. Surely, she couldn't be serious.

She matched my laugh with her own. "It's the best way. Hide in the open. Who is going to suspect we are two real vampires and that our story isn't just a game? We even use our real names. Makes it easier to find one another. Although I was annoyed at having to be Thorn69."

I shook my head. "It's a bit cheeky. Meeting at a vampire convention as well. Why not tell the world and have done with it?"

"Again, hide in the open. You will learn. Who is going to spot us in amongst the costumed fans? I have bought us some costumes, so we can blend in and act the part."

"Act the part," I said in disbelief, "you are the part."

"No, act the part as in a fan, silly. I am going as a seductive gothic vampire."

"Really. Do you actually need a costume?" I said.

"Oh V, you've no sense of adventure. You're going as a brooding teenage vampire, full of angst," she said, and stared over at me for a moment, her face frowning, "actually, maybe you don't need a costume either."

"Ha ha," I replied.

She smiled back, revelling in her little game and turned the music back up.

I sat in the passenger seat, looking out at the snow on the sides of the road. I was sad to be leaving the slopes behind but excited to be meeting another vampire, getting the truth and visiting Las Vegas.

Life at the ski resorts had been great. No complications of gang members and Hunters. I had a new life and identity. No one judged me as the bullied kid at school. I could be whoever I wanted to be. I had spent most of the daylight hours alone, skiing. I loved it as it pushed my body to its limits down the slopes, cutting in the bends and hurtling down the hills. The icy wind on my face and whistling in my ears. The force of the turns bracing through my legs. I couldn't believe how quickly I had learnt and how good I had become. I loved showing off and racing past other skiers and snowboarders.

On the days Thorn joined me on the slopes, we would race each other down the hills, daring one another to go faster. Other days, I would have to wait for the day to darken and Thorn to awake, but it was worth the wait. Thorn was a passionate woman and hardly a night went by without her showing it. At night, we would drive off to the neighbouring towns for her to feed and party. Other nights we spent training in physical combat or other skills. A few nights she went off alone, as I was tired from the day's skiing. We had slipped back into our regular patterns of behaviour we had formed in England.

The sadness I felt to be leaving was matched by the excitement of meeting another vampire and going to Las Vegas. Thorn promised me the answers I had craved since my psychic skills had picked up her memories of other vampires.

Back in Leeds, before my revenge on the O'Keefe gang, my psychic skills had kicked in. On that occasion, I had accidentally seen a flash of Thorn's memories. In her thoughts, I saw vampires like her, warm and passionate, fighting against knights with swords and shields, but there were also other vampires in her mind. They lurked in the shadows and had cold dead decaying flesh. I had seen other things as well, but the complete picture was hidden as Thorn ejected me from her memories. I am sure I saw fire and smoke.

This insight into her past triggered a multitude of questions. Who were the other types of vampires? The cold decaying ones. Who were the knights attacking them? Where were all the other vampires? Who was she? I hoped I would get these answers in Vegas from Cassius. I also looked forward to seeing the sights and enjoying the famous Vegas nightlife. Thorn appeared to be enjoying herself as well.

"You seem very happy? Is that the feed or going to Vegas?" I asked.

She laughed. "Both. The feed was great. A nice little pick me up and some measure of revenge for my lost money. Vegas will be fun as well. Can't wait to hit the poker tables. But mostly, I am looking forward to spending time with another vampire."

I felt a little hurt at her comments. "What about me?"

"Sorry, darling. I know you have changed through the needles, but it has only been two brief nights. I enjoyed it and we will do it again, but Cassius is a fully-fledged vampire with many lifetimes of experience. We share a history and understanding that only two vampires could have of one another. I haven't seen another vampire, apart from you, for over three years. Don't be hurt, you will become one of us soon," she said, and placed a hand on my arm and smiled. I understood her response and let my sudden indignation slide. Thorn carried on. "Meeting with Cassius will move our plans forward. He will help us find out the truth and get our revenge."

The charter plane picked us up at Calgary airport and flew us down to a private airstrip outside Vegas. During the flight, I studied documents on my tablet. Thorn had moved the training on to encompass a broad range of topics. I had learnt about explosives and how to make them. We had recently moved on to studying battle strategies and tactics. I read the 'Art of War' and the 'The Book of Five Rings,' and studied famous battles and the strategies used. I also got to play computer games, but only for educational purposes - battle simulation games controlling armies, formations and tactics to test my knowledge.

We touched down at the private airport in darkness, so Thorn could exit the plane without problems or suspicions. A white limo with tinted windows had chased us up the runway to greet us. Thorn checked through the windows and folded away her sunglasses and hat, happy the UV levels were safe. In her passenger bag, she always carried a scarf, sunblock, gloves, etc to ensure she would be fully protected if needed. Just in case we got delayed or re-routed. No one ever questioned her appearance or strange requests, as she had a certificate proving she suffered from a rare skin disease, which described her sensitivity to light. Plus, being rich, no one asked questions anyway. Only too happy to take the money and keep quiet.

We left the aeroplane and the black-suited driver escorted us into the back of the limo, while the aircrew removed our luggage and put it in the boot. We drove out of the airport, through Vegas City, and then onto the Las Vegas Strip.

Palm trees lined the road as we drove along the strip and underneath bridges connecting the two sides. To one side of the road, a roller coaster peeked out over the top of a hotel, while on the other side was a multitude of food courts offering popular choices of fast food, alongside flashing amusement arcades that lit the pavement. In front, massive hotels towered over the smaller clubs, bars and restaurants that packed the strip.

We drove on, following an advertising trailer for a lap dancing club, showing three scantily dressed girls posing provocatively on the back. We drove past the Monte Carlo hotel, and I stared at the bleached ornate arched entrance with sculptured angels on the top. Behind us, a red Ferrari cruised along, allowing everyone a chance to admire it. I stared out the open window; the wind blowing my hair backwards, waking me up from my long flight.

Up ahead, the fake Eiffel tower lit up the skyline, the bright yellow spotlights tracing its frame and peak. We drove past Planet Hollywood and the endless shopping malls. The casinos en route flashed enticing images of big money wins. Big screens showed dollar signs growing larger and flashing on the screens, roulette wheels spinning, cards flying across tables and slot machines spinning around to hit jackpot wins.

The billboards kept switching from adverts for gambling to adverts for stage shows with women in extravagant sequined garments dancing choreographed moves. World-famous acts were being advertised outside the top hotels; well-known singers, magicians and comedians.

Other cars cruised up and down the strip, with the passengers hanging out of the windows and craning their necks to take in the spectacle. In front, a taxi ferried its cargo to their entertainment for the evening. On the other side of the road, a pink stretched limo with two young women with heads through the sunroof, drinking champagne and squealing while the wind was flapping their hair back. We continued our drive along the strip in amongst the melee of cars.

Thorn slumped back into her seat with her eyes closed, allowing her senses to fully engage with the atmosphere beyond the limo. Even with my limited abilities, I could sense the vibrancy of the city, a bombardment of emotions from its inhabitants. Joy and loss, fear and laughter, love and hate; emotions at the extremes and all occurring moments apart. In one place, people were having the time of their lives, and right next to them, people were flushing their lives down the toilet.

We cruised past the Paris Hotel with the fake 'Arc de Triomphe' acting as a roundabout as the road swept around the hotel entrance and back out onto the strip. Next, we drove straight past the 'Eiffel Tower' straddling the Paris Hotel with its French flags flying and statues decorating the outside of the building. I swivelled just in time to see the huge Caesars Palace hotel with its Roman pillars and its roofs capped with triangular peaks. Caesar's Palace sprawled out over the strip with multiple hotels, casinos, theatres and restaurant buildings.

Vegas felt like a dream, such a long way from inner-city Leeds, the car accident with Giles and all the problems of the O'Keefe gang.

"Las Vegas. It feels alive. Every type of entertainment possible and every emotion played out night after night," Thorn said, grinning as she opened her sparkling eyes.

"I guess you've been here before?" I asked, looking out the window at another casino with flashing dollar signs.

"Oh, yeah. It's a wonderful playground. So many lost souls to feed on, people looking for a good time. Plus, the greed, the tragedy, and daily shows. What more could a vampire want? And Vegas is full of strange people. I can move about and hardly be noticed."

"Who is Cassius?" I asked, trying to catch her off guard.

"An old friend. He and I belonged to the House of Fire," she answered.

"House. Is he related to you?"

"Distantly. Houses were a way of forming alliances and organisational structure in the vampire world, to bring discipline and order. We served the same King and fought side by side."

"Against the humans?" I asked. At last, she had started to open up on her past.

"I will tell you more once we meet up with him. But yes, against humans wishing to destroy us like the Hunters. But also against other Vampire Houses. There have always been tensions and wars between vampires. Just as humans are always fighting one another."

"So, is Cassius like you, or like the other vampires I saw in your memories?" I asked, wanting to understand the images I had seen months ago.

Thorn's nose wrinkled up in disgust at the mention of the other vampires, and she looked out the window.

"I think that's enough questions for one day. We meet Cassius and work out our next moves. It will be best to hear it from him."

"But there are others different from you," I said, pushing the question forward.

"I said that is enough!" she snapped back, bolting across the seat, her red eyes mere inches from mine.

I flinched and bashed my head on the inside of the door. My vision span for a second from the impact.

"Okay, but I want answers eventually," I said, rubbing my head better as Thorn settled back into her seat.

"Be patient. Cassius will reveal all."

The dark decaying vampires remained a mystery, but their existence was obviously important, and my mentioning them had disturbed Thorn.

The white limo swept around to the front of a casino with a luxury five-star hotel on site. Thorn booked us into a suite on the top floor. As usual for Thorn's taste, the hotel suite was luxurious. The room had a view down Las Vegas strip with windows that tinted, which provided her with protection from UV, but still allowed a view of the sights during the day.

We dumped our bags at the base of the huge four-poster bed located against the beige and black striped walls. I looked longingly at the bed, looking forward to a good sleep and a warm embrace with Thorn before we searched for Cassius.

I stepped down into a lowered part with a semi-circle of leather sofas and picked up a remote control. I pressed a button, and a huge flat-screen TV rose out of the floor in front of the sofas. A message appeared on the screen, 'Welcome Ms T.Horn,' and the menu options scrolled down the left-hand side. I turned it off again, and it descended back into the floor.

I climbed out of the sunken semi-circle towards the windows, where a hot tub nestled into the corner. I eyed up the hot tub, imagining Thorn and me enjoying the warming bubbles massaging our naked bodies, and the cold champagne bubbles relaxing our minds at the same time. Our arms would be entwined and sipping from each other's glasses, then kissing and it escalating into more. It created a heady mixture of desires in my mind, and I liked the idea of relaxing after the long plane flight, enjoying the luxury alone with Thorn, before I heard the truth from Cassius.

As I stood over the hot tub working out the different settings for our romantic embrace, Thorn pulled off her grey jumper and untied her raven hair. She shook out her tousled locks as they cascaded down onto her shoulders. She reached into her handbag to fetch her wallet and then walked over and grabbed my hand.

"Playtime," she announced and led me out of the room and down into the casino.

She acted like an excited child on holiday, wanting to go straight to the beach. I allowed myself to go along with her excitement. We had plenty of time to enjoy the luxuries of the room together.

In the casino, the slot machines chimed away in a relentless cacophony as we walked across the plush red carpets and through the bright white lobby. Every type of person sat at the machines watching the whirling wheels, hoping for a match and a big money win. People wandered around looking at the machines and heading back and forth through the front entrance, comprising of two large glass doors that slid back to allow entry and exit from the Vegas night.

A platinum blonde showgirl, dressed in a white sequined top with a feathery white shirt, handed out flyers for the hotel's show. She stepped past a few people and handed a flyer to me.

"Come to the show," she said, and smiled, tilting one hip and looking from under false eyelashes.

Thorn held my hand and pulled me away from the showgirl, who waved as I went. We passed a small restaurant carved out in the corner of the room. It had a mirrored wall along the one side and the kitchen area with a bar counter at right angles to it. The smell of food triggered my hunger, and the sight of two plates of burger and fries being served to eagerly awaiting customers had me walking over. But Thorn led me on, hand in hand, towards the back of the casino.

The casino held an array of people; some starting the night with a little gambling before more formal events. The men were dressed in suits and dinner jackets. The women wore glamorous dresses and high heel shoes with hair glossed and curled, and makeup carefully applied. Others dressed for comfort in shorts and t-shirts, looking like they had been there all day with no intentions of leaving soon. Most people dressed somewhere in the middle, enjoying the gambling pre and post their evening meals.

In amongst the customers, security staff in red blazers and ties, with black trousers and shoes, walked the floors and spoke into radios. The waitresses wore red aprons, skimming the top of their black knee length skirts, and they dashed through the crowds while carrying trays of drinks. They nodded at the security guards as they went by and swerved around unobservant customers.

As we passed the roulette table, two men in dinner jackets shuffled betting chips and stacked them onto numbers and colours. A woman covered in a sparkly golden dress with blonde hair that was swept over to one side and pinned with a white flower, span the wheel at their request, smiling coyly at them as she did. The dealer threw in the ball, and it rolled, bounced and clattered around. We walked on, and I heard the groans of disappointed gamblers as the ball clanked to a stop. We then stopped at the craps table as the dice bounced down the table.

"Snake eyes," the shout came from the white shirted dealer.

Then on again, past the blackjack tables and headed directly to the poker games. Thorn circled around a few tables, watching each of the players and their piles of money. We watched as a few bets played out, and Thorn observed their money and playing abilities. We moved onto other tables, each time Thorn watching the money piles and focusing her senses on the players.

"These are no good. They are a mixture of tourists who can ill afford to lose their money, with a few local pro's trying to fleece them. I want an obvious target. Someone with deep pockets," she said.

We headed further in, looking for the bigger money tables, and we found her perfect spot. A man in his late forties, with slicked back hair, big black sunglasses, black suit and unbuttoned white shirt. In front of him, a perfectly stacked pile of chips, and in the middle of the table, a mountain of chips. Opposite, two opponents who had nothing left to bet. The slick-haired man flipped over his cards.

"Four Fours," he said, grinning at his opponents.

The man directly opposite pulled up the edge of his card on the table. He had wrinkled skin from constant tanning and had overly dyed jet black hair that matched his shirt. The other player wore a Hawaiian shirt and had thinning grey hair and fat jowly features. The second man didn't look at his cards but just stared at the slick-haired man and the two men that stood behind him.

Thorn nudged me and glanced at the two men hanging about in the background. They tried to blend in, but their eyes scouted around, bodyguards.

One stood near the slick-haired man, and the other a few paces back, trying to mingle in by leaning against a metal rail. The closest guard had red hair and freckles across the brow of his nose. His short sleeve black t-shirt exposed his thick forearms also covered in freckles and coarse red hair. He wore a square metal belt buckle fashioned from the USA flag and grey cowboy boots underneath his dark blue jeans.

The man at the back had a shaven head and dark skin. He had a barrel chest and massive pectoral and biceps pulling on his black shirt to open the collar wide. He wore black trousers and shiny black shoes to finish his outfit. The rigid posture of the men and muscular arms and necks gave away their profession.

The red-haired bodyguard shook his head at the other two card players. The overly tanned card player gritted his teeth, checked his cards again and stared back at the bodyguards. The red-haired guard stared and clenched his fist into a ball. The guard in black lifted his phone to his ear.

The tanned opponent banged the table with his fist.

"I'm out," he said and looked at the fat man in the Hawaiian shirt.

The man in the Hawaiian shirt finished his drink and pushed away from the table. He stood up and shook his head from side to side in disapproval.

The winning card player, the slick-haired man, laughed aloud while pulling his winnings back and stacked it up into neat piles. The two losers whispered to one another for a moment and glanced over. The slick-haired man seemed intent on savouring his victory.

"Come on, you might win it back... maybe," he said to his defeated opponents and sipped his whiskey.

The card dealer eyed him as he took back the cards and shuffled the pack. The slick haired man threw him a small chip as a tip. He then swept back his hair and adjusted his sunglasses as he looked about for other victims.

Around the table, other potential players walked past, hurrying on after seeing the man's pile of money and spotting the obvious bodyguards lurking behind. The two defeated opponents intervened with a few willing players by whispering in their ears. Their eyes cast over to the two bodyguards as they warned the new opponents away. We watched from a short distance as a lack of opponents frustrated slick hair, and he started talking to the potential players avoiding his table.

"You are all too scared. Look at all this money you could win," he said, gesturing at the pile of chips. He drank more whiskey and laughed. The red-haired guard whispered in his ear, but he pushed him away.

"Remember who you work for. No one can touch me," he snapped back.

I looked at Thorn as she watched his every move.

"He is part of a well known family. His brother is very rich and powerful. He is our perfect target," she said, without taking her eyes off him.

"Target? What's the plan?" I asked.

"We take all his money," she said and strolled across to the table and sat down.

Slick hair pulled down his sunglasses, and his eyes widened to take in the view. The usual reaction to Thorn's beauty. She exchanged a few words with the dealer, and a cashier assistant came over, took a swipe of her credit card and returned with a small metal case full of chips. Slick hair seemed even more surprised by the wealth than the beauty of his new opponent. He summoned over his bodyguard and whispered in his ear.

"Are you sure about this? He looks bad news," I said.

"He is. That's why he is perfect," she replied, grinning.

He looked over and raised his glass to Thorn. She gave a nod back. "Beautiful and wealthy, it almost seems a shame to relieve you of your money," he said.

Thorn smiled back shyly, playing up to his deluded first impression.

"I will give you a chance for being so charming," she replied.

The man smiled back. "May I have the pleasure of your name before we start? I am Victor Vitsco," he said, as if we should already know.

Thorn looked at him blankly. "I am Tracey."

"Well, pleased to meet you, Tracey. We could go for a drink and a meal afterwards."

"I doubt it. I will have all your money by then. And I don't pay for anyone."

Victor frowned for a moment, and then laughed. "You have spirit. Good, this will be fun."

They played and inevitably, Thorn began winning. Her psychic powers were an unfair advantage. The man started twitching, betting bigger and bigger to scare her off, but Thorn ordered more money each time and met whatever bet he could come up with. His pile of chips descended and Thorn's ascended.

However, his complete ruin would take time, and I wanted to see the rest of the casino. My stomach continued to rumble, and my mouth watered from the sights and smells of the restaurant. I stood behind her restlessly swapping my weight from one foot to another while clicking away on my phone. Thorn turned around and handed me a fist full of betting chips.

"You're making me nervous with all that fidgeting. Go off and have a bet or have a drink," she said, and waved me away.

I grabbed the chips and shoved them in my pockets.

"Will you be okay? I don't like the look of his bodyguards," I said, knowing she could handle herself, but I still liked to play the part of protector.

Her eyebrows flashed up, and she returned to her game.

I exchanged some chips for cash and walked back through the casino. I tried my luck at poker, hoping my psychic skills would help. But I had little luck. My psychic skills weren't advanced enough, and there was too much psychic pollution from the other customers, making it impossible to focus. I headed onwards past the noise of excited shouts and disappointed groans at the craps tables and roulette wheels.

I walked past the restaurant and the smell of the food wafting out from the kitchen called to me. However, I wanted to try the slot machines so pushed onto the front of the casino. The wheels whirled around again and again, but every time I seemed to be just on the brink of winning, it would disappear or need more money.

My stomach rumbled again, so I gave in as my pot of coins had drained into the machines. I went back to the corner restaurant and picked up a few flyers from the stall at the side. A waitress escorted me to a seat against the mirrored wall. I ordered a bottle of beer and steak and chips to kill the time and my empty stomach.

As I ate, I read the tourist flyers. I had seen the Paris Hotel with the Eiffel Tower brightly lit up on the way to the hotel. We had also passed the Venetian Hotel on the trip down the strip, with the fake Piazza San Marco and gondolas. I would visit them during the daytime hours while I waited for Thorn to rise at night.

I looked up from the flyers and saw two young women sitting a couple of tables away. One of them smiled. They were dressed and groomed glamorously for a night out in sparkly clingy dresses and makeup adorning their features. I looked around to see who they were looking at, but only my reflection in the mirror met my eyes. There was no one else. I immediately felt suspicious.

Why are they looking at me? What are they after?

I tried to concentrate on the remaining chunks of steak, but I occasionally caught their smiles again. Since my change, I felt uneasy with the female attention that I attracted. I had spent most of my life ignored, trying to blend into the background to go unnoticed by the bullies. Since Scarlett betrayed me with Barry and the Hunters, I suspected everyone. These girls might be genuine, or it could be a trap arranged by the Hunters or some other local gang. It didn't matter which, I belonged to Thorn anyway. With that thought, I finished my beer and food. As I walked past their table, I winked at them. They blushed and smiled coyly back. Maybe they really did fancy me after all.

I walked back past the roulette and craps tables with their highs and lows, and then past the other card tables to find Thorn. En route, a waitress stopped one of the male card dealers.

"Come and watch. Someone is taking down Victor Vitsco," she said, and he hurried after her.

I quickened my pace back to the table, but only saw a crowd instead. The crowd, two deep, had encircled the table, blocking sight of the action and drawing attention from the casino security. The red-jacketed guards watched the throng from a distance and above the table, the CCTV cameras pointed downward to survey the action. People peered over each other's shoulders and whispered to one another.

I stood at the back behind two men dressed in black dinner jackets, and I tried to look through the rows of bobbing heads. The pot in the middle had become a mountain of cascading chips. Slick hair had gambled away all but his last few chips, and Thorn still had a sizeable stack of chips. She had continued to clean him out on my walkabout.

"Does she realise who he is?" the man in front said to his friend.

"I don't know, but her luck will run out if she wins," the friend replied.

I laughed to myself at their concern for Thorn. If only they knew.

"Excuse me," I said, and pushed through the crowd to stand at her side. A few moans came from the spectators as I stepped through, but Thorn smiled and reached out and pulled me in next to her.

"My lucky charm has returned just in time," she said, looking up into my eyes.

Victor frowned. His sunglasses had been removed, and he knocked back all his whiskey, grimacing as it burnt on the back of his throat. He rounded all his chips up in a pile and shoved them into the centre.

"That's everything," he said and glared at her.

The bodyguard in black slipped around the back of the crowd and forced his way in just behind us. He leant forward and whispered in her ear.

"Let him win his money back and leave, Missy. You've won enough."

Thorn looked up into the man's glare. His massive muscular frame casting a shadow over the table. She nodded at him and smiled weakly.

The dealer looked back and forth between Thorn and Victor, waiting for some acknowledgement of what had just happened.

Thorn pushed her chips into the middle of the table to join the mountain of chips already in place.

"I match it. Let's see your cards," she said, sighed and cast her eyes down. The bodyguard nodded with approval, and she half smiled back.

Victor looked over at Thorn and back to the bodyguard, having noted the conversation and passing signals between them. He smiled, leaned back and flipped over his cards, four aces. The crowd gasped and muttered to one another. Thorn looked down disappointedly, shook her head and then stood up to leave. Victor grinned and reached out with his hands towards the chips to scoop them all in. Thorn, quick as a flash, leant forward and slapped his hands off the chips.

"Hands off my money, grease ball," she said and flipped over her cards, a royal flush. Thorn had won.

Chapter Three

Thorn raked the money back towards her, turning to ask the dealer for a bag. Most of the crowd gasped in surprise, but others smiled and clapped at her win, ecstatic at the toppling of the arrogant slick haired man.

Victor's face drained, and he stumbled from the table.

"She's a cheat, she's a cheat," he shouted and pointed at her.

Thorn laughed at him and continued scooping the chips towards her, dropping it into the waiting bag. I helped scoop in the chips while smiling and laughing at her victory.

The bodyguard behind us growled. "Stupid girl. You could have saved us all a lot of trouble. This will end badly."

"Let's hope so," Thorn replied, not even looking at him and the guard walked back to the other side.

Victor grabbed the red-haired bodyguard by the arm.

"Do something you idiot," he shouted.

The guard spoke into his ear and tried to lead him away, but Victor pushed him back, picked up his whiskey glass and hurled it at us. Thorn caught it without flinching and grinned at him. The majority of the crowd dispersed as Victor made a scene, but a few, including his recent opponents; the overly tanned man and the fat man in the Hawaiian shirt watched on with delight at his sudden misfortune. They smiled and then came over to thank Thorn by shaking her hand. She passed them each a one thousand dollar chip.

"For your misfortune," she said. They thanked her for it and walked off.

This incensed Victor even more. Thorn flicked a one dollar chip at him to add insult to injury.

"For you," she teased.

His bodyguards pulled him away from the table, and the Casino's security guards hurried over to help usher him out of the building, as he continued to spit words of abuse at Thorn and me.

"Do you know who I am, bitch? You will pay for this," he shouted, as the security guards dragged him to the exit, with his feet kicking at the air.

The black clothed bodyguard shook his head at us and hurried after his screaming boss, as the red jacketed security guards dumped him outside.

Thorn laughed and kissed me on the cheek.

"Excellent, let's cash up. We should have plenty of free cash to help pay for this little adventure. We can try out the hot tub now and celebrate your birthday properly," she said, pulling the drawstring of the bag together, and then flicking a thousand dollar tip to the dealer.

Thorn took the chips over to the cashiers protected in their glass cages and exchanged it for cash, which they placed into a metal briefcase. The thrill of the win had Thorn almost skipping to the lift with the briefcase in her hand. At last, I could get Thorn out of her clothes, into the hot tub, and then between the sheets of the four-poster bed. Then tomorrow we could get the truth from Cassius and move our plans forward.

In the room, Thorn placed the briefcase on the bed. I switched on the radio and then turned on the hot tub taps. She flipped open the lid of the briefcase, and I looked on amazed at the stacks of dollar bills. She pulled out a bundle of cash and then shoved it into my pocket.

"Spending money," she said.

She stripped off her white shirt, revealing her black spider web patterned underwear. Her black boots unzipped and thumped to the floor. Next, she slid her tight jeans over her buttocks and stepped out of them to show her perfect figure and white silk skin. My desire ignited as my sight bathed in her athletic body and ample curves. She pulled the champagne bottle out of the cold bucket, and deftly worked off the silver wrapper and popped the cork. The bubbles fizzed out down the bottle onto her hand before she poured it into the glass flutes. Vegas would be fun.

I unbuckled my jeans and dropped them to the floor and then stripped my t-shirt off, desperate to get her into the hot tub. This would be a new experience. Then a knock rattled the door. Thorn closed her eyes. I pulled my t-shirt and jeans back on and then opened the door. I wanted to get rid of them as soon as possible.

"No," she shouted.

The door bolted open and knocked me to the floor. Victors' two bodyguards stormed into the room, and the red-haired guard towered above me, pointing a pistol into my face. The black clothed man strode into the room with a gun aimed at Thorn. Both wore black blazers to conceal the gun holsters they now wore.

"Give us the money, bitch," he shouted, and his eyebrows rose at the exotic sight of her in her lingerie. His gun lowered for a few seconds, and then he shook his head and levelled his aim again.

"No way. I won it," she shouted back.

"Sorry, my client can't afford to lose that amount."

"Tough," Thorn said, and glared at them.

The black dressed bodyguard nodded to the red-haired guard, who had the gun thrust in my face. He pushed the barrel of the gun into the flesh of my forehead. The cold metal pressed in. I sat up pushing my head into it, meeting his threat and snarling at him. They had taken me by surprise, and I wanted a chance to even up the contest.

"My client is the brother of a very important man. He won't accept no for an answer. You want a safe stay in Vegas, then I suggest you do as I say. You obviously have enough money anyway," he said, glancing around the room.

"Yes, I am aware of your client and his brother. Take the money and pass a message to Mr. Vitsco Senior. I want this money returned and matched as a means of an apology within 24 hours."

The guard laughed. "You're serious. What is your name again?"

"My name is Thorn, and I will make you bleed," she said and pointed at the metal briefcase on the bed.

He walked over, keeping the gun aimed at Thorn the whole time. The cowboy pushed the pistol into my forehead and bared his teeth as I drove back, waiting for the signal to attack. My eyes bore into his, and he kept his fixed stare. The black clothed bodyguard reached the briefcase; closed it with one hand, picked it up and backed towards the door while keeping his eyes on her.

"Let's go," he shouted, and the red-haired guard gave his gun one last shove into my head and walked backwards to join his partner at the door. They kept their guns levelled at us until they slammed the door shut once in the corridor.

I sprung upright and strode towards the door, ready to take revenge and reclaim our money.

'Leave them,' her thoughts spoke into my mind.

I turned to her.

"You could have destroyed them. We could have beaten them," I said.

"No need to waste your energy, and why take risks? I am only letting one get back alive. Just giving them a head start."

I smiled and grabbed my jacket as Thorn dressed in a flash into her skinny jeans, knee boots, tight white t-shirt, and then waited at the door.

"No, just me. Stay here and relax. I need a feed and want to move quickly," she said and winked with her red vampire eyes.

"But I could help?"

"You can't risk the formula until we know why it killed Barry."

"But even without it, I am strong. I can fight."

"I know, my darling, but I want you safe. This will be easier by myself, and I can return to you quickly."

"Okay, enjoy," I said and waved her out.

"I will," she said, fangs bared and eyes red as she slipped out of the room.

I threw my jacket off and slumped onto the sofas. It annoyed me I wouldn't get revenge or at least see Thorn beat them.

The adrenaline still surged, and I couldn't relax, so I decided to enjoy the hot tub by myself. I undressed, climbed in and sipped at the glasses of cold champagne. Maybe another night we would get to enjoy it together and celebrate my birthday.

I switched on my iPad and routed my browsing session through several proxies across the Internet to cover my tracks and prevent anyone from working out my location. I wanted to view my social networking pages and the normal world. I hadn't been logged on to them since leaving England.

I sat back in surprise to see my pages were full of posts from family and friends.

"Happy Birthday. Hope you are okay where ever you are. Love Auntie Joyce."

"Happy Birthday. Come home. Love Dad."

"Happy Birthday Jonathan, I still love you. Scarlett."

She posted on my page, still acting as the perfect girlfriend. The Hunters still hoping they could use her to get me back. But Barry had told me the truth.

"It was all arranged, the mugging, the bullying and your girlfriend."

What did that actually mean? I had assumed, following Thorn's remarks, it meant Scarlett was one of them, a Hunter. Our relationship setting me up to take the vampire formula. It had made sense, as I could never accept a flame haired beauty like Scarlett fancying me. Back then, I had been a scrawny teenage boy. Maybe following the changes to my body, I could accept it.

I pictured Scarlett, her flame red hair and light green eyes. I had been ecstatic when we started dating. After the disasters of Leeds, everything went right when I dated Scarlett. I had become the envy of every male student in our sixth form, but it didn't last. I'd been destroyed when I found out she had slept with Barry, the man who mugged and then bullied me. It got worse. I had prepared to forgive her, but his confession about her betrayal had plunged my world into total darkness. However, he only said it was arranged. I had always assumed she played a part in the conspiracy to make me use the formula. I rubbed my thumb across her name. Maybe there could be another explanation. I started typing.

"*I miss you too xx.*" I posted to the comments.

I panicked. I might have given away my position. I turned off the iPad and switched on the TV instead.

I wanted to go to bed and put the day behind me, but my sleep patterns were shot to pieces by sleeping at random times. I poured myself more champagne, not wanting to waste the cold bubbles of alcohol and warm bubbles of the hot tub.

The bubbles in the hot tub rippled against my tired muscles and smoothed away the stress of the night. The cold bubbles of the champagne dulled my aching head, relaxing the rest of my mind and body. My eyes fluttered as the combination of the bubbles took its toll.

I stood in front of Scarlett's front door with red roses in my hand. I knocked and the door opened. Scarlett stood before me, hair dyed back to flame red and dressed in the red hot pants and the white t-shirt that she had worn on our first date.

"You've come back to me," she squealed with excitement and stepped through the doorway, putting her hands around my face and standing on tiptoes to kiss me.

"You've grown," she smiled, grabbed my hand and dragged me up the stairs to her bedroom, all the time glancing around, her face beaming with excitement.

She took the flowers and threw them on her dressing table, scattering her makeup. She pulled me close, kissing me passionately, grappling at my belt and loosening my trousers. My hands reached down to her red hot pants, unbuttoning and sliding them off to the floor. She stepped out of them and pulled off her t-shirt. I stripped off the rest of my clothes. My heart pounded and hands grasped at her body as we staggered over to the bed, exchanging frantic kisses. We crashed onto the bed, her legs wrapped around my body, and I kissed her neck as we made love. The heat between us was rising and in unison, we began gasping at the air. My passion drove my instincts, and the intensity of our lovemaking rocketed us both to climax. Scarlett's head tilted back, her neck wide open, her veins pulsating and her blood calling to me.

A thirst swept through me. My claws ripped through my fingers, tearing into the bedsheets. My eyes burnt and fangs cut through. Scarlett opened her eyes and face recoiled in horror. Her hands bolted up to stop me and her head turned away but exposed the tender part of her neck. I bolted down, brushed her hands away, sunk my fangs into her pale white neck, and sucked down her blood. Then I started choking.

Water hit the back of my throat, and I splashed my arms around. A glass smashed and I hauled my head out of the water. I leaned over the side, spluttered out the water onto the broken champagne glasses and breathed in deeply to calm myself down. I spat out the last of the unwanted liquid and sank back into the hot tub, grabbing the bottle as I went and poured the remaining alcohol down my throat. I stared out of the window at the cars driving down the strip and the lights from the other hotels and casinos illuminating the skyline. The water settled along with my heart rate and heaving chest. Time for bed.

I climbed out, dried off and slipped into the fresh cotton sheets of the four-poster bed. I wondered what my dream meant as the mattress moulded around me. My heart still raced from my erotic nightmare. Did the desire to drink blood exist as a human? I wasn't sure. Maybe it was just a dream and didn't hold any meaning at all. Yet, perhaps I had changed more than I realised. After some time, both my breathing and heart rate returned to normal. My eyes fluttered again, and I closed them, allowing my thoughts to drift away.

I needed some sleep, as tomorrow the vampire fan convention started. I would get to meet another vampire, Cassius, and get to unravel the mysteries Thorn had been keeping. Maybe I would discover more about the Hunters and the betrayal from Scarlett and my Dad. As I lay in bed wondering what I would discover, my thoughts scattered across the previous day and sleep overwhelmed me again. Thankfully, this time, I slept without nearly drowning and any more strange dreams.

Chapter Four

I woke up in the morning to find Thorn asleep at my side. Her blood stained white t-shirt draped over the sofa. She fed on someone last night. Only one of those guards made it back alive. The victim served two purposes: a deadly message and her dinner.

I dressed quietly in my jeans and a blue faded t-shirt and slipped out of the room to explore the city in the daylight. I left the hotel through the grand entrance of red carpets and marble columns. As I walked through the double doors, my brow sweated, and I pulled on my sunglasses to shield my eyes. I wished I had brought some shorts to wear instead of jeans. We had just come from the Canadian winter, and my wardrobe wasn't equipped for the Vegas heat. I would have to endure it for now or spend most of my time awake at night, which I could easily do with a vampire girlfriend.

I walked down the strip, looking at the map on the back of the brochures I got from the restaurant last night. I tried out a few slot machines in Caesar's Palace and Casino Royale. As they are such well-known casinos, I wanted to visit and gamble in each of them.

Next, I visited the Eiffel Tower replica and queued up to get the glass lift to the top. I seemed to be the only person by himself or herself. Couples stood together on either side of me in the queue. Somehow, I had got in between two couples who were out together and they spoke around me as if I didn't exist.

My turn came and I stepped inside with the two groups I had separated. I stood at the back to get out of their way. To one side, a young blonde woman with a good tan and her athletic looking boyfriend had their arms around one another. She rubbed her hand over his white polo shirt and onto the back of his shorts. He looked down at her, eyes glinting and smiling. She met his gaze, her eyes wide and pupils dilating into a demure smile. They leaned into each other, exchanged a few kisses, and then went back to caressing each other gently. I wished they would save it for their room, so I turned away, only to see the other couple holding hands. I closed my eyes to block it out. I wished Thorn could be here, not that we would have held hands or been openly affectionate, but at least I wouldn't feel out of place. Thorn's presence would have all the men looking around and then jealously over at me. We would be the star attraction, but instead, I hid away at the back of the lift, hoping no one noticed me.

The glass elevator arrived at the top, and I waited as the normal couples ambled their way out. I hurried to the edge to look at the view across Vegas and not to watch their public shows of affection.

The same kissing couple from the lift stood by my side, still more engrossed in each other than the view. I took a few photos of the Vegas strip and watched the planes take off from the international airport. I would show the photos to Thorn later, but it wasn't the same as her being here with me during the day.

"Hey, buddy. Could you take a photo of us together?" the man from the couple asked.

"Yeah, sure," I responded, trying to be polite and not draw attention to myself. I wanted to say get lost, but the unspoken social contract means you can't without attracting attention.

"It's our first holiday together," he said as they smiled at the camera.

I took the photo and handed the camera back, ready to move on.

"You here with anyone?" the woman asked, as if it was a crime to be single.

"She had a heavy night and is sleeping it off," I replied, which wasn't really a lie. I just swapped getting drunk for feeding on blood.

I smiled and went around the other side of the viewing platform. I didn't want to get into a deep conversation, or make friends and have to endure their normality any longer. Besides, I couldn't make friends. I was a wanted man.

I arrived at the other side only to be confronted by the other kissing couple from the lift. Happy romantic couples seemed to inhabit every space, taunting me with their normality as they enjoyed the sun and surroundings.

Thorn and I could come at night, but we never did normal couple things such as trips out or dates. At night, the agenda was training, partying or feeding. I had never asked to spend normal time as a couple. Thorn wasn't the sort of girl you took to the cinema, or for romantic walks in the moonlight. Sightseeing in Vegas wasn't on the agenda, and besides, Thorn had been alive for hundreds of years and had done and seen almost everything, anyway. I had nothing new to offer her, as she had done everything already. I remembered watching a history documentary about the English Civil War on the TV when Thorn sat beside me and started telling me they had it all wrong and switched it off.

I had enough of the view and took the lift back down, and then walked through the back of the hotel, out to the front with the 'Arc de Triomphe' acting as a roundabout for the arriving and departing cars at the front of the hotel. I walked across the road under the Arc and admired the intricate stonework patterns, then along the small Champs-Élysées with the water fountains, which split the road up to the Arc.

On the walk, I encountered more couples enjoying the fake Paris romantic setting, walking hand in hand or arms wrapped around one another, or stopping and kissing and taking selfies together on their smartphones. I could imagine them posting on the web with accompanying sloppy message - *'Perfect'* - so they could boast to their friends and family, a true facebrag moment.

I walked down the strip, into the Venetian Hotel, to the replica San Marco Piazza. As gondolas glided along the canals, I went over the crisscrossing bridges. To the sides of the piazza, restaurant customers sat in the sun drinking cold drinks and Italian style coffees.

A couple of the bridges looped towards one another, creating a higher bridge over the central canal. The two little bridges feeding into the main bridge were roped off. Inside the roped off section, they had laid seats out in rows facing into the apex bridge in the middle. Groups of smartly dressed people milled about at the seats and took photos of the surrounding buildings. Men wore suits and women in formal summer dresses and hats.

At the gondola station, a crowd of people encircled around and cameras flashed. Stepping out of a white gondola with golden patterns inlaid into the woodwork, a woman in a long white dress holding the hand of an older man wearing a morning suit, a Bride and her Father. Her raven hair peeked out from her veil and skin shone as pale as Thorn's. She smiled as the tourists congratulated her and she walked towards the seating area on the apex of the bridges.

Back at the seats, cameras flashed and the guests quickly took their positions. The Groom waited at the front with his best man while watching the Bride walked around the piazza and onto the bridges. He pulled at his suit, making last minute adjustments as the best man pulled out a box from his pocket and checked the rings one last time.

The music 'Here Comes the Bride' played over the speakers and the guests turned around to watch her walk through the aisle between the seats. Her mother wiped a tear from her eye. Her father smiled proudly at her side as he escorted her to the front. The Groom took her hand from her Father's, and the Priest began the proceedings. This would never happen to me now. I would never get married or have children. My path was set in another direction with Thorn, and I had to accept I would never live a normal life.

I couldn't watch anymore and walked away to the other side of the piazza, over another bridge, just as a gondola floated effortlessly along underneath. The striped topped man pushed the pole into the water, and the gondola moved on. In the seats, a man had his arm around a woman, and she snuggled against his chest, her hand rubbing his leg. I watched jealously of their normality as they enjoyed the warm sun and each other's wonderment of the fake Venice atmosphere.

I wanted to take a ride in a gondola but felt too out of place by myself. The sight of normal couples and the wedding made me think of what could have been with Scarlett. If our relationship had of been real, then we could have been floating down the canals or taking in the view on the Eiffel Tower, or maybe taking in a show at night, or enjoying the warm bubbles of the hot tub together and sipping cold champagne bubbles. I doubted any of these things would happen with Thorn.

I scanned the map listing the attractions and decided to visit the rollercoaster ride inside the Stratosphere hotel in the hope it would offer some relief. I grabbed a taxi and it drove back up the strip, passed the Eiffel Tower, Caesar's Palace and onwards to reach the hotel. The Stratosphere was an enormous tower with a metal sphere on the top. I made my way inside, looking forward to the adrenaline boost of the rollercoaster, and I hoped it would sweep away the shadows growing in my mind.

However, even the thrill of the ride didn't help as couples sat in seats in front and behind me and I sat by myself. I heard their excited screams as the ride twisted and turned, pushing our bodies through G–force. The rollercoaster finished, and the man in front clambered out and offered a helping hand to his girlfriend, who accepted with a trembling hand and giggling as she stepped onto the platform. He placed a steady arm around her, and they laughed excitedly to each other as they headed for the exit. I watched all around as couples and friends streamed out. I noticed a few glances over at me, the sad man by himself, and I glanced away, not wanting their pity.

Time had dragged into the late afternoon, and I took refuge in the all-you-can-eat buffet and comfort ate. I filled my stomach up with my body weight in ribs and pizza until the daylight faded. Binge eating had left me feeling uncomfortable. So I hailed a taxi back to the hotel, to be at Thorn's side when she awoke and enjoy my own strange relationship.

I arrived back at the hotel to find the Vampire conference had already started, as a few costumed clad fans followed the signs to the main room.

Those in attendance couldn't be actual vampires, as the last of the daylight still filtered through the windows. Thorn doubted if any other real vampires would attend apart from her and Cassius. She had said the main events started after dark, as you would imagine.

I went back upstairs, sneaked into the room, stripped off and slid between the sheets next to her. The heat glowed off her perfect body, and I took solace in its normality. I cuddled into her and waited for her to stir over the next few minutes, as Thorn loved to be woken with a cuddle. As the sunset, she rolled around and wrapped her arms around my waist, and buried her head into my shoulder, and then hooked her leg over mine.

I wanted more. I started kissing her on the forehead and running my hand gently down her spine. I wanted to be part of a couple after being surrounded by all these happy, human, romantic couples out in the daylight. Thorn got the message and responded to my signals by tracing her fingertips across my back, around my waist, and down to my legs. The reciprocation developed and grew until our flesh and sweat locked us together. I felt normal again as her eyes burnt red and fangs pierced the air as she peaked with desire. Then she bit into my neck to drink a little love blood. There is nothing like sex with a vampire to put your life back into perspective. I was a lucky man.

Afterwards, we showered and dressed in appropriate attire for the convention. Thorn pulled on a knee length black leather coat; knee high boots, black PVC corset and hair straightened into a bob. Her costume styled on a famous female vampire from the movies.

She walked over and my eyes transfixed on her. I remembered watching the film a couple of years ago after a bad day at school because of a nasty bullying incident at the hands of the O'Keefes. To see her dressed as the film character felt as if a dream had come true. Thorn stood in front of me and rubbed her hands through my hair, spiking it up with gel. I placed my hands on her hips and took sneaky glances down her cleavage bursting out of her PVC corset.

"When we get back," she said and winked.

"I said nothing. Are you reading my mind?"

"Don't need to read minds to tell what you're thinking," she replied, and kissed me on the cheek. I guess some things don't need saying to be understood.

I finished getting dressed as a famous TV vampire, all in black with a long coat, spiky hair, real bite marks on my neck, plus I carried a pair of false fangs. Thorn planned to use her own fangs to complete the effect, flaunting her true nature in front of the crowds. She was such a tease.

We walked down the stairs and towards the main conference hallway. Other fans dressed in vampire clothing walked ahead, and we followed them through the fake stone archway wrapped in fake ivy. On either side of the archway, two headstones carved with R.I.P. At the front, two young women dressed in skimpy vampire outfits, short black skirts and silky red mini capes, who bared their fake fangs and handed us maps of the conference. We walked through into a series of large interconnecting conference rooms and looked around the vampire and supernatural paraphernalia that covered and hung off the tables and stalls.

Thorn looked through the outfits hanging on display. Sexy vampire outfits in shiny materials, and more hardcore clothes of tight leather and rubber strapped together. She stopped at the vampire lingerie section and teased me with some of the vampire themed items. Some in lacy bat wings and fang patterned. Others with printed vampire characters or vampire lips baring fangs.

We moved on and she flicked through the DVDs on sale. She was an avid watcher of vampire films and TV shows. She thought it important to understand the human fascination with vampires. I saw the movie on sale of the character she had dressed like, which I had watched a couple of years ago. I bought it as a memento and put it into my jacket pocket.

"You realise some of these film characters are based on me," she said and smiled as she walked on.

The other attendees swished in and out of the crowds and meandered about shopping and running critical eyes over each other's costumes. Numerous Draculas walked past outfitted in black suits and capes, gelled backed hair and white makeup. Others dressed normally, but with sparkles pasted over their pale skin, or wearing T-shirts displaying their fan loyalty.

Fans had adorned themselves as gothic vampires, Victorian vampires, cowboy vampires and space vampires. A choice of every vampire tale and character, with every twist you could imagine. Some dressed as victims. I noticed a young blonde woman in a yellow cheerleader's outfit. Her skin powdered white, fang marks on her neck with traces of blood from the puncture marks. In amongst the variety of vampires, other fans dressed as werewolves, zombies, witches and fairies as the convention offered safe haven to any fan of the genre. The concoction of outfits in style and character surrounded us in a parallel world of the supernatural.

I smirked as Thorn and I wandered through the costumed crowds while viewing the goods on sale. In my mind, I laughed at the fact of standing next to an actual vampire and having been a vampire as well. I imagined the fan's fear or excitement if they knew the truth.

As we shopped, Thorn, as usual, attracted a sea of flowing heads drawn to her flawless beauty and perfect figure. Her costume, with her real fangs and red eyes, created an extra spark of interest and turned even more heads than normal. A few people asked to have photos with her. Some thought she had been hired as a model, advertising and bringing glamour to the event. She agreed to the photos and gave flashes of fangs and eyes to the delight of her audience. The proper models kitted out as sexy vampires viewed her with suspicion.

We scouted around, and Thorn searched through the minds of the crowd looking for her vampire friend, Cassius.

Suddenly, a couple dressed as vampires in trendy clothes and glittery makeup walked up to us, and the man held out his hand.

"Hi there, we met at the Eiffel Tower," he said. I recognised him as the athletic man and his blonde tanned girlfriend.

I took their picture at the top and endured their kissing in the lift. She had tried to cover up the tan with white powder and heavy black eye makeup.

"Hi," I replied.

"I see your girlfriend is feeling better. Nice costumes, by the way," the woman said, and Thorn stared at them as only Thorn could.

Even without using her vampire features, Thorn could give a stare that would frighten people. She was a dark lioness, and her power felt almost tangible when she allowed it to show. The couple stood transfixed for a few seconds by Thorn's glare until I nudged her with my elbow and she broke it off.

"Okay, good to see you again," the man replied as he snapped out of his trance and hurried away with his girlfriend.

I sniggered to myself. I felt jealous when I saw them earlier, wishing I could have a normal life like theirs, but here they were pretending to be vampires to escape their normal, mundane lives. I had the real thing.

We continued our search through the rest of the conference. As we walked through the bar, I caught the eye of a redhead girl dressed in a steampunk vampire outfit; tartan skirt, heavy laced-up black boots, and purple velvet corset. She looked over at me and smiled.

Scarlett? Please... could it be?

No, it wasn't, but my reaction surprised me. Only a few months ago, I thought she had betrayed me, and I wanted bloody revenge on her. Time away had dissipated those feelings and hope had returned. The sight of the redhead re-ignited my heart. I smiled back at the girl, still unused to the admiring glances I received. As in my mind, I couldn't shake off my image as the bullied teenage boy.

Thorn led us through the crowds, cutting a determined path through the swathes of costumed vampires and away from the redhead.

"He is here," she said, looking deep into the back of the room.

"Cool, let's go," I replied. Finally, the moment of truth had arrived. No more mysteries and we could take our first step on the path of revenge.

"No, I need to go alone. I haven't mentioned you before. I need to check it is safe. It would be too out of the ordinary for me to turn up with a human in tow."

"But you promised me the truth. You said he would help. You said tonight," I argued, glaring at her.

"No, I said we would meet him tonight. You must be patient. He will help. Just let me scout it out and clear the air with him first."

"Clear the air?"

"Yeah, I haven't seen him for a while. We have a lot to catch up on. Plus, we didn't exactly part on good terms."

"What?"

"Vampires fight a lot with each other. A lot of egos. I'm sure it will be fine. Go and amuse yourself with that redhead you saw earlier. I will be back before dawn."

"What?" I replied, open mouthed.

"The steampunk vampire. I quite fancy her myself. Go and have some fun. I will return."

"You okay with that?" I asked, surprised at her suggestion.

She smiled. "One skill you will need as a vampire is the art of seduction. You may have developed the looks, but you need to work a bit on your technique. You may even have the residual powers to entice and attract her."

"Really, what powers?" Now I was interested.

"We can send out powerful chemical signals, hormones that attract and entice. It's part of our weapons as predators. Talk to her and imagine your body seeping out signals to her. I have detected you emitting these signals whenever a girl catches your eye. You probably aren't aware. It's slight, but obviously one of the remnant powers leftover from the vampire formula."

The idea of such power excited me, but I had first-hand experience of Thorn's jealous streak. Back in London, she had killed me after I embraced and talked with Scarlett at a nightclub. Thankfully, the formula brought me back to life.

"Okay, but won't it upset you, me with another woman?" I asked, remembering her reaction. I didn't want to die again.

"That was different. You loved her still. Betrayal of the heart, not the body. You are young and you should experience and enjoy life. I shouldn't be the only woman you have ever known. We have hundreds of years to look forward to."

She looked deep into my eyes, hypnotising me with her stare before launching into a passionate kiss. I staggered, stunned by its vigour, but held upright in her embrace. I returned the kiss and a loud cheer arose around us.

"Go now and enjoy. I will see you soon," she said, turned and blended into the crowd towards a dark man heading through the main doors. I got just a glimpse. He filled the doorway with his head scraping underneath the frame. He wore dark clothing with a fake sword on his back and hair shaven at the sides, and I recognised his costume as a hybrid vampire hunter. The costume triggered the realisation that I had turned into a hybrid myself through the injections. Still majority human, but the remnant vampire powers enhanced me way beyond the average person.

A couple of guys slapped me on the back as Thorn walked away.

"Is she your girlfriend?" one asked with a big grin on his face.

The question was harmless and meant in good spirits, but recalled memories of the gang that bullied me back in college when I dated Scarlett. I could almost picture Barry's big forehead and evil grin. I knew what they were thinking. *How did you get a woman like that?*

"Yeah. So what?" I answered and shoved the guy off his feet, stumbling him into a couple of costumed Draculas.

Other fans dressed as 'Lost Boys' stepped in to calm it down as the Draculas shouted and pushed back at the man. I slipped away to follow Thorn and Cassius, and swerved through the crowd and away from the commotions behind me. I hoped it would hide my tracks from Thorn's psychic abilities. I steadied my mind, blocking out thoughts by filling it with junk as not to alert her to my presence. They stood just outside the front doors of the lobby in the dark of night, while I hid behind a marble pillar to listen.

"Does he know the truth yet?" Cassius asked.

"No."

"So he doesn't know we aren't vampires."

"The time isn't right. It's too much to take in straight off, and we need to be sure first that we can trust him," she answered, paused and looked about. "Not here. Let's go somewhere more private. We have years of news to talk about."

I followed, but just saw a blur of speed as they disappeared into the darkness.

I stood gazing out into the Vegas night, my head rattling from the surprise.

Not Vampires! What the hell are they? What the hell did I transform into?

Chapter Five

I sat on the steps outside the hotel, staring out into the night. I couldn't believe what I had just heard. *Not vampires.* My muscles tensed, anger and rage pouring through them. I wanted to shout and scream. How could she have lied to me? Everything I believed in had been a lie, but why? Why lie about being vampires? Unless they were something worse.

It was the only thing that made sense. I sat outside on the steps, running it over and over in my mind, but came to no conclusion. If they weren't vampires, what the hell were they and what the hell had I turned into? I had fangs, a thirst for blood, supernatural strength. Maybe aliens? No, that's stupid. Yeah, because vampires are so normal.

I wanted answers. I wanted the truth, but I knew I would get nothing until her return. Tomorrow I would confront her. For now, I had time to kill and thoughts to block out. I needed to keep busy. I re-entered the convention and sought out the steampunk vampire to test my undiscovered seduction skills and get a drink. If Thorn wanted me to test my seduction skills, then I would, and I no longer worried about the guilt it may bring. I would test them thoroughly and enjoy it too.

I walked back into the convention and skirted around the sides as the red jacketed security guards broke up the scuffle I caused. The big fat guy I pushed over was being dragged outside by two security guards, while a glittery vampire held a bloody tissue to his nose.

I headed back to the bar towards the red haired, steampunk vampire. She sat on a stool next to the bar with a drink in her hand, and I walked up next to her and ordered a beer. She looked around and smiled. Her long red hair had that just out of bed look. She wore heavy black makeup, and eyebrow and ear piercings adorned her face. She wore a figure hugging purple velvet corset and short tartan skirt with her black leather boots just covering her knees. I smiled back while visualising the chemical signals pouring out of my body, seeping into hers, and then triggering her chemical reaction.

"Hi," I said.

"Hi," she responded.

I stood at the bar, shifting my weight from foot to foot and tapping the bar with my fingers while thinking about what to say next.

"You by yourself? What happened to that woman you were with?" she asked.

She must have noticed us earlier. I suppose Thorn always stood out in the crowd.

"She has gone off with a friend for the night."

"Oh. So you here with anyone else?" she asked.

"No. Just left alone to fend for myself for the rest of the night. My name is V, sorry I mean Christopher," I said.

"V, is that your vampire name? Mine is Pandora."

I frowned at her, unsure what to say. Thorn told me there were no other vampires in the building.

"What's wrong?" she asked.

"You're a vampire?"

She looked puzzled and giggled.

"You are funny. Look, the place is full of vampires," she said, looking at the crowds of costumed fans.

I had been a fool. Of course, it was her name for the convention, a role-playing name.

"Of course, sorry. V stands for Vengeance."

"Cool name. Who do you want vengeance on?"

I didn't expect that. What could I say? But I could say what the hell I liked. It would just be role-play far as she knew.

"Let me buy you a drink and I will tell you all about it."

"Yeah. I'd love a drink," she replied, turning around and crossing her legs together. She tilted her head back and her flame red hair, like Scarlett's, flowed away from her face.

I ordered us a couple of beers and re-told her my story. I changed the part that I was Thorn's lover to just friends in order not to put her off. She drank quickly through the story, encouraging me to do the same as she finished hers off.

"Wow, that's a cool story. I love the way you have tied it into being here at the convention as well," she said and placed her hand on my knee.

"Thanks. What about you? Why are you here?" I asked.

"Amber is my other name, but let me tell you about Pandora," she said, downing another drink and waving me on to drink up. I bought another round of beers.

"I am Pandora, the vampire, and I am the chosen one. I must find the vampire prince and protect him from the shadow clans of the Isles of Blood. They want his blood to invoke the blood demons and destroy the vampire clans and reign as kings."

"Where do you think you will find this prince?"

"I think I already have," she answered, smirking and squeezing my leg.

I laughed, reached down and put my hand on top of hers.

"I like that. How would you protect this prince from all these other vampires? How can you be sure who is after him?" I asked.

"I plan to seduce him and lure him back to my bed chambers and keep him there all night until the danger has gone," she said and finished another beer.

"He'd be a lucky man."

"You are," she replied and slid off the barstool, placed her hand in mine and led me off through the convention.

We grabbed a taxi outside, scrambled into the back, and held hands, gazing at each other. The taxi arrived at her hotel and I paid. We caught the lift by ourselves and rode up to the fifth floor. On the way up, we embraced in a passionate drunken kiss and resumed a regular appearance as the doors opened.

Once in her room, she flicked on the lights and slammed the door shut. She flung herself at me by jumping up and wrapping her legs around my waist. I grabbed hold of her as she covered me with kisses. I carried her over to the bed, and we crashed onto it. We exchanged kisses, and her hands yanked at my belt. I aided her by unbuttoning and kicking off my trousers. I sat her up and peeled off her velvet corset, then unzipped her tartan skirt and flung it across the room.

She wore black suspenders and stockings underneath. I grinned and removed my t-shirt. Her eyes widened, and she smiled at my well-defined muscles. A reaction I wasn't expecting, having never stripped for anyone but Thorn. I climbed back onto the bed, and we carried on kissing, touching and it descending into frantic drunken sex.

Sex with Pandora was my first time with a human, and although drunken and awkward, it felt fantastic. On occasions, the sight of her red hair let my fantasies run free, allowing my imagination to envisage Scarlett lying beneath me. I still missed her and the life we could have had together. Afterwards, Amber and I chatted some more until we collapsed asleep, both tired and drunk.

The next morning, I stirred in bed from the light shining through the windows of the hotel room. My head fuzzy from drink, and I rolled over to protect my eyes and enjoy more sleep. The red hair of Pandora lay across the pillow, gently covering the top of her neck. Thorn had been right about my remnant power, and I had surprised myself with the ease with which I spoke to her. My confidence had brimmed when we talked, as I had correctly observed the positive body language signals. In the background, I sensed an underlying current of desire as we flirted. Pandora liked a drink. I couldn't be sure if I was trying to pick her up, or if she was getting me drunk on purpose to pick me up. Did it matter?

In the end, she had swept me along with the combination of drink and fantasy role-play. Maybe I didn't need to do more. Maybe that is how the power worked. Regardless, we had a wild night, unlike anything I had experienced with Thorn, because Pandora was human and the excitement and responses were more in tune. Having sex with a vampire, as a human, is fantastic, but always a little one sided. I could never be sure if Thorn really enjoyed it. Only the times as a vampire I felt an equal, as I could match her physical prowess, passion and stamina.

Pandora stirred and rolled over in the bed.

"Morning, V," she said.

Oh, I forgot I had told her my vampire name. Then, as the fog of my drunken memory cleared, I remembered I had told her all of it, knowing she thought it was just role-play like her identity of Pandora, the steampunk vampire. Likewise, she told me her story.

Her real name was Amber; she lived in a town half a day's drive from Vegas, where she worked as a waitress in a sports bar. She enjoyed watching vampire films and reading books. She took part in web chats and enjoyed the costume role-play idea. When she heard of the convention, she saved up and caught a coach down, hoping to meet like-minded people. She sat in the bar that night working up the courage to join some groups, but when I appeared, she changed her plans.

Her identity as Pandora was escapism, her way of escaping the harsh realities of the world and her situation. Funny, my identity was escapism as well from the gangs, except I couldn't take mine off and fold it away in a box. My escapism had become real, and I had fresh problems with the Hunter organisation manipulating me, and Thorn lying about her true nature. I still struggled to comprehend that she wasn't a vampire. What else could she be?

The night before, I had asked Pandora what other things looked and acted like vampires but weren't vampires. As she enjoyed this fantasy world, I thought she might know other creatures who acted the same way. She laughed at the complete immersion of my character V and had just poured me another drink from the minibar. She had said vampires in the stories are often described in many ways, and that Thorn sounded like a vampire to her.

In bed, Pandora's eyes half opened. Her smudged black eye makeup framed her sleepy eyes and red lipstick smeared on her lips from our passionate night together. I placed my hand on her hip and felt the suspenders and stockings she had revealed under her tartan skirt. I found her strangely alluring in her dishevelled state as memories of our frenetic drunken sex flashed back. She ran her hand down my arm, and her nails brushed lightly against my bicep.

"Glad you're still here," she said.

"Well, no point in rushing off. I don't need to be back now until sunset," I answered.

She laughed again, wriggled across the bed, wrapped her arms around my neck, and kissed me.

"Well, looks like we have some time to kill. The room is booked till one o'clock," she said.

I smiled and kissed her back to answer. I didn't need to get back. Thorn would be asleep until dark, and she wanted me to get some training in. This was her idea, not mine. I still needed some more practice, I justified to myself. Anyway, I didn't know who or what I would be going back to, vampire or something else? The deception annoyed me, and I felt no guilt in staying with Pandora. One bad turn deserved another.

At one o'clock, we booked out of the room and had a few hours to spend together before she caught her coach back home, and I would need to go back to the hotel. Her stomach rumbled, and she admitted she had lived off chocolate bars since arriving, as the trip had cost all of her savings. I promised her lunch if she did me a favour, which she readily agreed to. I hailed a taxi to the all-you-can-eat buffet, so she could fill up for her journey home. She made up for lost food, and I joined in to help recover from my hangover.

Once the meal was completed, she kept her promise by accompanying me on a gondola through the canals of the Venetian Hotel, with my arms around her while watching the people on the bridges as we glided underneath. Yesterday, I had watched other couples jealously and today I got to experience a taste of normality. As she turned to look at the scenery drift by, I imagined I was with Scarlett and that she had never betrayed me. I imagined our lives had taken a different course, and somehow we were now drifting down the real canals in Venice. Maybe on our honeymoon. Amber turned back around, shattering the illusion, but the trip was still enjoyable.

Afterwards, we headed to the bus station and sat in silence as we waited for our time to end. The call went out over the speaker at the bus station. Her coach was boarding.

We stood up out of the rows of grey plastic seats, and then hugged and squeezed each other tight. We kissed again, and she shoved a piece of paper into my hand.

"If you ever pass my way, be sure to drop in, V. I would love to show you about. Take you down to the Sports Bar where I work and introduce you to Gerry. He's like my surrogate father," she said.

"I will. If the chance ever arises." I placed the paper inside my wallet.

We exchanged another last kiss, and she walked off to the coach. I waved goodbye and left.

I had really enjoyed that night and day, and not just because of the sex, but the fact I could relax. There was no hidden agenda with Pandora. With Thorn, I always needed to be mindful of what I said and did. Doubts still crossed my mind about our relationship. She was a beautiful vampire that I saved from prison and in return, she promised to turn me into a vampire one day. I played some part in the puzzle of the vampire formula and her conflict with the Hunters. With Scarlett, I could never believe someone like her would have dated someone like me. I had found out the truth. I'd been lied to in order to manipulate me.

With Pandora, it was just two single people wanting some fun, no agendas, no unbelievable reason or strange coincidences, but just two lonely people having fun together. Even though I had used my powers to seduce her, I hadn't the next day.

I still had a few hours left before Thorn woke and I could get the truth. With time to kill, I toured around the rest of Vegas, shopping and gambling at the slot machines before finally heading back. I had walked off the regular tourist routes as I wandered around. I walked past the lap dancing club I saw advertised on the drive in, then passed a few small bars where locals gathered. As I strolled around the other sights, I remembered what Cassius had said to Thorn.

"So he doesn't know we aren't vampires."

What else could they be? None of it made any sense, but Thorn had promised me the answers. As the daylight faded, I headed back to get the truth once and for all.

Chapter Six

I walked back to give myself time to think and delay the confrontation with Thorn. Before I saw her, I had to get it straight in my head. I had to get an answer. As I walked back, I sensed something out of place and felt small sparks firing up my spine to tingle on my neck, like someone blowing on it. Maybe it was part of my psychic senses detecting something unusual. I glanced over my shoulder and used the reflection in cars and shop windows to get a picture without making it too obvious.

In the window of a shop, I saw a man with short cropped dark hair, dressed casually in jeans, t-shirt, sunglasses and a lightweight cream jacket. When I stopped, he looked at his phone, pretending to press some buttons. I walked on again, glancing side-ways into bars and shop windows. He still followed on. I took a right turn, but he went the other way. I relaxed and carried on up the street, but the strange feeling hadn't gone. I was either brilliant or paranoid.

I stopped and retrieved my phone to look at the maps and peeked back down the street. The man had gone straight on when I turned, but behind me, another man dressed casually in jeans, mirrored sunglasses and black jacket seemed to linger and talk into his phone. I paced quickly up the street, turning right at the top, passed the Starbucks and then went full circle back on to my previous route.

The second man followed. I stopped and held my phone, pretending to take photos, but I had flipped the camera to look back over my shoulder instead to watch him on the touchscreen. The second man was still following but trying to keep his distance. I strode straight over the crossing, then planned on turning right again at the next junction. The second man turned off but walked right past the first man in the cream jacket who had come back up the street. I noticed a small nod between them in a reflection of a parked car window. I walked off again with the first man in the cream jacket trailing. They were definitely following me.

I walked on, taking the next turn down the road, walking faster, but he kept up. We passed an alleyway and out came the second man with the black jacket, and the man with the cream jacket turned into the alley. I started taking random routes through the back streets to see if they kept appearing. They moved up closer and closer until I caught sight through an alleyway of the black jacketed man running down the street parallel to mine, in order to swap places again.

I sprinted off, pushing through the pedestrians on the sidewalk, trying to lose my stalkers and test my theory. The man in the cream jacket sprinted after me. I glanced behind to see the black jacketed man run out from an alleyway to the side of the other man. Their cover was blown, and they gave chase.

I darted across the busy road, rolling across a car bonnet and bouncing on the top of another, but the men kept chasing as cars screeched to a halt and horns beeped. I ran in no particular direction, knocking past people and pulling over bins to slow them down. I turned right into an alley to cut through the back streets so they would lose sight, but I ran into a high wall that blocked the alleyway and my path to freedom. I skidded to a halt, looking for somewhere to hide. I made a dash for a row of large skip bins, but as the men ran past, they caught sight of me and turned in. They had me cornered.

They strode down the alley, removing their sunglasses and checking behind them. I stood in the middle of the alleyway to confront them. The man in the cream jacket pulled his watch to his mouth and spoke into a concealed microphone.

I considered my options. I could run at them and try to barge past, or wait and see what they wanted.

"All alone, little boy? No mummy to protect you?" the man in the cream jacket said.

"Mummy. What are you talking about?" I replied.

"Your substitute Mummy, Thorn. That's what the psych profile says. Is she not here to protect you from the nasty men?"

"I can look after myself and don't you dare talk about my mum."

"Mummy's boy is getting upset," the brown haired man in the black jacket said.

"Going to take the formula, are you? Look about you, it's daylight, won't work silly little boy. Going to have to face us man to man," he said, smirking at his colleague.

They were wrong about the formula. It would work in the daylight. I just hadn't used it or carried it since witnessing Barry transform into a hideous monster, so the result was the same.

"Thorn isn't my mum. She is my lover," I said, and puffed out my chest and smiled.

"Oh, Vampire toy are you. A walking, talking snack and plaything for Thorn."

I was growing bored with their insults and attempts to make me lose my temper.

"What do you want?" I asked, cutting to the point.

They grinned.

"You know who we are and what we want," the dark haired man in the cream jacket said, as his brown haired friend checked behind them again.

"Hunters?" I asked.

"Yes. We want you to come back with us. Tell us where Thorn and the formula are."

"Why? It's your fault I am in this situation. You arranged it all."

They looked at each other and shrugged shoulders.

"I don't know about that. I just have my orders. You can ask my boss back at the base. I am here to take you back. By force if necessary," he said, and they walked forward until they stood just a few steps away.

"Sorry, I am not going anywhere with you two. They probably want to cut me open."

"I don't know or care," the black jacket man shrugged, "It's your choice. The easy or hard way? Let's face it, without the formula or vampire mummy, you're just a boy."

They obviously weren't aware of the changes the formula had left behind or were trying to scare me. I had to choose - easy or hard. Let them take me or fight, but they were Hunters. They had trained to fight vampires. What could I do against them? I was just a teenager, but I had vowed that day I killed Barry and became Vengeance that I would never back away from a fight again. I wanted vengeance, and it would start here.

The cream jacket hunter turned and looked as I raised my eyebrows in pretend recognition of someone behind them. No more words. I front kicked him in the stomach, knocking him over. The other hunter jumped forwards tackling me to the floor and punching at my head. I dodged, kicked my legs up in the air, and then slammed them down while I pushed up with my body and pitched him off to the side. The cream jacket hunter ran back as I rolled over and stood up. I sprinted to the blocked end of the alley, and he chased me to the end. I ran up the wall, somersaulted backwards and grabbed his head, and then slammed it onto the floor on my descent. His head made a sickening crack against the concrete floor as blood spurted out over the bottom of my black jeans.

He lay motionless, with blood pouring from his head and pooling around his body. I couldn't believe what I had just done. My remaining vampire instincts knew what to do. I had reacted with deadly precision.

The remaining hunter looked on horrified at his fallen colleague and whipped out his gun and aimed.

"Stop, or I will shoot," he shouted, still glancing over at the bleeding hunter.

I placed my hands on my head, and he waved me away from the body over to the wall. "Move now," he shouted again, and then walked behind me and crouched down by the man's head and placed a hand on his neck.

"Luke. Luke. Are you okay?" he said, fingers on the man's neck. There was no reply. "He's dead. You killed him. You bastard."

The Hunter raced over and thumped me on the head with the butt of the gun. I staggered into the wall and collapsed to my knees.

"Up. Now," he shouted, waving the gun upwards.

I stood up again, my head spinning.

"Turn around, face the wall."

I followed the order, hands against the wall, holding myself upright. The gun pressed against the back of my head, shoving my forehead into the wall.

"He's dead. You killed Luke. He was my best friend. What am I going to tell his wife? It's his anniversary next week."

"Self defence!" I said, thinking he really wanted an answer. I hadn't intended to kill anyone.

"You think you're funny. I should blow your brains out," he said, and I felt the gun push further against the back of my head as he tightened his grip.

"Your bosses aren't going to be happy? I thought you needed to bring me back alive."

Silence for a few moments until the pressure of the gun decreased.

"Yes, alive but for how long? That will be revenge enough once they get their hands on you. Maybe they will let me join in. I am going to let you live, but you will wish I hadn't. You will pay for what you have done today. And the others that you and that bitch killed before."

He removed the gun from my head.

"Hands down," he said, voice shaking, and I heard the handcuffs clicking open, ready to restrain me.

I put my hands down as instructed. As the cold metal of the handcuffs touched, I twisted my wrists over. I grabbed his arm and pulled him into me, using his inward force to pivot away from the wall. He stumbled into the wall and shot against the brickwork. The bullet ricocheted off into his foot. He yelled in agony, as he went crashing down and spilt the gun from his grip. I scooped it up and levelled it at him. I wanted to blow his brains out, but I paused. I had killed the other one already, but that counted as self-defence. This would be cold blooded murder, but it wouldn't be the first time.

"Tell your friends I am not a bullied school kid anymore. You come for me, then someone will get hurt. I am no mummy's boy that you can scare or bully. I will bust you up, formula or no formula. Ask your friend lying in his own blood," I said, and then pistol whipped him in the back of the head, knocking him out cold. I let him live to act as a warning to the others.

I stuffed the gun in the back of my jeans, with my shirt concealing its existence. I ran from the alley, fearful the police would have been called to the gunshot. A few streets over, I grabbed a taxi back to the hotel to warn Thorn of the danger. We were being hunted.

Chapter Seven

I stumbled my way up to the room just as darkness fell. My head still hurt, but fear drove me onwards. The answers to vampires or not vampires could wait. I just wanted to be back in her arms and feel safe again. There would be time enough for the truth. For now, I had to warn her.

The key card slipped into the door slot, and I pulled it out, triggering the green light to flash in acceptance. I pushed the door open, preparing to find Thorn awake. A hand grabbed my arm, flung me over their shoulder, sending me crashing to the floor against the base of the bed. The door slammed and Thorn stormed over. She still wore the film vampire costume of tight PVC corset, catsuit, and black leather boots. Her hair had shaken loose of the straight bob and back into her tousled raven locks.

"Where the hell have you been?" she shouted. "I have been waiting all day and night in this costume for you, as I promised." She grabbed a white bag off the side table by the door and threw it at me, "this is for you, happy birthday."

Inside, I found a gold necklace with a pair of golden fangs suspended between the two chains. I pulled myself back together and sat up against the base of the bed. It didn't matter I had upset her, or that she had been waiting for me. She told me to go off with Pandora. Worse of all, she had lied to me. *"So, he doesn't know we aren't vampires."* I remembered Cassius saying to her and my anger took hold instead of guilt, or fear of being hunted. I pulled the gun out, aiming it straight at her. Her face froze in surprise and then eyes burnt a fiery red and fangs cut through her gums.

"Don't you dare make me the bad man," I said. "I am sick of your lies. I want the truth right now, or one of us dies."

"The truth," she shouted.

"Yes, the truth. I heard you and Cassius talking. What are you if you aren't a vampire?"

She glazed over, face in shock, vampire features retreating and she stared for a moment.

"Where did you get that gun?" she asked.

Changing the subject. *Typical.*

"Hunters. Now tell me the truth."

She checked outside the door.

"They gave you this gun? Are you betraying me?" she said, eyes reverting to red.

"No. I took it from them."

She sighed in relief, and her eyes switched back to sky blue again.

"Sorry V, but this will have to wait. We must leave immediately."

I kept the gun aimed as she started packing her clothes.

"No, I want answers right now," I shouted.

"Don't be foolish. The Hunters are coming. We need to leave and find Cassius, safety in numbers. He has agreed to tell you everything tonight. I promise we will answer all your questions," she said as she flung her clothes into the bag and started packing my clothes as well.

"Come on. Get a move on," she insisted without looking at me as she busied herself getting our stuff together as if the gun and our argument didn't matter.

She was probably right; I had come back tonight to warn her so we could escape. I put the gun back into my jeans and started gathering up my gear. Thorn smiled and then slapped my bum as she walked past.

"Hey," I said.

"Once we speak with Cassius, you can tell me where you have been all day," she said.

"You're jealous. Again!"

She frowned, re-emerging her vampire features, and then a knock thundered on the door. Perfect timing. Her rage had returned.

I looked at Thorn, waiting for the all clear, having learnt my lesson last time with the bodyguards stealing our money. She closed her eyes to focus her psychic senses through the door.

"It's okay. I am expecting them," she said.

I walked over and opened it.

At the door, a man in his fifties stood wearing a smart grey suit. He had grey hair and a bushy moustache. Flanking him stood two bodyguards in black suits. Behind them stood the red-haired bodyguard who took our money, and Victor, the slick-haired man she had won it from. The red-haired cowboy started shaking in fear at the sight of Thorn.

"Come in, Mr. Vitsco," Thorn said, standing there like she had no cares in the world.

I moved out of the way as Mr. Vitsco walked past me with arms stretched out to Thorn, and they exchanged kisses to the side of each other's cheeks.

"Good to see you again, Thorn. I like the outfit," he said, eyeing her up and down.

"It's for the convention," she replied.

"That is very cheeky of you, Thorn. I don't think it's meant for actual vampires," he said.

"You know me, Francesco. I like to flaunt it," she replied.

He smiled back and nodded with a small chuckle to himself.

"I remember only too well," he said, "Thorn, I must apologise for my brother. He is an idiot," he added, looking back at the door.

The brother, Victor, limped in, sporting a black eye and bruised cheeks.

He looked at Thorn. "I am sorry," he said and skulked back out the door again. Thorn never mentioned beating him up, and I guessed his own brother had arranged it.

"The money boys," Mr. Vitsco said, and the two bodyguards walked either side of him and placed the metal briefcases on the floor, twisted them around and opened them up. I had never seen so much money in my life. Bundles of cash crammed into the metal briefcases.

"Half a million dollars in total. Quarter a million, your original win and the other quarter as an apology from my brother," Mr. Vitsco said.

Thorn nodded and signalled me to take the cases. I clipped them both down and carried them to the bed.

"Thorn, I hope that concludes this incident. But should you really be gambling in Vegas? It is unfair considering your talents," Mr. Vitsco said.

"Maybe. But the other syndicates would be unhappy to hear your brother reneged on his bets. You would have more than me to worry about," she answered.

"True. You have a safe journey. Come and visit sometime, but please find another unsuspecting idiot next time. We should be friends, not enemies," he said and signalled his men to leave.

I glared at the red-haired bodyguard as he left and shut the door. I still wanted revenge for him shoving the pistol in my face the other night. He wouldn't ever bother us again if the terrified look on his face was any indication. Thorn must have given him a real horror show when she fed on the other guard.

Thorn stood directly behind me as I turned back, and I jumped back into the door in surprise. She had pulled on her long black leather coat and had all the briefcases and our suitcases at her feet.

"Let's go. This money will come in handy en route. We can pay by cash and avoid any tracking," she said.

She picked up the cases and headed for the door, and I followed on carrying the others. We paid the hotel bill in cash, and then went around the corner and stole a car. We loaded up and headed off to find Cassius.

On route, I told her what had happened with the Hunters in the alleyway. She remarked how far I come to take down two Hunters. The Hunters were highly trained to fight vampires, they were usually ex-military, or mercenaries, and for me to beat them in my human form was significant.

We drove down the strip illuminated by the bright lights of the casinos and then passed the replica Eiffel Tower, all lit up with bright yellow lights.

"Shame we couldn't stay for longer. I wanted to take you around the sights. Go up the Tower and take in the view and go on the gondolas at night," she said with a disappointed smile.

Shock at her statement must have shown.

"What?" she asked, double-taking my angry expression.

"You promised not to read my mind anymore."

"I haven't," she replied indignantly, and we carried on in silence.

The car rattled along the road out of the Vegas Strip. I watched in the mirror as it faded into the background and the lights merged. We never got to share the hot tub and champagne together.

We drove into Vegas city, and then finally out to the trailer park where Cassius lived.

"Why all the way out here? Isn't he stopping in a hotel?" I asked.

"You've seen him?"

"Yes."

"He isn't exactly inconspicuous. If ever someone looked like a vampire, it was Cassius. He stays away from people as much as possible. It is easier for him that way."

We reached *Happy Trails Park*, clinging to the edge of Vegas and behind it, the desert stretched out to the horizon. It was the kind of place that people low on their luck and struggling to leave Vegas lived. That meant hopeless gamblers, addicts, and adult workers.

The car swung through the welcome arch and curtains flickered on a few trailers as we weaved through the strange community. A man carrying a bottle in a brown bag stumbled across in front of the car. His clothes were filthy, face unshaven, and eyes absent.

"Nice place your friend is staying at."

"Perfect place, you mean. No one around here asks questions."

We rumbled along the dirt road towards the back of the park, passing the inhabitants starting their nightly routines of getting ready for work or getting high. We reached the back of the park with a chain link metal fence running around the perimeter. Along the sides of the metal fence, a few dried up bushes that broke up the fence line, but they were nothing more than dried up tangles of sticks in the ground. The place felt like a prison, and I guessed that was how it felt for many of its inhabitants.

In the corner nestled in against the fence, a trailer with a big black van parked directly behind it at right angles. We were nearly there. I would have another piece of the puzzle and some more of the truth. I felt excited about what they could really be if not vampires. They must be something even stranger.

"This is it," Thorn said and pulled in on the right hand side of the trailer.

I climbed out of the car, with it between me and the trailer door, and scanned about. Something seemed wrong. I sniffed the air, and the smell of decaying flesh curled my nose. Thorn copied, sniffed the air and shut her eyes to focus on the rest of her superior senses.

"Quickly," she shouted and pointed at the door of the trailer.

From behind the other trailers, a group of ten creatures charged out with swords and guns at the ready. The creatures had grey decaying skin, yellow fangs and bloodshot, dead, black eyes and wore dirty, ragged clothes.

Thorn unleashed her vampire powers; claws out, fangs gleaming white and eyes blood red. She ducked under the first swipe of the blade swinging at her head and rammed the creature back into the dirt with her on top. Then she grabbed the blade and rolled off onto her feet.

Behind me, a creature attacked. I turned and blocked the punch. It bruised my arm and forced me backwards as two other decaying creatures joined in. Shots fired and bullets exploded onto the sides of the trailer with glowing blue liquid, just missing Thorn. I reached for my gun in the back of my jeans and shot the creature firing at her. It staggered backwards, dropping a strange gun to the floor.

The creature in front leapt forward, scratching at my face. I fired several shots into its torso. It slowed it down, and I stepped back to gain some ground. It charged again. I jumped forward, drop-kicking it back into the two following creatures. I crashed to the floor. Another creature flashed around the side, sword in hand and swiped down onto my prone position. I rolled out of the way and under the car for protection.

Thorn fought two of the creatures on either side of her. From my position under the car, I watched their feet moved backwards and forwards. The creature that had attacked me dropped to the floor and started crawling towards me under the car, growling and snapping its fangs. I took my chances and kicked through the knee of the creature fighting Thorn on the other side of the car. The bone snapped and it crashed to the floor, spilling its sword. I rolled out, grabbed its sword and swiped back at the creature's claws thrashing at my leg from under the car.

The sword cut its hand off, but then I felt a bite on my shoulder. The creature with the smashed knee. I plunged the sword under my arm and into its body. It screamed, releasing its bite. I stood up and looked down at it. I recognised the creature from Thorn's memories, one of the dead and decaying vampires. It had the fangs, claws and transformed eyes similar to Thorn's, but they were weaker, colder, broken and rotten. Their skin was filthy and cold to the touch. Their eyes black with bloodshot veins, instead of pure blood red. The claws and fangs were a discoloured nicotine yellow. I drove the sword further through its heart. It grabbed at the blade, fighting for its life as it disintegrated into a mound of ash. I guessed the swords were silver, but the handles were just metal for them to use it.

Thorn dispatched another opponent and shouted at me, "Duck!"

I did, and she swiped over my head, decapitating a vampire behind me. Its body came crashing to the floor and disintegrated to ash across my back. She ran up the car bonnet, jumped and somersaulted with the sword cutting through the putrid flesh of a creature as she landed. Fighting in her tight PVC vampire costume, she reminded me of the film character she was portraying.

The trailer door burst off its hinges as Cassius charged out with sword in hand. He barged past and attacked the other decomposing vampires. I followed in, firing bullets into the creatures and aiming at the heart in the hope it would cause maximum damage.

I reached for the strange gun, scooping it up and shooting at the vampires. The bullets hit a cold vampire and punctured the dead flesh, allowing the liquid to drain inside the wound. Then shards of light radiated from the inside of its body, as a furnace burned the flesh into lava. The heat reached a blinding level, and I shielded my eyes as the flaming vampire exploded into ash and drifted away in the hot desert air. The remaining vampires protected themselves from the explosion of ash. Then fled into the dark corners of the trailer park and scaled the wire fences. I dropped the strange gun clattering to the dusty ground and slumped down, holding the bite wound on my shoulder.

Thorn came back with Cassius at her side and stood in front of me. He looked even scarier face-to-face. His big muscular frame and brooding dark stare, casting a shadow even without the presence of any light.

Thorn pointed at the fleeing, decaying creatures. "The truth. They are vampires."

"We are Dragans," Cassius said and growled.

Chapter Eight

"Inside human. I will take care of your bite," Cassius said, and hauled me to my feet and helped me into the trailer.

Inside, I slumped onto the sofa and grabbed at my bite mark. Cassius rummaged around the messy trailer. Finally, he pulled a big bag and sorted through its contents, fishing out a first aid kit.

"We shouldn't stay too long. They will be back," Thorn said, looking out the window.

"Yes, let me bandage this little one and we can be on our way," he replied.

"Who you calling little?" I said, feeling the need to respond to his comment.

"You are the little one," he said again, "remove your top so I can clean the wound." I pulled off my black top, and he cleaned away the blood with a sterile wipe. "Normally, a vampire bite will get infected as they carry all sorts of bacteria, but we have it early. Plus, I sense you are stronger and more resilient than a normal human. Yes, I definitely get the feeling of power from your body."

I craned my neck to stare up at him. He crowded the small trailer with his vast dark frame. He was a giant of a man, and I understood what Thorn had said about him. Had I never known about the existence of vampires and met him, I would have sensed something unusual and terrifying about him. I was expecting a normal introduction, not fighting off decaying vampires. So if Thorn and he weren't vampires, but Dragans, then what the hell is a Dragan?

His hazel eyes narrowed as he stared down at me, and his voice bellowed up from the darkness. "A Dragan is an old creature. Before vampires," he said. I guessed he could read minds as well. "I will explain it on the way."

Thorn had already made her way to Cassius' van, getting our cases and throwing them in the back. Cassius finished applying the bandage and put away the first aid kit. He zipped up the bag, slung it over his shoulder and helped me out of my seat. I pulled my top gently back on over the wound. We left the trailer, and Cassius threw his bag into the van with our cases and climbed into the driver's seat.

The van was black with tinted windows. Behind the front seats was a wooden panel with a door for access to the back of the van. I guessed the back of the van acted as a bolthole from the Sun. There were three seats in the front, two passengers and the driver's seat. I slid along the black leather seats and sat between Cassius and Thorn.

He started the engine and pulled away from the trailer park, weaving us back through the dirt road and the other trailers, and then onto the highway. I stared at him, wondering what the hell was a Dragan. He didn't flinch from my stare, staying focused on the road.

"Tell me then, the whole truth. If they are vampires, and you are Dragans, why are they after you? Why do you seem so similar? They are like dead, decaying versions," I said, staring at Cassius impatiently for answers.

"I will tell you the truth. It will be easier for me to tell you than Thorn," he said.

Thorn angled her body away and stared out the window, watching the dark desert go by.

"It's a long story, but we have plenty of time on the road. For now, just listen and don't ask any questions until the end. You understand?" he said, frowning at me.

"Yes. I am all ears," I replied.

"A long time ago, a power existed in the world within certain people. We would probably call them 'Mages.' They could use this power, this magic for good and evil. Also linked to each Mage and were Dragons from where the magic channelled."

"Dragons?"

"Yes. Christianity despised magic and dragons and set out to annihilate it all from the Earth. They did a good job as soon only four dragons and four mages survived."

I listened intently as Thorn continued to stare out the window. I could see her face drained of colour and saddened by the story.

"One mage had an idea for escape. They gathered together on a high mountain to hear him out."

I nodded, willing him on while trying to work out what dragons had to do with them and vampires.

"He offered them a way out from being hunted down and wiped out by the humans. They couldn't hide forever as the size of a dragon was too revealing, and the Mages' magic was the only means of protection and could be reported back to someone. Plus, with the execution of so many Mages and Dragons, magic was dying. Time was running out."

He paused and took a slug of water.

"And what next?" I asked impatiently.

"A pact. He could use the last of the magic to create a new creature, a hybrid from Dragon and Mage. He had already tested it with a wolf and a man and it worked."

"You mean werewolves?" I said, excited at this revelation.

"Yes. They had an agreement and each Mage paired with their Dragon. Together, they conjured up the last of the magic in the world and channelled it into themselves over two stormy nights and two blazing hot days."

He took another drink, checked the road sign and turned off onto another highway.

"Sorry, I got distracted. From the smoke and ash, a rose a new creature, four of them called 'Dragans."

"You two are a Mage and Dragon hybrid then. That is what I turn into, not a vampire."

"Questions at the end, remember? The Dragans needed to change partners to keep the gene pool as diverse as possible. Dragan children had been born through various partnerships. However, jealousy and love got in the way, and war broke out amongst the Dragans. One of the Dragans discovered their blood still ran with magic. He found that after feeding on a human, if he was to give the human his blood when near death, it would turn into a weaker copy of himself. He used this new knowledge to create an army of the 'Turned' and attacked the other Dragan houses."

Those creatures I fought were the Turned. It was starting to make sense.

"Of course, the others soon realised this secret and raised their own armies. Many Dragans died until a truce was called and the Earth carved up into four parts, four houses to rule each domain. However, the damage was done. The Turned had grown in great numbers and eventually turned on their masters, nearly destroying the entire Dragan race. Today, there must only be less than ten of us in the world and the Turned still hunt us. Ask your questions now."

"Those creatures were the Turned?" I said, and he nodded in reply.

"You are both Dragans. When I change, I turn into a Dragan."

"Yes," he answered again.

"So the Turned are vampires and we aren't."

"The word vampire comes from humans to describe the creatures of the night feeding on their blood. In the stories, they are always the undead, cold and decaying. That isn't us. We are warm and still alive. Humans use the word vampires to describe both the Turned and us, but we don't like to think of ourselves as vampires. We are Dragans," he said.

I looked him squarely in the eye.

"You are a vampire," I said honestly

"It's a matter of opinion," Cassius said.

I laughed. As far as I was concerned and the rest of humanity, they were still vampires. Apparently, a better class of vampire and they considered themselves far superior, but still a vampire. Maybe they were the first vampires, but still vampires.

I nodded over at Thorn, who still stared out the window. I noticed, in the window's reflection, a red tear rolling down her face. Cassius gave a half smile as a sign of recognition.

"Thorn is a first generation born Dragan. She had a husband and young baby when a rival Dragan's Turned army, destroyed her home, killed her husband and baby, and then killed her mother and father. Thorn and I escaped."

I looked over at her and placed a consoling hand on her shoulder. It had never occurred to me she had ever experienced that kind of pain and suffering.

"Thorn retaliated and destroyed her enemies," he said.

I went to withdraw my hand as fear gripped me of her true nature, her true power. Her hand grabbed mine and held it tight as she turned back around to face me.

"It's a story I can't tell. That's why I needed Cassius," she said, her voice choking and a red tear rolling down her face. I reached out, captured the tear on my thumb and wiped it off her face. She smiled gratefully and continued her story.

"We created the Turned, and they finally turned against us all. It's our fault they plague the world, and we have been locked in a war with them ever since. They want to capture us and discover our secrets to make themselves stronger."

I nodded, understanding why they attacked.

"The Turned don't have our strength, speed or psychic abilities, and they want them. The Turned can replicate themselves as well, but they then become a copy of a copy and as such, the power reduces even further. They can create three generations of copies, as the fourth never survives, as the third copy is too weak to create from. Their weakness makes them easier to kill. Silver and UV, like us, but also flames and crucifixes will damage and kill them. As you can imagine, a hybrid of a Dragon doesn't fear the flames. The crucifixes sting us a little, but they will burn and kill a Turned if held in place long enough," Thorn said.

"What generation were the ones who attacked us?" I asked.

"Mostly third generation and a couple of second gen. First generation Turned come from Dragans and we don't do that anymore. The Turned keep first generations safe, as they are the strongest source to be copied from. To win the war, we need to eliminate the first generation to prevent any more second generations and so on," Thorn answered.

"What about Dragans? Is ten the end of the line?" I asked, trying to skirt around the memory of her dead family.

"We have tried to have more. It seems we have become infertile somehow. No Dragans are being born. No Dragan pregnancies anymore," she said, and her lips and eyes turned down.

"You are the last of the line?"

"Yes. We are the end unless we find a cure. The formula changes you into a Dragan, even if only for one night at a time. The Turned want that formula to become like us. Maybe we could use it to find a cure for our fertility issues. The Hunters want it as a weapon. But there is more," Thorn said.

I looked at her, perplexed; how much stranger could this get?

"When I was captured and placed in the prison. It was by a group of Hunters and Turned working together that have allied themselves against the remaining Dragans. Both Hunters and Turned, wanting our powers for themselves. This new threat is worse than anything we have faced before."

"Why would the Hunters work with the Turned? Surely they should hunt them as well?"

"They did hunt Turned and Dragan. It was a three-way stalemate. Now they work together."

"So, what is your plan? What are you going to do about it?" I asked.

"Now I am free. I am raising an army. I am looking for the last of the Dragans to form a strike force. The werewolves will probably join us as they hate the Turned and the Hunters. But most importantly, we have you."

I looked at her uneasily; suddenly aware I stood at the centre of an oncoming storm.

"Why me? Why am I important?"

"Because you can transform into a Dragan. They haven't been able to find anyone to do this before. You are one of a kind, unique. Your body holds the secrets for all of us. Your ability to transform could hold the key to both their quest for our powers and our cure for infertility."

I slumped in my seat. I just thought I'd come along for the ride, swept up by the events enveloping me, but discovered I was the key to winning a war.

I stared at the dark road ahead. "Where are we going?"

"Seattle. I own a majority share in a biotech research centre. They will check the formula and take samples to determine how the formula works, and why it only seems to work on you and failed on Barry. We need to find out what the formula is doing to you if some of the residual powers remain. Plus, is it still safe for you to use it?"

I nodded and it made sense. However, my head hurt not only from the attack but also from my new knowledge.

"When were you going to tell me this?" I asked.

"We didn't plan on the Turned attacking. We meant to tell you at the trailer park originally," Thorn said.

I felt exhausted taking in all the information. She would have to explain it all over again tomorrow. My eyes flickered as the long day took its toll. I blinked hard, trying to keep my eyes open.

"Rest, it is a lot to understand, and you've had a rough day," Thorn said, and pulled me over to rest my head on her shoulder as she wrapped her arm around me.

Her high heat felt comforting and encouraged me to drift off to sleep as Cassius drove us down the long, dark highway. I finally had the truth about vampires and hunters, and the reason for the formula, but I didn't feel any better for knowing.

Chapter Nine

The constant hum of the engine decreased and eventually stopped, waking me from my sleep. My head lay on Thorn's lap, and her hand stroked my hair. I sat up and looked around. In front, a red neon sign, "Nelson's Diner," glowed in the darkness. The diner sat on the side of the main highway with a small concrete parking area scattered with an assortment of cars, pickup trucks and other vans. The surrounding dirt patches provided extra parking for a couple of trucks.

Inside the diner, it looked clean and crisp. They had decorated the walls and seating in red and white, with a retro fifties theme - an old jukebox and posters of classic Hollywood film stars on the walls. The waitresses wore in a red striped fifties dress, carrying a large plates of food. My mouth watered and my empty stomach rattled despite the two recent sessions at the all-you-can-eat buffet. My body needed more food than normal to keep going. I assumed it must be another side effect of being partly Dragan.

"We are taking a break. You probably need some food as well," Thorn said.

Cassius climbed out. I turned to wait for Thorn to get out, so I could slide across the passenger seat and clamber out of the van. She didn't move but just stared at me, face frowning.

"What is it?" I asked, rubbing the sleep from my eyes.

"Where were you all day?"

She wasn't going to forget. I didn't think it mattered anymore, considering everything else that had happened.

"Thorn, please. Just let it go," I pleaded, still bewildered by the revelations.

"Truth, Jon. I want the truth. I have told you everything. Now it's your turn."

I bolted upright, startled that she called me Jon. She hadn't used my old name since the day in the woods when I killed Barry. From that moment on, V for Vengeance had been born, and since then she had always called me by my vampire name. Her calling me Jon was significant, a reminder of times past and how we came to meet. I rolled my eyes up to the ceiling.

"You know where I was. You told me to practice."

"No, I said, practice your seduction skills. Not spend all night and day with a wannabe," Thorn said.

I tried to remember what she had said.

"That isn't what you meant. You know it. Like you said, we have eternity together."

She released a low growl.

"Thorn, I am tired and hungry. You know it's only ever going to be you. Like you said, body not mind."

She huffed and looked out the window.

"You were there for a long time. That was more than just practice. You were supposed to come back the same night. I was waiting for you as promised. I thought you loved me."

"I had just found out you weren't vampires and that you had been lying to me."

"So you admit it being more than just practice then," she said.

I put my hands on my head. I wasn't going to win this argument; everything I said just dug myself deeper into a hole. I should have felt guilty for spending all that time with Amber, but I enjoyed it and was angry at Thorn for lying to me.

I slid across to the other side of the seat, clambered out of the driver's side and shut the door. I didn't want to argue anymore. Thorn stood face to face with me as I turned around. She grabbed my arm and pinned me to the truck.

"I want the truth," she shouted.

"Thorn! You just turned my life upside down again in the last few hours. Stories of Dragans, the Turned, and vampire wars. You just told me I am the key. The future may depend on me. Give me a break."

She grabbed my throat and lifted me off my feet, pushing me up the truck. I kicked and grabbed at her arms but to no avail. My punches and kicks bounced off her supernaturally strong muscles.

"I will break your neck. Now tell me the truth. Remember, I said your body is important. As long as I have your body, I don't necessarily need it alive."

I punched her in the face, angered by her comments. She was no better than the Hunters.

"That's the truth, isn't it? I am just a commodity. A science experiment you need to control," I said through my strangled throat.

The bruise on her face healed, and she growled through bared fangs. I had got myself into trouble again.

"Thorn, leave him. You are making a scene," Cassius shouted, as he appeared to our side, and looked back into the diner where a couple of faces squinted into the darkness.

"Cassius, you know better than to get in my way. Remember who I am," she snarled back.

"Yes, I do, but I also know you. For some reason, you like this human else you wouldn't get so angry, and he wouldn't be alive," he said, and he turned to me, "Little one, I would explain yourself quickly."

Thorn released her grip, and I slumped to the floor. She leant over me and glared before reaching down and hauling me to my feet. Cassius had gone again, and Thorn stood with her arms crossed and scowled.

"If I tell you the truth, you will kill me," I said.

"What choice do you have?"

I had to come clean and tell her everything.

"Truth is we stayed in her room till midday and I took her to lunch. We went on the gondolas as well. I enjoyed it. It was uncomplicated and normal."

"You mean normal because she is human."

"Yeah. I have never been with a human before, and you know that. You have had several lifetimes before me. I am sorry if it upsets you, but I thought I had your permission."

Silence hung in the air between us as Thorn's eyes connected to mine.

"Maybe. I just didn't expect you to stay so long and enjoy it so much. I thought you would rush back to me. I was waiting for you and wanted to hear how it went and then reclaim you as my own," she said.

"I was angry after I heard you and Cassius talking, and I didn't want to come back till I was ready."

She relaxed, her arms uncrossed and nodded in acknowledgement.

"I understand. It must have been a shock after all this time."

I stepped forward, and we hugged. I leant back and looked into her blue eyes.

"So you really do like me," I said, grinning.

"Where is the necklace I bought you?" she asked, and I fetched it out of my coat pocket and handed it over. She pulled out the gold chain with the fangs suspended in the middle and placed it around my neck.

"Thank you," I replied and kissed her on the cheek.

"Shut up, and let's get something to eat," she said and led the way into the diner.

While we grabbed something to eat in the diner, Thorn planned the route on her tablet, finding us a motel to stop in before daylight. Both Thorn and Cassius ordered rare steaks to help with their thirst. The waitress looked at us suspiciously, not surprisingly with the rare steaks and the fancy dress outfits giving away our true identities. I still wore my black outfit and leather coat with spiked hair. Thorn was in her PVC corset and catsuit with black leather boots, and Cassius in his black trousers and red top. We looked quite a sight.

I flicked on my iPad and found a message from Scarlett. I couldn't read it with Thorn next to me, so I decided to wait until she fell asleep before viewing it. We finished up and got back into the van. Thorn and Cassius took it in turns to drive for the rest of the night until we pulled into a motel to sleep away the daylight hours.

Cassius took the room a couple of doors down, and Thorn and I another room. Before we went to sleep for the day, Cassius investigated the strange gun the Turned had used against us. He dismantled it on the bed, sorted through the parts and then examined the bullets. The gun looked bigger than an average pistol, with the barrel wider to house the large rounds. The bullets magazine connected on top of the gun, allowing gravity to drop them into the chamber. Cassius unclipped the magazine and popped out the bullets.

He shook the bullets and the blue liquid inside faintly glowed.

"I guess from the death of the vampire back at the trailer park, these bullets contain something lethal to us. The liquid glows when excited."

He shook it more violently, and as the blue liquid glowed, it seared his hands.

He continued with his observations. "UV bullets. The impact and firing at high velocity would be enough to create the chemical reaction and give off the UV light. The bullet will drive into the skin delivering its contents, into the vampire or us, making it impossible to remove before the plastic casings break, seeping the liquid into the body while emitting harmful UV rays. A perfect delivery system."

"We will need to be careful. We need to prepare some armour and protection. In the meantime we can use this against the Turned," Thorn said, looking at Cassius.

Cassius nodded.

"You keep the gun and examine it some more. It will prove an excellent weapon against other Turned," Thorn said.

"Okay. I will see you two tonight. It's good to have some company finally. So try to stay friends in the meantime," Cassius said.

We said goodbye and ran back to the room as the dawn lit up the motel parking lot.

The journey in the van had been silent since our altercation in the car park of the diner. Although we had apologised to one another, we both brewed with anger. I had stayed annoyed that she had kept secrets from me for so long. Thorn was still angry I had been off enjoying myself more than she had expected.

In the journey's silence, guilt played on my mind. I hadn't thought about my night of passion, as the attack of the Hunters, the visit from Mr. Vitsco and the ambush of the Turned had overtaken that event. I had decided to apologise to Thorn properly when we got to the motel, but I still wanted to know why the secrets were for so long.

Thorn flung herself on the bed as I shut the door to the motel room behind us.

"Thorn," I said and grabbed her attention and perched on the bed beside her.

"Can this wait?" she asked.

"No. I want to apologise."

"Okay. Apology accepted... I suppose I did encourage you."

"I still have questions about the Dragans and the Turned. Why didn't you tell me this before?"

"I don't really like talking about it. Secondly, it's a lot to take in. Vampires are one thing, but to be told of Dragans, the Turned and an impending war, which you may be the key to, is another thing altogether. I thought it best a bit at a time. I had to be sure you could handle yourself and understanding the truth."

I half smiled in agreement. It made sense, as I was struggling to understand. If I had been told about Dragans and a Vampire war the first time I met her, then I would have run a mile.

"Enough talking. I kept this costume on for a reason," she said, and grabbed my shirt, pulled me down onto her and kissed me. "The best part of arguing is making up."

Chapter Ten

After sleeping through the middle of the day, I woke up with Thorn at my side. I needed some fresh air and hot sun on my skin before another night of driving in the dark. I showered, changed clothes into something less conspicuous; jeans, red t-shirt and trainers, then swooped up my iPad before creeping out the door. The sun warmed my face, and I took in a deep breath of fresh air.

I looked around to find out where we had stopped, as I hadn't paid attention on our arrival last night. On the top of the Motel were pictures of the moon and stars that had been painted across it. Plus a sign written in silver moonlight letters, "Night Motel." Next door, a diner with a big Sun painted on the front and fluffy white clouds painted around it called, "Day Diner."

My stomach rumbled and my watch ticked two o'clock signalling time to eat, and I strolled across the car park and through the doors of the diner. The diner continued the sunshine theme inside with bright colours, sunny landscape murals and menu themed food, "Fluffy cloud pancakes," and, "Sunny Orange juice." I ordered the big American breakfast with both included, from Susie, the young waitress, and then connected to their wi-fi. I wanted to read the messages from Scarlett and find out what she had to say for herself. I had the truth from Thorn, but I had questions and still wanted revenge on Scarlett and my Dad for setting me up. I quickly clicked through to the messages, expecting to encounter more tricks.

Jon,

I wanted to tell you this in person, but I missed my chance at the nightclub. I guess that will never happen now unless I give you a reason to come home and leave that thing you are hooked up with.

I never betrayed you. Something didn't seem right the days after the incident with Barry at the party. My memories were confused, and I felt exhausted the next day. Mary convinced me to take a test. They slipped something into my drink. Speak to Mary.

I needed you to know that. I am grateful for your act of revenge on Barry and his gang. I guess you had something to do with the attacks in

Leeds as well.

I sensed from bumping into you at the nightclub that you weren't happy and wanted to come back.

You can come back. Your Dad was devastated when you left. He wants the chance to explain everything. He says he can help if you return home.

Please, just call us. Let us know you are safe.

Love

Scarlett.

The message surprised me. I read it several times trying to decide if the contents were genuine or another trick. I had used my anger at her and my Dad to drive me on all this time. It had been the thing to fully push me into Thorn's arms once and for all. The acceptance of my destiny and the reason I had become Vengeance. As far as I was concerned, Jonathan Harper had died, but I was wavering again. The recent news of my central part in a war between the Turned and Dragans had made me question my decision. I didn't know friend from foe, or what side I should be on. I still had Mary's phone number and impulsively hit the dial button next to her name. The phone rang.

"Hello," Mary answered.

"Mary. It's Jon."

"Jon? Where the hell have you been?"

"No time for questions. Did they drug Scarlett?"

"Yes. Now tell me...," and I hung up, knowing the number showed up as private, and she couldn't call me back.

It might be true. Maybe Scarlett hadn't betrayed me. I wished I could go straight back into her arms, stare into her beautiful green eyes and kiss her ruby lips. I wanted to take revenge on the gang all over again. Make them suffer this time instead of the quick and easy deaths I had given them. I wanted to return and speak to my Dad as well. I wanted the truth to find out his involvement with the Hunters. Maybe he was innocent as well.

I had the truth from Thorn, but I needed to know who had set this up and what part Scarlett and my Dad had played. I needed to return to England, but I couldn't. For better or for worse, I followed Thorn. We were on our way to find out the truth behind the formula, and then possibly I could convince her to return to England to face Scarlett, Dad and the Hunters. In the meantime, it would have been wrong to give Scarlett false hope, so I replied to her message.

Scarlett,

I am sorry I never trusted you. It's too late for me now. I can't come back. I have made my decisions and my life is much more complicated than it seems.

J

I wiped a tear from my eye, switched off the iPad and drank the rest of my coffee.

"You okay?" Susie asked as she cleared away the plates.

She displayed that look again, her eyes dilating and her tongue moistening her lips. Another young woman drawn in by the Dragan power. Another example of how easy it is for them to hunt and control. How much of Thorn's power of seduction had clouded my judgements over our months together?

"Just some unexpected news," I replied, and laid some cash down on the table to cover the bill and tip.

I decided not to share the news about Scarlett with Thorn, as her jealous streak would be too much to cope with. I stayed outside, enjoying the sunlight and studying more battle tactics on my iPad. Occasionally, I drifted off into daydreams of my previous life with Scarlett. Plotting ways we could be together again, but none of them ended well. It would be impossible without a sacrifice. Thorn would never let me go without a fight. My transformation made me too valuable regardless if she loved me or not. I finished reading and went back to sleep away the rest of the daylight hours next to Thorn, while trying desperately not to think of Scarlett in case Thorn could hear my thoughts.

The darkness came around again. After rising, Thorn dressed in a more subdued outfit than her vampire costume. She put on skinny blue jeans, a black t-shirt but kept the black leather knee length boots on over the jeans. Cassius sat waiting in the van, ready to go. He had changed out of his costume into a black tracksuit with a hood and white trainers. He still looked menacing, no matter what he wore.

We hit the road again, and I talked most of the way, getting them to go over the whole Dragan and Turned history continuously. It kept thoughts of Scarlett out of my mind and prevented any accidental mind reading. Plus, I wanted to check I really understood everything about them.

We bounced along in the van down the dark, desolate highway. The headlights showed the endless straight road ahead, with only sparse bushes and rocks randomly lining the edges. I sat in the middle of the two Dragans, Thorn and Cassius.

"So you two are Dragans. A hybrid," I said.

"Yes," Thorn replied.

"I turned into a Dragan."

"Yes."

"You don't look much like dragons."

"The first of our kind did. When they transformed, as we do, their skin would produce scales, they would have talons instead of claws, and their eyes would burn with golden fire, but it also drained them of energy. Their first born couldn't reproduce the same change and no Dragan since has been able to."

I continued with the questions. "Dragans created the Turned by nearly killing humans and then feeding them their blood, which contains magic?"

"Yes."

"The Turned and the Hunters are working together to unlock your secrets."

"Yes, how many times do we have to run through this?" Thorn said, rubbing her temples.

"I just want to understand. So why now? Why are the Turned and Hunters working together now?"

"I guess the advent of DNA sequencing and advances in technology has made it more likely to unravel our secrets. Previously, it wasn't possible to unlock our powers. Opportunity creates curious bedfellows."

I allowed it to sink in and a flash of Amber's and Scarlett's smiling faces flitted across my mind. I needed to keep talking; fearful Thorn would pick up on my thoughts.

"Who leads the Turned?"

Thorn looked away.

"Bramel leads the Turned," Cassius answered. "He runs the show. He was one of the first to turn on his Dragan masters, and he quickly gained support from the other Turned. The other Turned have had their civil wars as well, but Bramel took ultimate charge."

"Was it Bramel that captured you?" I asked Thorn.

"No, it was Carmella, one of his generals. I killed at least ten of them and five hunters before they imprisoned me," she answered, trying to excuse her capture.

I tried to think of more questions.

"Why silver, daylight and crucifixes?"

"Silver was the only thing that could penetrate Dragon scales. Sunlight burns as the magic used was dark and the transformation completed at night. Crucifixes work as it was Christianity that drove us out and killed our ancestors," Thorn replied.

I sat in silence while trying to think of something else to say to keep my mind occupied and keep the thoughts of Amber and Scarlett out.

"V, I realise it's a lot to take in. It may feel even more confusing with the vampire bite, as your body could be fighting off infection. The head injury could cause some concussion, as well. It will make sense, and your body will repair. But trust me and stick with it," she said, brushing her hand through my hair.

I smiled back. "I will."

I stared ahead as we continued on the endless straight, dark road to Seattle. I couldn't hold off thoughts of Scarlett and memories of my night with Amber any longer. Thorn and Cassius had promised to stay out of my mind. I had to hope they would keep to their word.

We drove on the highway for a few more hours with Thorn and Cassius swapping over until we pulled over to another diner to rest and feed. I went into the diner to order while Cassius and Thorn took in the night air. Thorn had been feeling cooped up in the truck all night, as it reminded her of the prison cell. She wanted to burn off a bit of energy and find some animal to feed on. I glimpsed them before they shot off in a blur into the remote countryside.

The car park was empty, and the diner had seen better days. The windows were smashed and boarded up. The sign was missing letters due to broken bulbs, "B G MA 'S DIN R." From the blank spaces, I made out the missing letters to read "BIG MAX's DINER." I gently opened the door as it wobbled on its hinges. The door hit a bell that tinkled and swung off its loose screws. I was afraid it would fall to the floor.

Inside the diner, it shone clean, but it was clearly broken down. The tables and chairs looked like someone had smashed them up, patched back together and cleaned up. The chair legs were a patchwork of wood holding them together. The white plastic tables were chipped and yellow burn marks created dips in the surfaces. The black and white chequered floor was marked with burns and scuffs, and a few loose tiles curled up at the edges.

In the centre of the diner, a solid metal serving counter carried its own damage of dents and cuts. The bottles of sauces and menus sparsely scattered about different tables. The photos on the walls had missing panes of glass or only rectangular grease marks to show where photos once stood. I looked around for signs of other customers, but I saw none. A woman's head with brown hair tied back popped out from a door behind the counter.

"Grab a seat. I will be straight with you," she said, eyes wide and smiled.

I wandered down a few tables and sat down next to one of the few unbroken windows so I could look outside.

The waitress walked over; she wore blue jeans, a white t-shirt and black waist apron. She looked mid-twenties but carried a weariness about her. She stared with her brown eyes scrunching up. I ordered a burger and fries and water. She kept staring at me, and her face frowned, nose flared, and she sniffed the air. She wrote the order down and rushed back around the counter and into the kitchen area. I heard words exchanged between her and a man in the kitchen.

The kitchen door flung open and a big blond man, with a hairnet sagging at the back of his long hair, thundered out and marched towards me. He towered nearly as tall and wide as Cassius and looked as scary, with muscles bulging, tattoo sleeves on both arms and bristling fluffy sideburns. He stood just to the side of me, sniffing the air, and his grey eyes stared at me. I sniffed back, wondering what he could smell. Something strange, something musky, wafted up my nostrils. He pulled off his white greasy stained apron and threw it on the table behind.

"Get out scum," he shouted, and his veins raged red.

I sat still, trying to work it out. He grabbed me by the shirt collars, dragged me from the table, and hauled me along the diner. He reacted stronger and quicker than I expected, even for a man of his size. I lashed out and hit his face hard enough to knock most people out cold. He staggered and swung a punch back. I jumped back onto a table. He stomped forward and punched through the table, cracking it in half. I leapt from my breaking platform to the next table, and he did it again, creating a path of destruction.

The woman had raced back and flashed a light into my face. I jumped down from the table and front kicked the mad man backwards. He stayed on his feet, grabbed a chair and threw it at me. I ducked and recovered as he launched forward and grabbed me with both hands around the throat, ramming me back into a table and chairs.

We rolled over the top, scattering the menus and napkins across the floor. I unleashed an elbow onto his arm, loosening his death grip, and then I followed up with a headbutt on the nose. He shouted as blood ran from his nose, but carried on with his brutal attack as he smashed in punches. I blocked each blow against my forearms, shielding my face but sending shockwaves through me.

The woman hurried around the side and shone the light into my face again. At which point, he halted and stood up. They stood over me with the light shining down into my face. An ultraviolet light! He pulled out a crucifix hanging from a gold chain and pushed it into my face.

"I am not a vampire," I shouted.

They both looked down, foreheads scrunched and mouths open.

"You smell like one. You're nearly as strong as a vampire," he said.

"Yeah, well, it's complicated. You aren't normal yourself. No man can fight like that," I said, and I sniffed at the air again. Something seemed strange about him.

The bell rang, and the man crumpled to the floor as Thorn stood over him. The waitress flashed the UV light around into Thorn's face. Her skin burnt and she dived away to the floor. Cassius quickly disarmed the waitress and shoved her down into a seat. He smashed the torch into pieces against the counter. The blond man slowly regained his breath and knelt up to see Cassius staring down at him, his eyes burning red.

"Wolf. Control yourself. We are Dragans. The old alliance is still in place," he said and growled.

The man relaxed and looked at me.

"This one. I thought he was a vampire," he said.

"Something in-between human and Dragan. He can be trusted. He has a vampire bite which you might have detected," he said.

Thorn got back up, her face healing from the burns.

"My apologies," the blond man said to me and stood up slowly. "You should have told me you were with the Dragans."

He reached down and helped me to my feet.

I shrugged my shoulders. "I didn't know I needed to. I just came in for some food."

"My name is Max. I am a werewolf."

I shook his hand. "Hi, I am V. I don't know what I am."

"This is Eleanor," he said, looking down at the waitress cowering in her seat.

Max turned around and looked at Thorn.

"I am Thorn," she said. The name shook him and he took a small step backwards out of some unknown respect.

"I... I... am honoured to meet you," he said and bowed slightly.

"Cassius," Cassius said, and leant forward and shook Max's hand.

"Get these people a drink, El. We have a lot to discuss. I have only ever met one Dragan before, two years ago, a man called Cyrus," Max said.

Both Thorn and Cassius turned to one another and frowned.

"We know Cyrus. I guess he mentioned us as well," Thorn said.

"Yes. I understand you were opposing houses in the last wars. If it helps, I think he is ready to put the past behind him. We all face a greater threat with the rise of the Turned."

Cassius and Thorn nodded in agreement.

"Take a seat, please," Max said and ushered us to one of the undamaged tables.

Max cleaned up some of the broken tables and chairs, then picked up the scattered menus and napkins off the floor. Eleanor regained her composure and slid out from the table to fetch us some drinks.

"I guess you are still hungry. It's on the house," Max said as he returned to our table.

"Yes please," I answered, and Max headed back into the kitchen to cook my food.

Thorn, Cassius, and I sat in silence for a few moments.

"You okay?" Thorn asked and put her hand on my leg.

"Yeah, he took me by surprise," I replied, rubbing my bruised body and sore muscles.

"Sniff the air, can you smell something?' Thorn asked.

I took a long snort of air into my nose and detected that distinctive musky smell again. When Max first appeared, I noticed it.

"I smell something musky."

"Werewolf," Thorn replied. "Remember how it smells. It will be important to be alerted when a werewolf is around."

"We have an alliance, though."

"Alliances come and go. It seems the wolves struggle to tell you apart from a Turned. You need to be wary, just in case this happens again."

"Can Dragans beat werewolves?" I asked.

Thorn waved her hand mid-air to signal uncertainty.

"It depends. This is how it works. Werewolf in human form can match a 2nd generation Turned. Werewolf in wolf form can beat a 1st generation

Turned, but not a Dragan. However, once a month at the full moon, a werewolf's power reaches its maximum, at which point it matches our own. On those nights, they must change into a werewolf and remain in that form for the entire night. We must respect their power. They make good allies but powerful enemies," she said. I nodded and breathed in the werewolf's smell, remembering the hierarchy of power.

With my order cooked, Max brought the burger on one plate, fries on another, and joined us at the table. Moments later, Eleanor came out with a banana milkshake for me.

"So what are you three doing travelling this road? Where are you going?"

Cassius and Thorn stared at each other, and I just buried my mouth around my burger. I left Thorn to tell our story or give a convincing lie.

"We are looking for others like us or like you to join our war against the Turned," Thorn said.

"Why this road?"

"V and I met up with Cassius in Vegas but ran into some trouble with the Turned and Hunters. We needed to flee quickly and this was the best route."

"Okay. I am ready to join you in the fight. I hate the Turned. Eleanor's family was killed by the Turned. I saved her from them," Max said.

"We are always looking for powerful warriors to join the fight," Thorn said.

"Are there any others?"

"We are still looking at the moment. In the meantime, we are learning about the Turned and Hunter Alliance."

"And the boy, V, what is he, you said Human and Dragan?" Max asked, nodding over at me.

"Boy!" I replied. It was bad enough with Cassius calling me, little one, without being referred to as the Boy.

"He is Human and Dragan. The Hunters have experimented on him. It was V that rescued me from a research lab where they were experimenting and studying my powers and blood. But they hadn't expected the Dragan bond that was created between us."

"What experiments?" Max asked.

Thorn looked over, remaining silent for a moment.

"That is all I will say until we know you better."

Max nodded. "I understand. In war, secrets are a must."

Cassius interjected, changing the subject. "So Cyrus came through town. Do you know where he went?"

"He didn't say. We just exchanged stories and news on the Turned. He said all the Dragans had gone into hiding. Either running from the Turned or hiding from one another, fearful of the old blood feuds. From the clothes, kit and map he carried, it looked like he was heading into Canada, the west coast."

Thorn's eyes rolled as we had just come from the same part of the world while skiing. I continued eating a handful of fries and washing it down with the last of my banana milkshake.

"Thanks, Max, this is great," I said.

Max nodded in appreciation and spoke to Thorn and Cassius. "You two look hungry as well."

Although I had let Thorn take some blood in the other night at the hotel, it wasn't enough. Cassius' thirst sparked in his hazel eyes every time Eleanor walked into the room. Something Max must have noticed.

"We could do with something. If you have animal blood, we can use it. We scouted the area outside, but we couldn't find any prey before your fight alerted us," Thorn said.

"No, you wouldn't find anything around here. I am afraid my werewolf half has scared it all away. However, there is another option. As you can see, my diner has been smashed up a bit recently, even before mine and the Boy's little dance," he said and looked at the boarded up windows we had noticed on our arrival.

"A mile north is a roadhouse bar. They come down here still drunk and cause trouble. Nothing I can't usually handle, but I live here and have to be careful."

"What are you suggesting?" Thorn asked.

"I have given them a beating before, but they returned in the dead of night and smashed the place up before I had a chance to stop them. They have scared away all my other customers. I can't afford to keep the place running and fix it up."

"Go up there and transform and rip them a new throat," Cassius suggested.

"Easily done, I know, but I live here and don't want to be a killer. You guys, on the other hand, need a feed and have no such worries," he said.

"It would be our pleasure," Thorn replied with a hungry smile.

Max handed them a few photos of the troublemakers. "I got photos for the police, but they weren't interested. I think some of the troublemakers are family. If you take care of them and leave the rest a warning, it would do us both a favour. The roadhouse is called the 'Cattle Horns.' it's easy to spot, there are massive cow horns on the roof."

"Look after our little one. He needs his bandages changing," Cassius said, looking at me as he stood up. Little one, I was sure he only said it to annoy me.

Thorn kissed me on the cheek and followed Cassius. The door banged on its hinges, and the bell rang as the two Dragan's disappeared into the night.

Max followed his orders and brought out the first aid box.

"Take your shirt off, so we can take care of these wounds and bite mark," he said.

I agreed and stripped off.

He pulled the bandages off, and a lump of yellow puss and skin stuck to them. He threw it in a bin, cleaned up my wounds and replaced the bandages.

"So who are you really? I never heard of Dragans bringing a human around with them before."

"It's complicated. I guess you sensed something about me when I came in."

"Yes. You smell a bit like a Dragan, but not quite. It's similar to a Turned, but your skin and smell are still human. It was unusual. I assumed you must be some sort of Turned. Maybe a 1st generation."

"No. I guess I am a Human – Dragan hybrid at the moment. But one day Thorn has promised to make me like her."

"Really?" he said surprised, eyebrows raised.

"Yeah. One day. When the time is right."

"How?" he asked. "Dragans can only change people into Turned. New Dragans can only be born."

I stared at him in a trance as the information sunk in. She only promised to make me a vampire one day, never a Dragan. She couldn't turn me into a Dragan; it was impossible. I didn't want to become one of those dead decaying creatures that attacked me in the dark. They were her enemy. She would never turn me into one of those creatures, as I would be another foe. What was I then? Just the result of an experiment. A chance to stop her enemies and use the research for her own agenda. I had been a fool. The truth had been staring me in the face for the last day and I hadn't realised. I had even said I was just an experiment, even if I had only said it to annoy her. We were travelling to another lab to test the formula and to test me.

"No, I am sure there is another reason," I said, hoping something would spring to mind. I didn't want to show my shock at the revelation.

"I am sure there is, you should talk to her. Listen, I am allied with the

Dragans, but they are dangerous. There is a war coming, and you need to understand what you are and where you stand with them. You are just a young boy, after all. I would hate to see you get caught up in trouble if it was avoidable. It may feel great to run with Dragans, but think about where it will all end," he said.

I glazed over, staring into space, trying to work out my next move while he bandaged me up. He packed away the first aid box and walked back into the kitchen to prepare me some food for the road. I gently pulled my shirt back on, trying to avoid disturbing the bandage. He came back and handed me a bag of food, and I went to ask him more questions, but Thorn and Cassius re-entered the diner with the bell tinkling their arrival.

"Thanks for the tip, Max," Thorn said, her face glowing from her feed and the excitement, "we have taken care of your problem. I doubt if they will come here again."

"Thank you," he said, and walked over and shook their hands.

"We must get going. Be ready when the call comes. We will need everyone to fight the Turned," Thorn said.

I walked past and he stretched out a hand. We shook hands and he leant into my ear.

"Take care. You are a brave warrior. Change the bandage every day," he whispered and patted my arm.

We got back in the van and continued driving north past the roadhouse. Outside the roadhouse, styled like a large western saloon with massive horns on the roof, two ambulances and three sheriffs' cars parked up with lights flashing. The sign of the roadhouse, 'Cattle Horns,' hung down from one tip of the horns, as the other end had broken loose. Scattered around outside, people pressed bandages against wounds, and the paramedics assisted and treated injuries. The motorbikes and cars out front had been smashed and torn apart. Thorn and Cassius had really gone to work on the place, and they high-fived each other as we sped past.

Thorn drove fast, intoxicated by the blood and cranked up the music loud. I slumped into the door and stared out the window, trying to work out my friends from my enemies.

Scarlett hadn't betrayed me. Mary had confirmed that on the phone call. It wasn't a setup unless Mary had been involved. Maybe that was what Barry meant by saying it was all arranged, including your girlfriend, as the attack on her was supposed to send me over the edge, not her betrayal. Thorn had jumped to conclusions about Scarlett's involvement that made me believe she worked for the Hunters. She probably did that on purpose, as Scarlett was her competition.

I had to speak to my Dad. He knew more of what was happening than anyone else. The way he acted implied his involvement had been deep and pre-arranged. Hopefully, like Scarlett, he had a good excuse, something I hadn't thought about. I had to find out what really happened in England that led me on this path. Was it just an accident, or did the ones I love betray me?

I shut my eyes and pretended to be asleep as Thorn drove, letting my mind wander across all the information, trying to make sense of it. With my eyes closed, sleep easily found its way to me.

I was stood in Scarlett's house and following her into her bedroom. She took the flowers and threw them on her dressing table, scattering her makeup. She pulled me close, kissing me passionately, grappling at my belt and loosening my trousers. My hands reached down to her red hot pants, unbuttoning and sliding them off to the floor. She stepped out of them and pulled off her t-shirt. I stripped off the rest of my clothes. My heart pounded and hands grasped at her body as we staggered over to the bed, exchanging frantic kisses. We crashed onto the bed, her legs wrapped around my body, and I kissed her neck as we made love. The heat between us was rising and in unison, we began gasping at the air. My passion drove my instincts, and the intensity of our lovemaking rocketed us both to climax. Scarlett's head tilted back, her neck wide open, her veins pulsating and her blood calling to me.

My dream was repeating, but I couldn't stop it and didn't want to.

A thirst swept through me. My claws ripped through my fingers, tearing into the bedsheets. My eyes burnt and fangs cut through. Scarlett opened her eyes and face recoiled in horror. Her hands bolted up to stop me, and her head turned away but exposed the tender part of her neck. I bolted down, brushed her hands away, sunk my fangs into her pale white neck, and sucked down her blood. I drained her dry, savouring every last drop. I stood up, looked at her dead lifeless body, and wiped my mouth clean of her blood. Vengeance at last.

I jerked awake again from the repeated nightmare, and a comforting hand wrapped around my shoulder.
"Shhh, it just a dream, sweetheart. Go back to sleep and dream pleasant dreams. Dream of us together," Thorn whispered hypnotically into my ear,

and I followed her orders before I had the time to think about what the dream meant. Soon I slipped back to sleep again, reliving my best memories of us together in her underground chamber and between the silky red sheets.

Chapter Eleven

Thorn woke me as we pulled into the car parking lot of another characterless motel, 'The Rested Traveller.' The typical half-filled motel. Most rooms were black and silent, but always one with the light on and TV flickering late in the night.

"Hey sleepy, come on, we are resting up for the day. Last time, we should be there in a few hours tomorrow night."

I climbed out, booked in and went to the room with Thorn. She checked all the curtains and taped them in place, then got into bed. By the side of the bed, she laid out her black combat clothes and mask just in case she needed to make a getaway in the sunlight. After sleeping most of the night, I felt too awake to go back to bed. Instead, I watched TV while waiting for the sunrise.

Thorn slept beside me on the bed, and I watched her as she rested. She had filled my dreams with wonderful memories of us together, but the reoccurring nightmare of attacking Scarlett as a vampire still lingered. My increasing appetite and dreams of attacking and feeding worried me. Could I trust myself around humans? Was the Dragan part of me taking control? I didn't know. The other night, I hadn't tried to drink from Amber. I was probably okay, and it was just a dream.

The sun rose and I abandoned my soul searching and strolled up the road to a small diner for some breakfast. I devoured the pancakes and crispy bacon and turned on my iPad to check my messages again. Immediately, another message from Scarlett popped up. I shouldn't have read it. The messages kept upsetting me and causing me to doubt myself, but I couldn't help it. The message flag flashed up like an itch I had to scratch.

Dear Jon,

I spoke to your dad. He wants to meet. He says he can explain everything.
Tell you all about the vampires, the formula and the Hunters. He is desperate to tell you his side of the story. To tell you the truth.

Love Scarlett.

I still couldn't decide if it was a trap or not. I wanted the truth from both of them, Dad and Scarlett. Thorn would never leave to go back to England, and she would probably kill Scarlett if they ever crossed paths again. It wasn't the only thing making me re-think. Max had opened my eyes to the continued deceit. I still wasn't getting the full story from Thorn and Cassius. She had no intention of making me like her, a Dragan; she couldn't. My transformation ability remained just another weapon. The key to her war with the Turned. Why didn't she come clean the other night instead of letting these doubts cloud my thoughts?

I brought up the map of the area on my iPad. One more night and we would be in Seattle, and it would be too late. During the daylight, I had my best chance. I would have a ten hours' head start if I left now.

I flicked across the map and recognised the name of a town, Twin Falls, Amber's hometown. When we drove past it, I must have been asleep. I searched through my jacket pocket for my wallet and inside the scrap of paper with her name, address and telephone number. Perfect.

I drained my coffee cup and ran back to the motel. Inside the room, I repeated a song in my mind over and over again, as to mask my real intentions. Thorn rolled over and the blankets on the bed slid down her body, revealing her naked bosom. It transfixed me for a moment, and I waited for her to settle. I padded across the threadbare carpet into the shower room, washed and changed clothes, pulling on a pair of jeans, a red t-shirt, boots and a black leather jacket. I didn't want to make my exit too obvious.

Thorn stayed asleep. I didn't want to look at her for too long, else I would change my mind. Her raven tousled hair lay on the pillow, revealing the side of her neck. The blankets rolled down to her waist, as she always gets too hot when she sleeps.

I took in the sight of her flawless pale skin and the curve of her spine. I couldn't help but remember all the times I slid under the sheets behind her and hugged her warm body for comfort. She would wrap her arm around my embracing arm and scuttle her hips back into me. When the night came, she would roll over, and we would make love without saying a word.

My body wanted to sneak into bed with her and relive those memories. *Just one more time.* I might never get to feel her warmth again. I might never get to make love to her again and be seduced by her supernatural powers. Her raven hair bellowing, her lips red, and body glistening warm and firm to the touch. My desires stirred, but I had to find the truth. Even without her powers, her body had a hold over me. Thorn would always be a killer, but also one hell of a woman.

I must have been mad to walk out on her, but I couldn't carry on without knowing the truth of what happened with Scarlett and my Dad. Thorn had been lying to me all this time. It was one lie after another. I gritted my teeth and clenched my fists to cement my resolve. I swiped a briefcase full of cash and walked outside. As I left, I said a silent goodbye. I would miss her, and I might never see her again.

I pushed my sunglasses on and wiped a tear threatening my eye when I noticed someone in a new silver Chevrolet about to drive away. I dashed over wildly, waving my hands and briefcase in the air to get their attention. The man in the driver's seat slowly smoked a cigarette and watched me in the wing mirror as I ran over.

I skidded to a halt at his door and checked back to the motel room for any movement. Nothing stirred inside.

"You going south?" I asked.

The man blew smoke out and ran a hand through his thick black hair.

"Yeah," he said in a strong New York accent.

"Can I grab a ride to the next town, please?" I asked, and then checked the motel room again, half hoping she would come out and stop me.

"Sorry, it's a drive away I am taking to Vegas. I am not supposed to pick up travellers."

I hadn't thought this through properly and stared at the ground for inspiration and saw the briefcase. The answer was held in my hands.

"$1000 help?" I asked and looked back up.

His eyebrows flashed above his sunglasses. "$1000 always helps, jump in. My name is Steve, by the way."

I ran around and jumped into the passenger's seat. Steve flicked his cigarette out the window and held his hand out. I clicked open the briefcase enough to get my hand in, without him seeing inside, and pulled out a wad of cash. I quickly counted the notes and slapped them into his hand.

"Let's go," I said, not wanting to hang about.

He nodded, checked the road looked clear and pulled away to head back south.

"So what's your name?" he asked.

I looked over my shoulder and watched the motel disappear into the background.

"Christopher Lee," I said.

He laughed. "Like the actor that played Dracula?"

"Yeah, just like that."

"So what's your story? Who you running from?" he said, looking out of the mirror as we drove down the highway.

"I prefer not to talk about it," I replied.

"Come on. It's a couple of hours to the next town."

I opened the briefcase slightly and grabbed some cash. I counted out more money.

"Here is another thousand dollars for no questions. Just drive," I offered.

Steve took the money and leafed through it as we drove down the long, straight road.

"Deal," he said, and cranked up the stereo to occupy himself as he drove.

He forced country and western music on me for the rest of the journey. I thought of paying him more to turn it off, but at least it kept him busy.

As we drove, I couldn't help think of Thorn and how angry she would be that I had left her. When I first runaway with Thorn in England, I spent many weeks plotting an escape plan. I had worked out routes, bought weapons and stored up cash already to make a daring dash back to the research centre and the Hunters. I believed they offered safety, and I had made a mistake setting Thorn free and becoming her lover and trainee.

I never put my escape plan into action, as the time never seemed right, or I lacked the courage. I am not sure which. However, I had just left spontaneously, with no extensive planning. I had just changed my clothes, stole the money and bought a lift away from her. I hadn't really thought how to get away from the motel, and I'd been lucky someone was travelling south. Since I changed from Jon to Vengeance, I had changed a lot.

On the drive to the next town, I couldn't think of anything else but Thorn. I tried to think of what to do next, but her face kept reappearing in my thoughts. My mind switched from regret at leaving her, guilt from stealing her money, and the idea of how much it would cost to get Steve to turn around. But it won't change the facts that she had lied to me.

Finally, after a few hours, we pulled into the next town on the route and Steve dropped me off. I wandered through the streets looking for somewhere to eat and settled on buying a sandwich to munch on the way. I found a local car salesroom and paid cash for an old red Ford. I hooked up my iPad as a GPS and hit the road again. I had about five hours left before Thorn woke and realised I'd gone. I had left no note, as couldn't risk her finding it before I got far enough away.

I drove on, knocking back high-energy drinks to stay awake; the GPS said it would only take two and a half hours. The roads cut through empty scrubland with only rocks, dust and withered bushes lining the road and stretching off to either side. The occasional car came the other way, breaking up the monotony. It went on and on in a straight line, with the scenery repeating itself over and over again, as if in a computer game loop. I felt like I wasn't going anywhere, but thankfully the GPS showed my progress and gave me confidence I was heading in the right direction.

I finally arrived at Amber's hometown, Twin Falls. I wound down the window, pleased to be back in civilisation after the endlessly straight highways and their empty landscapes.

The sights and smells of the town streamed in through the window, and the warm air hit me. I welcomed the senses of other people, even if it was the hum of car engines and sights of office buildings and shops. I drove through the green traffic signals on the straight sunny streets with its buildings spaced out, and it felt in stark contrast to the grey overcrowded narrow streets of London and Leeds. I immediately liked the place, and it justified my decision to leave Thorn and seek Amber in Twin Falls.

I parked up on the opposite side of the road to a small brown block of apartments. The street was spaced out with other apartment buildings, two local food shops and a Starbucks on the corner. Cars rolled gently down the street, and people walked in and out of the apartment buildings.

I turned the GPS off on the iPad and tucked it under the driver's seat. I watched Amber's apartment building and saw an old woman making her way up the steps to the doors. I jumped out, locked the car, and ran up the steps to follow the old woman. She unlocked the inside door, and I tailgated through the doors and climbed the stairs. I scanned all the numbers until I finally saw Amber's number 52. I brushed myself down and knocked on the door. I hoped she meant to drop by anytime. Footsteps thudded, and the door opened up. Amber stood there in surf shorts, a baggy white t-shirt, and her red hair messed up. I smiled, and her mouth dropped open.

"What the hell are you doing here?" she asked.

"Well, you said to drop by if in the neighbourhood, so I did."

"Yeah, I know, but I never thought you would," she replied, looking befuddled at my sudden appearance.

I thought she would be over the moon to see me. Maybe I didn't understand what happened in Vegas. It could have been a one-night stand and had nothing to do with my powers.

"Should I leave then?" I asked, and thought about using the seductive powers, but in the cold light of a normal day, I didn't feel right about tricking her. Luckily, she smiled with her face blushing red. I caught a quick flash of her memories from our last encounter in Vegas.

"Of course not, it's just a pleasant surprise," she said and stepped aside to let me in.

I walked through into the dark and messy apartment. The kitchen sides covered in dirty plates, mugs and a vast number of empty beer cans and spirit bottles.

"Heavy night. I was still sleeping it off," she said, rubbing her eyes. "Make yourself comfortable. I will just get changed."

She shut the door and raced off to her room, and I heard the shuffling of clothes and thumping of drawers. I pulled back the curtains, allowing in the sunlight and revealing the extent of the mess. I cleared away the drinks cans and put all the dirty crockery by the kitchen sink.

After a couple of minutes, she came back dressed in jeans and a clean, tight purple shirt. She had combed her hair and applied some basic makeup.

"Sorry to drop in without warning. I need a favour. Can I stop for a couple of nights until I sort out some onwards travel plans?" I asked.

"Of course. Where are you going?"

"Back home. Back to England."

Chapter Twelve

Inevitably, the last shreds of sunlight disappeared from the window. Amber pulled the curtains across, and we ordered some takeaway pizza. With the darkness, Thorn would have woken and wondered where I had gone. I could only imagine the scenes playing out with her and Cassius hundreds of miles away. Thorn would waking up and looking around for me. Then checking outside and calling my phone, speaking with Cassius and asking around the motel. How long would it take her to realise I had gone and not just out of the room? The missing quarter of a million dollars in the metal briefcase would have been the giveaway.

I should be safe at Amber's, as they would have had no idea of my location. My departure was such a spur of the moment plan I didn't leave any clues behind. I had turned my phone off in the car on my escape. She couldn't call me or get my phone traced. Yet, I feared she would appear at any moment with her fangs and claws, ready to take revenge.

Since running away with Thorn, this would only be the second time I'd been without her for the entire night. The first time had been the other night in Vegas with Amber. Just then, a knock rattled the door and Amber sprung to her feet to answer it.

"No," I shouted, and followed behind her.

She looked at me wide-eyed and then frowned.

"It's just the pizza," she replied and opened the door.

On the other side, a young man in a blue uniform handed over the pizza box.

I slumped back down onto the sofa and poured myself a glass of soda.

"Who did you think it was?" she asked, walking back and then sitting beside me.

"I thought it was my friends. We didn't part on good terms," I answered and tore off a slice of hot BBQ pizza from the opened box.

"I guessed something had happened for you to appear at my doorstep."

"Sorry, you are the only person I know in America. I hope you don't mind. I will make it up to you, I promise. I will pay my way and then some. It's just until I sort out my onward travel plans," I said.

She smiled and blushed. "No worries, it's great to see you again."

We ate and talked for a while, and I enjoyed her company. Amber told me about her town and her life. She'd left college with little education as her parents moved around a lot. Her dad followed construction work due to regularly losing his job because of being drunk. Her mum picked up odd jobs whenever they moved.

Her parents had moved on again six months ago after he lost another job, but Amber stayed in Twin Falls. She had a job at a local bar as a waitress and wanted to put down some roots. She intended to save up and go back to college to study accountancy. I discovered her age, twenty-two years old, and when she asked me my age, I lied and told her twenty-one when, in fact, I had only just turned eighteen when skiing in Canada. The changes in my body from the formula made me look older. To match that, my fake ID of Christopher Lee said twenty-one to cover up the maturity of my looks. I thought she would be unhappy to discover my true age.

As we spoke, she moved further down the sofa, placing her hands on my legs and shuffling in next to me. I held fast, pretending nothing was happening, but I recognised the look in her eyes.

She knelt up on the sofa, dived in, and kissed me. I remained still for a moment, only giving a little response. She leant back and frowned. Yet again, I hadn't really thought it through. The night in Vegas had been great, but so much had happened since. Maybe I could justify it to myself as had been told to practise my seduction skills by Thorn, but this would be different. I didn't know what I expected to happen when I visited Amber, but I should have realised this would be the outcome, especially as I had provoked her with my powers back in Vegas.

I felt guilty about being with Amber, which seemed strange, as I had already abandoned Thorn hundreds of miles away. But it was too late for guilt or remorse. I had made my decision. Either way, I was damned if I did and damned if I didn't. I might as well enjoy myself and gain some pleasure from my guilt. I smiled and leant forward to kiss her, and she readily responded.

Amber worked nearby in a bar and managed to swing the next two days off. I had plenty to prepare for my trip back to England, and she wanted to spend all her time with me. I had left Thorn's company with only the clothes I wore, but luckily, I had remembered my passport. The next morning, I drove us into town and bought my aeroplane tickets with cash. I would pick them up at the airport.

Amber gave me the tour around town, and I tried to enjoy myself as much as possible. I wanted Amber to enjoy the visit and repay her hospitality. We went to the ice rink, and I surprised myself at how quickly I took to the ice. I could balance and skate around pretty well. Amber couldn't believe it was my first time. Yet another improvement from my formula altered body. Everything had improved.

I chased after her on the ice rink and grabbed her waist with both hands. She laughed and leant back onto my shoulder and kissed me, her red hair floating in my face. We then skated around the rink holding hands and weaving in and out of the other skaters. We jumped off the ice, our faces rosy red and hearts pumping. Then we went and warmed up with large mugs of hot coffee and shared a chocolate muffin.

Next, we went bowling. Amber scored over two hundred, but again I did better than expected and could have won, but I purposely threw a few balls away as not to show off. We asked one of the staff to take a photo of us together, using my smartphone. Then we went to the burger restaurant next door and enjoyed a late lunch.

Shopping next, I drove us down to 'Magic Valley Mall' in Twin Falls downtown. I needed some clothes for the next few days until I returned to England. I just bought a few pairs of jeans, t-shirts and fleeces to combat the cold weather I would face on returning to England in the winter. I treated Amber to new clothes as well. I sorted through the clothes in the shop, helping her to choose and kept picking things I thought would suit her. She didn't like them much, and I realised they were the sort of clothes Scarlett would wear. I was trying to get Amber to dress like Scarlett, to compliment her red hair and to make myself a Scarlett clone.

I continued to splash my cash out, buying her new clothes for normal wear and for her alter ego of Pandora. Whatever she wanted. I stopped trying to help her decide, realising she had her own tastes. Amber held my hand as we walked around the shops and smiled at people she knew, happy to show off her bags of shopping and her new boyfriend.

After shopping, we went to the bar she worked at, "Home Run Sports Bar." The bar counter was at the front to the left side of the two glass entrance doors. Surrounding the bar were brown booths along the walls and tables and chairs filled in the gaps.

The bar had a baseball theme, as the name suggested. Pictures of baseball players decorated the walls and posters from famous teams and victories. The bar owner was called 'Gerry,' and he was a big middle-aged man wearing a Chicago Cubs baseball shirt and hat. He had a fluffy grey goatee and big sad brown eyes. We ordered a couple of beers and sat on the red leather stools at the bar.

"Gerry, this is Chris," Amber said.

"Chris, we heard about you. An app games developer," Gerry said, shaking my hand across the bar.

I stared confused, not remembering what cover identity I had given in my drunkenness.

"Yeah," I replied and went along with it.

"So, why are you here? Hope you are looking after our Amber."

"I am stopping over for a few days before I go home. I am being nice," I said, unsure why I needed to justify myself to her employer.

"Look at everything he bought me," Amber said and held up the bags as to prove my niceness.

Over in the corner, a group of five men and one woman stared over. They wore denim and leathers, and I guessed the Harley Davidson motorbikes outside belonged to them. My senses twitched when they leant in to talk to one another.

"I think it best not to show off too much, Amber. I don't like the look of them," I said, lowering her shopping out of sight.

"They know me, that's all." She shrugged it off and waved over.

One of them reluctantly waved back.

"He might be right, Amber. Best to keep a lid on it. They ain't a pleasant bunch and are connected to that biker gang."

The biggest one proved my point when he stood up from his seat and strode over. He had to lean back to gain his balance, and his gut wobbled out in front as he waddled over. He wore old denim trousers and jacket, a dirty black t-shirt, with a scruffy beard and shaven head. He rested his gut against the bar to take the weight off his back and breathed heavily from shifting his bulk down the bar.

"So who's your friend?" he asked Amber.

Amber smiled and held my hand. "This is Chris. I told you about him the other day."

He sniffed. "The rich one?"

"Yeah, look at the stuff he bought me," she said, holding up the bags.

He nodded at all the shopping and turned around to his friends and smiled. They grinned back.

"So, rich kid, you gonna buy us all a drink?"

Gerry jumped straight in. "I don't want any trouble."

"Trouble? Us? No, we are just asking for a drink from the rich kid."

I rolled my eyes. They thought they could intimidate me. There were five of them, and all looked rough and nasty. I am sure they would fight dirty, and the drink had numbed their senses enough not to feel it. They saw easy pickings, a young man at the bar with his girlfriend.

The remnant vampire rage inside tightened my muscles, ready to fight. I could probably take all of them on and win with ease. If I could beat two

Hunters, then these slobs would be no problem. But what was the point? Thorn had taught me to pick my battles. I had plenty of money, but I could do without drawing attention to myself. An unknown young man beating five people would attract someone's interest. I would have to find another way.

"Of course I will buy you a drink. Amber has often spoken about her regulars and how nice you are to her," I lied. "Get these guys and girl a drink, please, Gerry."

"Okay," Gerry replied, "the usual drinks, Burt?"

"Yeap, a beer each followed by a double Jack Daniels chaser."

"Enjoy," I smiled at him and leafed the money onto the bar from a roll of cash.

Burt stared. "You know, I think a rich kid like you should stay here and buy us drinks all night."

Now he was pushing it.

"Well, thank you for the kind offer, but Amber and I have plans tonight," I said.

Burt grabbed my wrist. "I insist."

I stared back and waited for a moment to pass.

"The thing about money isn't the money but the power it can buy. Power to make friends or break friends. I could easily get some big and nasty friends of mine to pay a visit. You have a drink now, go and enjoy it," I said and glared at him. My minor psychic senses picked up changes in emotions as his aggression drifted away.

"Thanks for the drinks, rich kid," he said and picked up the tray of drinks and walked back.

Amber rubbed my arm. "Sorry, I didn't know that would happen. Maybe we should go."

"It's not a problem. We will finish our drinks first," I replied and went back to our conversation with Gerry. All the time, I imagined myself running over and flying into the group with a brutal attack. My instincts were to fight. Yet, I had to learn to control my temper if I wanted to avoid unwanted attention from the wrong people, Hunters.

Before driving back to the apartment, we loaded up a supermarket trolley to fill her bare cupboards up with food and beer. I enjoyed spending money on her and not just as a repayment, but it felt good to see the money being put to good use. The joy it brought her rubbed off and allowed me to escape my worries. When I enjoyed Amber's company, I didn't think about Thorn, Scarlett, vampires and the Hunters. I was just a boy hanging out with a girl.

However, my stay at her place came at another price. Just like Thorn said, I may need my powers at some point to win favours. The night back in Vegas, I enjoyed it, but I now felt guilty about using her and cheating on Thorn. But not guilty enough apparently as I requested she dressed back up as Pandora, the steampunk vampire, for our intimate night together. A request she readily accepted wearing the new assembly of lingerie and clothes I bought for her during the day; purple and violet basque, fishnet stockings, suspenders and a studded leather collar.

As Amber walked over and straddled my lap in her new steampunk vampire outfit, I decided I might as well enjoy my guilt about leaving Thorn.

"My dark prince," she said.

"My protector," I replied, reliving the role-playing we enjoyed in Vegas together.

The role-playing carried out to its ultimate climax, and afterwards, we crashed out asleep in her bedroom.

I walked around the London house at night calling to Thorn.

"Where are you? Thorn, where are you?" I shouted, but I couldn't find her. The lights wouldn't turn on and the shadows seemed to have taken a life of their own.

"Thorn, where are you?" I shouted in fear, wanting her to come and protect me.

I climbed the stairs of the basement into the hallway and crept up the stairs to the first floor. I heard scratching at the doors outside and heard footsteps running around the outside of the house.

"Thorn, I need you. Something is happening," I shouted again, fearful of the shadows.

My blood pumped harder as black shapes ran from room to room.

"Thorn, don't hide, it's me, V."

I walked to the door and went to open it. It bashed back, knocking me to the floor. Out of the room, a dark shape loomed over me, and the lights switched on. In front stood a Turned vampire, its skin decaying. Suddenly, behind me, two other Turned vampires appeared. Then more came out of each room and surrounded me. They growled and slashed the air in front of my face. I tried to push back, but claws sliced my hands open and blood poured out. From the corner of my eye, I saw Thorn walking down the stairs.

"Thorn, help me, please," I screamed, reaching out to her with bloody

hands, but she just laughed and kept walking.

The Turned vampires grabbed at my arms and legs to pin me down. The one in front dived in and bit into my neck, and I screamed for Thorn again.

I woke with a jolt of adrenaline buzzing through me. It took a few seconds to remember everything that happened and to work out I had dreamt it. The clock clicked over to 3 am and I couldn't get back to sleep. My sleep patterns hadn't adjusted to living my life the right way round after months of being awake with Thorn during the night. Plus, the dream had woken me with such a scare I couldn't relax.

Amber lay next to me, naked. I slipped out of the sheets, stepped over her basque and opened the door with the fishnet stockings hanging off the handle. On the sofa in the living room, I moved her studded collar to one side and pushed aside my jeans and t-shirt to make space.

I sat back on the sofa, wondering what Thorn would be doing. I guessed she had arrived in Seattle and would be working with the researchers to examine my blood samples and the formula. Or maybe she'd gone out partying and feeding. I didn't know and it worried me. I switched on the TV and watched some trash until I drifted off to sleep again.

The next morning, I let Amber decide how we would spend our last day together. She never had much money since being in Twin Falls and had yet to see the sights. We drove off to see the local waterfalls, 'Shoshone Falls,' and rented out two kayaks and paddled around the base of the falls. I took some pictures on my phone of the spray and caught a rainbow effect through the water mist and streaming sunshine.

Afterwards, we had a picnic on the riverside, watching the water meander and other tourists paddling down the river. Once we finished lunch, we drove down to the 'Perrine Bridge,' and went on a zip wire, where we did tricks hanging upside down and spinning around as we shot along the wire to the ground below. Amber recorded her journey down on a helmet camera.

I was buzzing by the time we left to head back into town for dinner at the pizza restaurant. It had been the kind of romantic fun filled day, which I had always wanted to spend with Scarlett or Thorn. The opportunity, the money, or location had never worked together to let it happen. I should have had a wild time in Vegas, but it never worked out. In London, with Scarlett, money and confidence had prevented anything beyond going to the cinema and days in each other's houses.

We finished dinner and went back to the apartment to spend as much of the night together as possible. She changed clothes into Pandora and asked if we could play out scenes from her favourite vampire book. I agreed and surprisingly enjoyed it, and it delighted Amber to have someone to share her passion for vampires with.

We had spent two memorable nights and two happy days pretending to be an average couple having fun and spending time together, even if it was pretending to be vampires. I still caught occasional flashes of Scarlett when looking at her and making love to her. If I spent any more time with her, I might never have left. I might forget the past and my search for the truth, and settle down with Amber using the money I had taken and my new talents to get by. Maybe in another lifetime.

The following day, I prepared to leave. I stood in the doorway with my clothes packed and the metal briefcase full of cash.

Amber wore her lacy red pants and white t-shirt straight from bed. Her messy red hair rolled onto her shoulders, and her eyes were sleepy and watery. We embraced and kissed.

"This is for you," I said and handed over the metal briefcase.

She took it in both hands and then placed it on the table and opened it up. She knew I had a lot of cash with me, but had no idea until then how much. Her eyes widened to take it all in.

"How… how much is here?" she asked.

"It was a quarter of a million. We spent a bit and I have taken twenty thousand," I replied.

"Are you sure? But why? I won't be paid for," she said, hands on hips.

"I can't take it all back through customs. It will cause too many problems. I can't pay it into a bank account either without it being suspicious. You buy yourself somewhere nice to live, get a nice car or go back to college. I may need your help again in the future, so it would be good to know you are okay."

She smiled.

"Goodbye," I said and kissed her again.

"It has been great having you here. I still haven't made too many friends. You don't have to leave. Stay."

She hadn't formed her own group of friends yet and spent most of her time working or hanging out in the bar with Gerry. I guess she wanted company just as much as anything else.

"We have spoken about this. Part of me wants to stay, and I have enjoyed it, but I have responsibilities. I have people relying on me. I can't just leave them."

She had made the offer a couple of times since I arrived. On the second night after we relived our role-play from Vegas, she had asked me to stay. Then again, the last night back in the apartment. Each day I spent with her increased her feelings towards me. I guessed my seduction powers were affecting her more than I realised, as I didn't yet have control over them. It was hard not to get caught up in the intensity of the moment.

"You mean the games company," she said. I had kept up the persona of Christopher Lee, the game's developer.

"Yes, sorry. I have been away too long already," I replied.

"Sort things out and come back. I know more is going on than you are telling me. The whole thing with your friends and this money, it doesn't make sense. I am not stupid."

"You're right, there is something else happening, but I can't explain it. Amber, you enjoy your life. I may return one day and tell you the truth, but I can't promise."

"Okay," she said, relaxing her arms to her side and looking away for a second.

We hugged and kissed one last time. I opened the door and walked through. Amber stood in the doorway and waved me goodbye, her eyes building up with tears.

"Bye, Pandora."

"Bye, V."

I walked down the stairs with my suitcase in hand and wiped my eye with the other. Thorn had taught me to build up my contacts and to create a network to support me. Strange how much I had learnt from Thorn and now used it against her. Yet, I didn't expect it to be such a pull on my emotions. I got into the car and drove away quickly before I changed my mind. It would be too easy to stay and start again, but I had to face my future head on.

Since fleeing from Thorn, I had guessed she would try to call me, then scream and shout at me down the phone, so I had turned it off when I had left her. She might trace it, as she had a network of contacts everywhere and I couldn't take the risk. For the last two days in Amber's company, I had remained in my little bubble of ignorance at Thorn's reaction, but on the way to the airport, curiosity got the better of me. I turned on my phone.

After a couple of minutes, the phone beeped continuously with text and voicemail messages. She would have someone tracing the phone, waiting for it to register on the network. Then someone would come after me, or she would come herself as soon as the location was revealed. I read the text messages. The contents were as I expected. The messages started concerned, but quickly broke down into torrents of threats and came back to concern again. I listened to the voicemails as well. The same again starting with "Where are you?" "You okay? Has something happened?" and ending in "where's my money? You better get back here straight away or I will … *something, something very unpleasant,*" and back to "just call me, please."

As I would be traced anyway, I called her to make peace. Thorn was a drug. I was addicted and couldn't stop wanting her even though it would be deadly. The phone rang only for a short time.

"V, it's Cassius. Tell us where you are," he said.

"Sorry, not going to happen. I want to speak with Thorn."

"I am not sure it's a good idea."

"I know she wants to kill me. She has done it before. It's always her answer."

I heard the phone passing over and her angry, yet controlled voice spoke.

"Why did you leave me?"

"Do you remember what you promised when we first met?"

"Of course. I promised to make you not scared anymore. I have taught you to fight and look after yourself, and this is how you repay me," her voice snapped, and I could imagine her vampire features; fangs, blood red eyes and claws breaking out from her rage.

"Yes, you did. You also promised to make me a vampire one day."

The phone fell silent at the other end. I followed up.

"You were going to make me into one of the Turned? Or is this just another lie?"

"V, listen to me. I told you what you wanted to hear. What would make sense at the time. I not going to make you one of them, you know that surely."

"So what do you have planned for me except for the experiments in Seattle? Beyond that, what use am I to you?"

Her voice softened, and I sensed her transformation back to normal. "At first, it was just an excuse to escape and steal the formula. I trained you up to keep you safe, but things changed."

"Oh, let me guess, you grew to like me. Sounds perfect."

"It's true and you know it. The formula is created from my blood. A special bond has been formed between us. You know it to be true. That wasn't the only thing to change. You have changed, as well. Your body has altered. You are a hybrid Human-Dragan at the moment."

"I know, but when the needles run out, what next? Will the formula eventually kill me? Will I spend the rest of my life as a hybrid, not belonging in either world? What happened to spending eternity together?"

"I know. I was lying at the time, but the truth is we don't know what effect the formula has on you. Each one seems to push you further towards being a Dragan. The point of going to Seattle was to find out if the formula was safe for you to use and what would happen to you long term. The decision would have been yours to make."

I sat silently in the car, trying to think of an answer. The conversation hadn't gone as I had planned. I couldn't be sure of anything or anyone. The revelations of Dragans and the Turned had completely disrupted my new reality. The news of Scarlett's innocence at the same time had been the last straw. I had to get everything straight on my own.

"Okay. Maybe it makes sense, but I am not coming back. You have the formula. Get them to run the tests they need, and I will be in touch once I have taken care of some other business."

"V, don't be silly. Come back to me. We can work through this together. Remember the vampire bite and your concussion? You're confused and scared, that is all. I can make it all better. I promise."

"No way. I need to work it out for myself. I need time away from you to think straight, as your powers affect me. They cloud my judgement. I have seen its effect on people first hand. I have to work it out alone to be sure it is the right thing and not just a trick."

"It's not a trick. Unlike you, I can control my powers."

This was probably true. I apparently couldn't stop the powers from affecting Amber.

"How can I be sure? No, time alone is the only way. Get it clear in my head, see how I feel, then I will know for sure."

"But V, we need samples from you to finish the testing."

"I will send some in the post. Text me your address."

"I will. You are going back to England, aren't you?"

"Call me when you have the results. Bye."

I hung up, not wanting to deny or confirm my next move, but Thorn knew.

I stopped off at some shops and bought a small airtight container, cut my arm and poured in some blood. Put it inside a padded envelope and sent it off to the address I had received. Hopefully, that would be enough to get some answers. In the meantime, I would get the truth from Scarlett and my Dad.

I drove to the main airport in Vegas and abandoned the car. I checked in with no trouble, as my fake passport of Christopher Lee still worked.

We took off from Las Vegas Airport, and as we rose into the sky, the lights of Vegas shone out in the desert. The Fake Eiffel Tower lit up with yellow bulbs. The casino lights flashed, and cars streamed up and down the strip. Vegas had been exciting, even if it hadn't gone as I expected. I wanted for Thorn and I to enjoy it together, but we spent more time apart in Vegas than together. Instead, Vegas held other memories for me. But, I had to put those memories away and focus on the future.

On the flight back, I rehearsed my speeches to Scarlett and my Dad. What my questions would be. Also, how would I explain what I had become? How much I could tell them just in case they really did work for the Hunters?

Chapter Thirteen

I arrived early in the morning, staring out of the window as the plane banked. I pressed my face to the glass to spot the landmarks. The 'River Thames' snaked its way through the city and the 'London Eye' stood proudly on the riverbank. The light bounced off the millennium dome and then the arch of Wembley Stadium. We landed at Heathrow Airport, and I pulled on a warm winter coat ready for the cold British weather. I left the plane and passed through customs with no problems. I exchanged most of my currency back to British pounds and then caught a train and a taxi back to the house I had shared with Thorn. It felt good to be home.

The house hadn't changed; a three bedroom house on an ordinary housing estate. Nothing unusual, nothing to make it stand out as the house of a vampire, I mean Dragan. I still hadn't got used to the idea that Thorn and Cassius weren't vampires but Dragans.

I jumped the back gate, found the hiding place for the key under a paving slab in the greenhouse, and let myself in through the back door. The house had been cleaned and tidied since we left. The post cleared away and the plants watered. The cleaners had done a good job.

I immediately headed for the door leading down into the basement, Thorn's daytime hideaway. I entered the combination, opened the door and walked down the wooden stairs. The lights flashed on, illuminating the room and it shining red from the spotlights bouncing off the painted walls. I turned the stereo on and one of Thorn's favourite dance albums played in the background.

I walked across the exposed oak floorboards to the large king size bed in the middle of the room facing a TV screen. I ran my fingers across the velvety red blanket on the top of it; just as I had done the first time I arrived. The room held so many wonderful memories of being with Thorn. Plus a couple of bad ones as well, like the time she took too much blood and crushed my bones. The formula had saved my life that night, and afterwards, Thorn and I went on a night time adventure, tackling a gang and rescuing a group of girls in a nearby warehouse. I smiled at the good memory, and I wondered how Annabel and Lucinda were getting on with Miss Jones.

I pressed the button under the side of the bed, and the picture of the vampire and werewolf fighting slid across the wall, revealing the extensive weapons rack behind it. I took out a couple of pistols, the silver knife, and the UV torch for protection against the Turned. I also pulled out a long, sheathed sword at the back and placed the weapons on the bed.

I loaded the pistols, checked the torch and unsheathed the sword, swinging it about. I would need weapons. The messages from Scarlett might just be a trap, but I had to find the truth. With my new psychic and seductive powers, I could force the answers from her. I switched off the music and climbed into bed to sleep out of habit and jet lag.

I woke up later than I expected. Something was comforting about being back in the bed I had shared with Thorn, as if I had come home. So many great memories, like waking up in her arms and enjoying each other's bodies before embarking on our nightly adventures. At night, we would train in martial arts, and Thorn would need to hunt. We would often end up in fights in local nightclubs and pubs as she looked for prey.

I had been away from Thorn a few days, during which time Amber had kept me occupied. Now alone again, I had nothing to distract me from her absence. An emptiness dwelled within that I couldn't ignore, and it wasn't just the fantastic sex, but the other things we did together. Thorn was my mentor, as well as my lover, and I missed her guidance. I also missed the fun we had together. Thorn loved watching vampire films. She would pick holes in the plot and say what she would have done as if in their place. She enjoyed playing computer games against me. We had often battled against each other in fighting games and war games by pitting armies against one another. I enjoyed her telling me about the actual history of the world she had lived through, like the two world wars when she had worked as an assassin for the British Government.

Yet I had abandoned her in America, and it wasn't until now I realised how much I missed her. Her absence left a void in my life. I didn't expect it to be the normal things together that I missed. I hadn't understood what I had until it had gone.

The clock read 6 pm and I had missed Scarlett leaving college. I climbed out of bed and looked in the mirror. The soft features of a teenage boy had gone to be replaced by a strong, taut jawline, and my eyes were turning an icy blue as well. The formula had changed me, but so had those vital teenage years and months of hard physical training.

I would drive around to Scarlett's house and look out for her instead. I got dressed and put on the gun holster under a leather jacket. Then I stashed the rest of the weapons in a black sports bag and put them in the boot of the car. I drove the BMW with ease through the local streets and onto the main roads heading back to the area I lived in with Dad. I would visit him next if I couldn't find Scarlett.

It didn't take long to get through the traffic, so I took in a few sights on the way. I parked up and walked into the park where I first turned into a Dragan and killed the gang. Flowers had been tied to the railings of the playground, and a police incident sign requesting witnesses to the murders sat outside the playground gate. A memorial plaque had been put up on a tree. The plaque described a different set of people to the ones that preyed on the local youth. They weren't the ones that had mugged and bullied me into utter despair. Wasn't it always the same on the news, parents telling the world their children were full of potential and lighted up everyone's world? Never that they were a horrid bully that had terrorised the neighbourhood.

I remembered the beating and them forcing the injection on me, as they thought it was for diabetes and would make me sick. I relived my transformation into a killing machine. The formula killed me as it changed my body, but then it resurrected me as a vampire, I thought, but actually a Dragan. My memories replayed the thrill of the chase as I exacted my revenge. The smell of their fear and the sight of their hearts pumping a yellow pulse out into the gloom were still tangible in my memories. In the park, I had ripped their bodies to pieces and drank my first blood.

Next, I drove past the research lab where Thorn had been imprisoned, and my Dad worked. The building was charred with black marks from the flames, and the windows were boarded up. Vegetation had reclaimed the ground as weeds and grass cracked the concrete walkways. The guards had gone and the big metal gates locked tight. It looked empty.

After taking my revenge on the gang and feeding on their blood, Thorn's image had called to me. I had been connected to her. I sprinted to the research centre to be with her in my Dragan form. My Dad let me in, and I had overwhelmed the guards in the basement lab. Then I scared my Dad away so I could get to Thorn alone. She had waited for me, stripped naked and lured me into bed to seal our bond. On our escape, we stole ten more needles filled with the formula, which had been left in the lab. Then we had started the fire to destroy the research.

I drove to the college next with its gates locked firmly shut, as I expected, but I wanted to look at it anyway. As with both the park and the research centre, an array of both good and bad memories flashed back.

I remembered meeting Scarlett for the first time. Her flame red hair blazed like a beacon in the sixth form common room. I had been lucky to be introduced to her, and we became friends when realising we had lived in the same area in Leeds. Our friendship developed until it eventually turned into something more and we admitted our feelings for one another.

However, not long afterwards, the mugging came at the hands and feet of Barry and his gang. Then the film of my mugging had been broadcast around the college, which my peers used to bully me. The students laughed at me and I hid away. To finish it off, I received a picture of Scarlett and Barry together. I thought Scarlett had betrayed me and slept with Barry while I convalesced at home, battered and bruised. Recently, I found out the gang had drugged her. I turned around and drove off to Scarlett's house, wanting to find out the truth. Had she been part of the plan or another victim?

Her house looked the same, a neat and tidy semi-detached on the new estate. The estate was a strange maze of almost identical houses, with a distinct lack of parking demonstrated by the cars mounted on the pavements and doubling up onto driveways. The streets weaved through the estate, leading to dead ends and blocked off roads with metal bollards preventing car access to the next street along. I turned the wrong way a couple of times and got stuck. I had always walked to her house before and did not need to remember the route for cars. Finally, I navigated my way in the dark onto the right route to reach her.

Her house was in the middle of the street, with cars parked on driveways and bumped up on kerbs between houses. Her mum's Black Mini cooper parked on their small driveway. I guessed they still lived there. I parked down the road and waited for any signs of life. As I waited, I rehearsed my speech over and over. I couldn't wait all night, and I was building myself up to meet her when a young man walked past, up to her front door and rang the bell.

I recognised him. He'd been in the group who had tried to chat up Scarlett on our first day at college in the sixth form room. He had good muscles and showed off his designer wear and cool gadgets. He had been the first to incite the bullying when the film clip of my mugging broadcasted across the college. He was jealous I was going out with Scarlett despite his superior good looks and money. I hated him. What was he doing calling around Scarlett's house?

Scarlett, red haired again, came to the front door, kissed him on the cheek and pulled on a red coat over her white t-shirt and jeans. She closed the door and walked off into the night, holding hands with the young man. I couldn't believe it. I gripped the steering wheel tight and clenched my jaw. They walked right past the car but didn't see me as the windows were tinted. On the messages she sent, I thought she was heartbroken and saving herself in case I ever came back. She had already moved on and onto one of my tormentors as well.

I swung the car around and drove slowly on, waiting for a spot to talk to her. The estate was a maze of streets and alleys, and I had to pick my spot carefully and quickly. They walked across the road and through a back alley. From their route, I guessed they were heading to the cinema. I could cut them off at a quiet spot. I knew the back alleys well from my time visiting her, and I drove the car calmly around, trying not to draw any attention to myself. My previous detours served me well as I remembered the right route through the estate, and I pulled in by the alleyway I expected them to walk out from.

It wasn't long before two shapes walked down the alleyway. The young man was dressed in boots, blue jeans and a black puffer jacket, and Scarlett was in her red coat and jeans. Their breath froze before them as they walked down the alley at the side of the houses, and then across the closed ending of the street and towards another alleyway down the edge of a house. They walked arm in arm, Scarlett laughing and smiling at his side. I thought she missed me. I thought she cared for me. Didn't take her long to find someone else and he was one of them as well. One of those guys she said she had nothing in common with.

They walked past the car and Scarlett frowned at the sight; I guessed she had remembered it from earlier. I got out of the car and walked up behind them, checking about for any onlookers. Scarlett turned around as the car door clunked into place, and I stood in a dark spot between the lights.

She looked straight through me with no recognition on her face at all. She walked on another couple of paces and swung back around.

"Do I know you?" she asked.

Her boyfriend glared at me.

"I should hope so," I said, and I realised even my voice had changed, deeper, more coarse than before. I stepped into the light for her to get a better view.

"Jon, is it you?" she asked, and I nodded and smiled.

She released the arm of her boyfriend and launched at me for a hug.

I gratefully received it and winked over at the boyfriend, who clenched his fists and jaw.

"I remember you, northern boy. You got beaten up and ran away. You lost your chance with Scarlett. She is my girlfriend now," he said, stepping towards me.

I remembered being scared and intimidated by him when I started college, and I felt the anger brew up and emotions burn with energy just as

Thorn had taught me. I pulled Scarlett around to one side and walked over.

"You don't scare me," he said and swung a punch.

It hit me square on, but my head just absorbed it, and I stared back. I'd become used to fighting hunters, vampires and werewolves. He was just an average human. I punched him back in the jaw and he flew off his feet onto the rough pavement.

"Jon, leave him," Scarlett shouted.

I left him to his pain and walked back to Scarlett.

"Get in the car," I shouted and pointed over to it.

Scarlett walked across to the car as her boyfriend dragged himself to his feet and pulled out a knife.

"Come back here, this ain't finished," he shouted, blood running from his nose.

"Yes, it is," I replied, spinning back, pulling the gun from its holster and aiming it at his head. He shuddered, dropped the knife and ran.

"In the car," I shouted, and she obeyed.

I got back into the car, turned it about and raced off out of the estate to somewhere quiet before he raised the alarm. It wasn't far from the cinema, and I drove into its large car park and pulled into a dark quiet corner out of sight, well away from the other cars and the furthest distance possible from the cinema.

It would be unlikely anyone would park near us and there would be no passer-bys. Scarlett remained quiet in the car, just staring at me as I drove. Once parked, she unbuckled her seat belt and turned sideways on to face me. I did the same.

The time away from her had eroded my memories and some of my feelings for her, but sitting next to her again made it all flood back. My heart pounded in my chest and a teenage nervousness seeped back into my system.

"Jon. Where have you been? What happened to you?" she asked, and then scanned around looking into the back seats, "is she with you?"

"I am here by myself. I guess you deserve an explanation, but I have questions of my own as well."

"Okay, fire away. I don't see what I know will help."

"Who hired you?" I asked.

Her eyebrows arched, and she glared. "Say that again."

"Who hired you?"

"I don't know what you are talking about. Are you crazy?"

I sensed no deception from her.

"The Hunters, did they hire you to be my girlfriend?"

"What the hell are you talking about? I assume the Hunters are those guys that came after you and spoke to me after you killed Barry's gang. That was the first time I had ever met them."

"Then why did you date me?" I asked.

"Because I liked you, you idiot! I am wondering why."

I sensed only the truth and no deception. My small psychic abilities were picking up anger and confusion, nothing else. If it were true, I would have expected fear and panic that I had discovered her true identity.

I looked back out the window and sighed. All this time I had been wrong about her, and I wondered if I had been wrong about my father as well.

"My turn," she said, and I nodded in agreement. "What the hell happened to you?"

"The night Barry's gang mugged me, I met a vampire imprisoned in my Dad's lab. She told me about a formula that could transform me into a vampire for the night. When I walked into the lab, my Dad hid away some needles, and I guessed it was them."

She looked at me, absorbing it all, not flinching from the strangeness of my story.

"After the bullying at college, and when I thought you had betrayed me with Barry, I confronted them in the park. I turned into a vampire and killed them all, except Barry."

I kept using the word vampire, knowing it was easier to understand than to explain about Dragans and Turned. Suddenly it clicked into place why Thorn had done the same.

"You are a vampire?"

"No, I changed into one just for the night. I then rescued the vampire from the lab, and we went on the run. After that is when we met at the nightclub. Then I went to Leeds to take revenge on the O'Keefe's. Next, I finally found Barry and finished him off as well. Since then, Thorn and I have been travelling."

"Thorn, that's her name? The one with the red eyes and fangs."

"Yes."

"Why are you back?"

I thought it was obvious. "I got your messages. I wanted to know the truth from you and my Dad. I thought you both betrayed me, and it drove me away."

Scarlett shook her head. "You're not happy with Thorn?"

"I don't know. She has so many secrets and told me so many lies, it's hard to know where to begin. I have to set things straight, clear up the mess I left behind. Maybe if I understand my past, I could choose my future."

Scarlett reached forward and grasped my hand. "I never betrayed you. You know that now. They slipped something into my drink."

I put my hand on top of hers. "I am sorry I didn't trust you. I am sorry I didn't wait to find out the truth before I acted."

"I am not sorry you killed them. I just wish I hadn't lost you," she said.

We sat there looking into each other's eyes, and Scarlett leant forward with eyes closed, searching for a kiss. I leant back and let go of her hand. It felt wrong kissing her. A betrayal of Thorn with my heart. Being with Amber had been different.

"You want to come with me to speak with my Dad?" I asked, trying to change the subject.

She opened her eyes and slumped backwards. Her cheeks flushed, turning the same colour as her hair. She looked away from me.

"Your Dad moved back to Leeds as the research centre was destroyed in a fire. I believe he is back in your old house. He hasn't had to worry about the O'Keefes anymore since you paid them a visit."

It pleased me to hear that his life in Leeds had been untroubled by the O'Keefe's, or what was left of their family.

"I am heading up to meet him. You coming?" I said.

"Oh, so you want me to go with you, and nothing else?" she asked, her voice sharp.

"Sorry, I am not ready to carry on where we left off just yet. I have a commitment to Thorn."

"Then why come back and find me? How did you think I would react?" she said.

"I wanted the truth. I wanted to know if there could be a chance."

"What, just in case your dead lover gives you the elbow? What am I, your backup?"

"No, you're not. She isn't dead. It doesn't work like that."

"If you think I will wait forever, then you'd better think again."

"I can see you wasted no time getting a boyfriend. One of them as well."

She slapped me across the face and I let her.

"I waited for ages, but you said you weren't coming back on that message. I had to get on with my life," she yelled.

I had sent her that message. I remembered thinking it would be for the best, but I hadn't expected to feel so jealous, or for her to move on so quickly.

"But him. He bullied me."

"I know, I am sorry. He said in that school it was a case of being a bully or be bullied," she answered.

"Yeah, seemed like such a nice guy carrying around a knife," I replied.

Her eyes widened, and she breathed in sharply. "Says the man carrying a gun."

"It's for protection in case the Hunters come after me."

"After what you did to Barry's gang, I think his knife was for protection as well."

She turned back in her seat, slumped down and stared out into the dark.

I tried to convince her. "I do need a friend, as I don't have many. It would be great if my friend came and helped me out."

Her face softened as she relaxed. "Okay. When?"

"Now," I answered.

"Now?"

"Yes, I want to get moving. Your boyfriend is bound to have called the police. It's not safe for me here, and probably not safe for you either once the Hunters find out I am back in town. They may use you to get to me."

"Okay. I need to go home and collect some things."

"No, I will buy you new stuff. Let's just leave. Call your mum and let her know you will be alright, then switch your phone off," I said.

"No need. She is away with her boyfriend all week. Just drive."

I started the car and headed out of the car park and onto the motorway back to Leeds. Back home to where it all started. Back to get the truth from my Dad.

Chapter Fourteen

We arrived in Leeds about four hours later. On the drive, Scarlett fished for more information on Thorn and what I had been up to with her. I kept my answers to a few words, still wary of Scarlett's true intentions and wanting to avoid another argument. I explained the Hunters wanted me back to carry on their experiments. My ability to transform had become the key to a war between the vampires. Best to keep it simple, I decided. I didn't mention Amber or the details of my relationship with Thorn, but Scarlett knew about Thorn and I.

With that thought, I sympathised with Thorn's dilemma of how much to tell me when we first met. I didn't want to discuss Dragans and the Turned. It would be too much to comprehend. I freaked out on hearing it all and realised I had overreacted to everything since. If I had stayed, maybe I would have calmed down and worked it all out. *Too late*, I had run away, leaving Thorn and Cassius to visit the research centre in Seattle.

I had booked Scarlett and me into a room each at a hotel on the outskirts of town, next door to a Snowdome and shopping centre. We arrived at the hotel as the in-car clock edged towards midnight. I walked Scarlett to her room and then moved quickly onwards to avoid any lingering thoughts of going inside.

The next day we met downstairs for breakfast with Scarlett still dressed in the same clothes, jeans, a white t-shirt and red coat from the night before. The first job of the day would be getting Scarlett kitted out with new clothes and other essentials.

We walked around the shopping centre next door to the hotel. I helped to pick out new clothes, and it felt like old times together, reminding me of our time together at college. It also felt a little weird having just done the same thing with Amber in America. I felt good buying her clothes, and I happily paid for whatever she wanted. We had already visited a few of shops and bought a few outfits to get her through the next couple of days, a few pairs of jeans, t-shirts, fleeces and socks. She teased me in the lingerie section, flaunting the sexy lacy underwear at me. She held up a combination of red pants, bra, suspenders and stockings.

"What do you think? Would I look good in these?" she asked.

My eyes flashed wide at the sight, and un-requested mental images of her in the sexy lingerie jumped into my mind.

"Yeah, great," I said and looked away, trying desperately to shake the image in order to restrain the temptation.

It wasn't like in America, with Amber, when I would get to experience it firsthand. I dare not look else my resolve would crumble. I promised myself to be strong and try to keep to my commitment to Thorn. Amber had been just training. Scarlett would be the real thing. At least this is how I had justified it to myself.

"What about the black ones with the pink lace?" she asked, grinning.

"Just get all of it," I said, flustered, and shoved a handful of notes into her hand and walked away. "Meet you outside."

I walked out of the shop to get some air and calm down. I breathed in slowly, trying not to think of Scarlett in the sexy lingerie. The images wouldn't leave my mind, so I did the next best thing and thought of Thorn in them instead. It helped take my mind off Scarlett, but did nothing to calm me down. About ten minutes later, Scarlett strolled out of the shop, carrying another bag.

"I got three types. Naughty, nice and strict. Which one should I wear tonight?"

I picked up her other bags and walked off, trying to ignore her question. She walked fast and caught up with me.

"You've no sense of humour. She sucked it all out of you?" she asked and laughed.

I didn't want to argue, so I smiled instead and shook my head.

"You haven't changed," I replied.

We roamed through the shopping mall back to the car when Scarlett glared over at a gang of ten girls and five boys about our age. The boys dressed in baggy jeans, hooded tops and baseball caps. The girls were in tight jeans and jackets with lots of gold jewellery.

The gang had sprawled themselves over a couple of benches facing a set of railings on the first floor of the mall. They had also dragged some of the chrome seats away from the cafe. They sat on top of the bench, with feet resting on the bench seat. Others were leaning against the railings and staring around the mall. A couple of the girls were sitting on the boy's laps, and giggling and messing about. Tinny music pumped out of one of their phones, and a couple of them tapped their feet and shuffled their bodies along to the undecipherable tune. The other shoppers looked over and strode away to get out of their reach. Even the security guards seemed to ignore them and walked on to escape responsibility for their behaviour.

Scarlett's body tensed, and her pace increased as I sensed fear in her thoughts as well.

"What's the matter?" I asked.

She glared back at them and started walking around to the other side of the mall to avoid them. I halted and turned her around to face me.

"What is it?" I asked again.

"Them," she shook her head towards them, "they were the gang that used to bully me."

"Really!" I answered.

I shoved the bags into her hands and marched towards them. *My name is Vengeance.*

Scarlett ran behind, loaded down with bags and pulled on my arm. "No, Jon, don't. Leave them, it isn't worth it."

"It is. Don't worry. You will enjoy this. I know I will."

"I won't, it's not me, Jon. It's not you either," she said.

"Not me. Are you joking? You know what I am capable of and what I have done. Jon has gone. I am Vengeance, and I will exact vengeance for you and all of those other people who will never get the chance," I said, and snatched my arm out of her grip and marched on.

The group, alerted by the argument, had looked over and got to their feet as we approached. The boys walked to the front, puffing their chests out and pulling down their hoodies. They glared as I approached, trying to threaten me with their aggressive stance. I stood a step away and Scarlett ran to my side.

"Do you recognise this girl?" I said and looked at Scarlett, whose face had gone bright red.

They all looked over at her.

"No, and so what?" said a lad in the middle, obviously the leader. He stood as tall as me, but fat and out of shape, but used his sheer mass to intimidate.

"Her name is Scarlett. She used to go to your school. She may have looked a little different back then. Brown hair and glasses," I said.

"I remember that slag," one girl said and glared at us.

I focused my eyes on the girl and felt Scarlett tugging on my arm to leave.

The girl chewed her gum. "You remember me, Scarlett. I was the one who used to make your life hell, you fat slag."

Scarlett recoiled into herself and dropped her face down to the floor.

"Scarlett is my friend, and she wants you all to apologise," I replied.

They all burst out laughing, and I glared as I waited for them to settle.

"Screw you. Leave your shopping and run off else we will give you a kicking," the lad said, and the rest of his crew all circled behind him with fists clenched.

I raised my eyebrows, unsurprised at their reaction, just like the O'Keefe gang trying to bluff their way out of a strange situation.

"The O'Keefe gang tried to scare me off in a similar way. You know the O'Keefe's?"

A look of recognition crossed their faces, followed by a moment of hesitation. They knew the O'Keefes; they were gang rivals. They would also know what happened to the O'Keefes when I last came to Leeds and took revenge for the bullying I suffered all my life at school. I had killed the father, son and the visiting friend. I bit the ear off the other brother as well.

"Who are you?" the gang leader asked.

"I am Jonathan Harper," I replied, hoping they may have heard of my name following the deaths of the O'Keefe's at my hands. The leader of the gang rocked back slightly, acknowledgement of my name and its deeds. A few others started looking around for an escape. But as he rocked, he felt the gang behind him, and the desire to look strong overwhelmed any fear.

"Lies. Jonathan Harper is long gone," he said.

"You're right. I am Vengeance," I replied, raising my voice.

I had got bored with waiting. I launched forward and head butted him straight onto the nose. He fell backwards, taking down other gang members with him. I swivelled around and punched another to the floor. The lead girl picked up a chair and swung it at me. I kicked it out of her hands and she stumbled back into the railings.

The boys regained their composure and another one swung a wild punch. I ducked and grabbed him around the waist and lifted him above my head, then threw him at the rest of the gang. They toppled to the floor like nine pins and scrambled away, leaving just the girl who had led the bullying on Scarlett. I grabbed her by the throat and shoved her over the railings, ready to drop her onto the ground below.

"No, no, I'm sorry," she screamed through strangled breath as she looked wide eyed at the ground.

"See, I told you it would be fun," I said to Scarlett.

"No. Leave her," Scarlett shouted and grabbed my other arm. "Don't do this. You have done enough already."

I bore my eyes into the girl's petrified face as it turned blue. I wanted to shove her over the top and watch her smash to the floor, but Scarlett's pleas of mercy interrupted my instincts to kill. She dropped in a heap and gasped for air after I withdrew my hand.

Scarlett tugged at my arm again, and I turned around and walked away. I took a few paces, but Scarlett hadn't followed. She stood over the girl on the floor, leant over her, grabbed the railings for leverage and kneed the girl straight in the face. The girl's head rattled off the railing, and she slumped to the floor unconscious while blood dripped from her nose. Scarlett picked up her shopping and walked over.

"Too good an opportunity to pass up," she said as she walked past and returned to looking in the shop windows. I couldn't believe Scarlett had done that to someone. I had told her she would enjoy it, but it was a heat of the moment statement. She had always been so gentle. My darkness and violence must have affected her.

With clothes bought and having grabbed some lunch, I drove us into Leeds and to my old house to get some answers from my Dad.

On the way, Scarlett stared out the window, avoiding all eye contact and disengaging from the conversation.

"What is it?" I asked, trying to break the silence.

"Why did you attack them?" she asked, turning to face me.

"Because of revenge. You deserve justice."

"But you would have killed her."

I didn't know if I would have or not. I had acted on instinct and let the heat of the moment guide me. My Dragan instincts to kill had overwhelmed my human side.

"Well, you joined in as well," I said, trying to divert her anger on to herself.

"I know, but it was wrong. Jon, you must realise it was wrong."

"Wrong? Why? It's justice."

Scarlett stared at me, her eyes watery and curled down.

"What happened to that boy I fell in love with?"

I grunted with displeasure at her question.

"The world turned against him, and he fought back."

"I know it must have been rough, and your choices seemed obvious at the time, but you can change again," she said.

I wished it could be true, but the transformation couldn't be reversed. The physical changes were permanent, and with them came an instinct to fight and kill. The events since had left emotional scars that I had suffered at my own and others hands. The killing of my tormentors as a vampire, and the murder of Barry with my own human hands couldn't be washed away from my memories.

"Too late. I have seen too much and changed too much. I am a wanted man, and I might be the key to the oncoming vampire civil war. They won't let me go back to a normal life. I have no choice but to embrace it and fight back," I said.

"There is always a choice," she muttered and turned to face out the window again. We carried on the rest of the journey in silence.

We reached my old house with my Dad's car parked in the drive, and I pulled the BMW over to the side of the road. The house looked back to normal as the windows were back in place, and the 'for sale' sign had been taken down. The front garden looked tidy and the grass cut.

I scanned about before going to meet him. I doubted the Hunters would still be watching out for me after a year. I put my sunglasses on and walked down the road, scanning the houses either side. Then we walked through the gate and along the path to the front door. Scarlett stood behind me and held my hand, giving it a reassuring squeeze, as I knocked on the door, then pressed the bell. A few moments later, I heard his slippers dragging along the floor.

After discovering Scarlett was innocent, I decided I should give my Dad the benefit of the doubt. He could have a reasonable explanation for his actions.

The door opened, and my Dad stared out, shielding his eyes from the low sun. Last time I had seen my Dad had been in the lab just before I freed Thorn. Dad wasn't tall, just about average height, and I was shorter than him back then, but now I looked down at him. His face was unshaven and hair wilder than usual, with more grey in it than I remembered.

"Hello, who is it?" he asked, looking up at me.

I pulled off the sunglasses and smiled.

"Dad, it's me, Jonathan," I said.

He stepped back to take in the complete picture and shook his head.

"No, it can't be. You're too tall, too broad. The body shape and skeletal structure is all wrong. Who are you?"

"Dad, it's me. The formula has done this. It's changed me."

Scarlett poked her head around the side and waved.

"It's definitely him," she said.

His mouth dropped wide open. He poked his fingers under his glasses and rubbed his eyes, then narrowed his gaze to focus in on my features.

"You best come in, son. I will get us some coffee," he said and quickly shuffled down the hallway to the kitchen.

I stood, arms open, ready for the big reunion. Scarlett rubbed my arm. "It's a shock, that's all. You really do look different. Give him a chance."

We followed in and Scarlett shut the door behind us. I peeked into the front room, and it was clean and tidy, but it had never been when I lived with him. On the windowsill sat the picture of my Mum. Next to it a picture of me in my school uniform. The photo had been taken only a few weeks before we ended up leaving Leeds because of the harassment from the O'Keefe gang. I looked so young. The change in my appearance was more surprising than I realised. I had been so used to seeing my features and size change. I didn't realise how startling it was in such a small amount of time. No wonder he didn't recognise me.

We walked into the kitchen as the kettle bubbled and boil away, while Dad clunked some mugs together and fetched out the milk. He placed the coffee down on the kitchen table as we each took a seat.

"You going to tell me where you have been and what you've been doing with Subject X."

"Dad, her name is Thorn. Besides, I think you should start. I want the truth about the experiments, the Hunters and the formula. Did you set me up? Was the whole thing planned, from the car accident, the job offer, the mugging, leaving the formula out and everything else to force me to test out your work?" I asked, speaking calmly and concisely, repeating the speeches I had practised on the plane journey. I kept it simple, avoiding anything that could provoke an argument, or give away too many details that could compromise others: Thorn, Cassius and Max.

"I realise it must seem that way," he said, "from the beginning then. The car accident with the gang and Giles, I know nothing about it. The job offer, I had been offered it a few weeks before and turned it down. We had no reason to leave Leeds before the accident. Things were bad with the gang, but you only needed to get by for another six months until you were free of them."

"The packed boxes of textbooks, Dad. You were already packing away."

"Hey... Oh them. I was donating them to a local university."

Such an easy explanation after all this time. I felt embarrassed to have asked.

"Okay, so London then and the mugging," I said, moving on to the next point.

"The night you came to the lab, I'd had a visitor moments before, my boss, Gabriel Fenwick. He told me the research had gone well, and they had combined it with other research to create a potential working solution. Then he showed me the two red needles in his hands. Next, the phone rang and it was you. I told Gabriel what had happened, and he suggested I brought you downstairs while I made arrangements. Then I went up to fetch you. By the time we came back downstairs, he had gone, but he left the needles with the formula on the bench. I shoved them away, hoping you hadn't noticed them and went to make the phone call."

"You left me in a room next to a psychic, psychotic vampire," I said.

"I am sorry. I got flustered. The news of a working formula and then your sudden phone call threw my focus. Anyway, she had never done that before. She had always been quiet and subdued before."

His story seemed plausible, and I couldn't sense anything abnormal in his behaviour or emotions from my psychic powers. However, Thorn, quiet and subdued seemed unlike her. I thought she would have fought them fang and claw.

"So what did you research in Leeds that made you so important?" I asked.

"I have done similar research before, but it was on a werewolf instead."

"A werewolf?"

"Yes, I had successfully isolated the werewolf genetics and created a delivery system into a host," he said, and a small smiled appeared.

"You tried this on someone?"

"No, they do all the research in isolation to others. Someone high up combines it all together to make the final product. When I came down to London, I had just carried on the same research, but against the vampire instead. I had submitted a report on my findings only a week before the incident."

"And?"

"And that is it. Someone must have combined several strands of research and created the final formula. I was as shocked as anyone to find it in the lab, then I was terrified to tell them I had lost it, or it was stolen."

"But you had ten more needles the next time I came down."

"I know. By the time you came back down into the lab, after injecting the vampire formula, they were all sat on the side. They sent them to me to test, as their experiments had failed elsewhere."

"So, just a coincidence, then?"

"I have had plenty of time to think about it. The first time I am convinced was planned. The second time could have been bad luck on their part."

"What happened after I left?" I asked, pushing for more information.

"They interrogated me for days about what I knew and where you were hiding. Finally, they let me go. I kept my job and they posted me back to Leeds, but downgraded my role, keeping me away from the important stuff. I stayed with them in the hope I could find out the truth one day."

The revelations had taken me no further forward with finding out who controlled it all, but at least my Dad wasn't part of the scheme against me. He was just another victim of the Hunters, the same as Scarlett.

"And you, son, what happened to you?"

I poured down my coffee and unleashed the truth on them both. The training with Thorn, the revenge on the O'Keefe's and Barry's death with him turning into a monster. Off to Vegas with Thorn and meeting Cassius. Then fighting the Hunters and the Turned, and meeting a werewolf.

Finally, my coming back to England. I explained the differences between the Dragans and Turned. I felt my Dad could cope with the whole truth and so could Scarlett now, as she had time to get used to the idea of vampires. I changed the story a little, not mentioning Amber and steering clear of my intimate relationship with Thorn.

Dad nodded along with interest.

"I heard about the O'Keefe's and we assumed it was you. I hoped I had been mistaken," he said.

"I went for revenge. I wanted to give them a beating and warn them off. But they threatened to kill me and I had no choice," I said, not quite believing my lie.

Dad studied me for a moment.

"It doesn't surprise me about Barry turning into a monster," he said.

"Why?" I asked, surprised at his matter of fact answer and pleased he hadn't pushed about the O'Keefe incident.

"The same method I used on the werewolf didn't work. Thorn's code was more complex. I realised it had to be encoded to a specific person's DNA to work. I used my DNA to create the right formula to get it to work, but I kept it secret as I worried about how they would use it. I gave just the genetic code of the new strand without mentioning it would only work on a matching code. As my son, your DNA would be similar and hence the formula would work," he said.

He'd been clever to keep the truth of the formula a secret, but I wondered if they knew this.

"Is that why I was used to test it?" I asked.

"Could be. They must have worked out the formula was encoded to my DNA and why it had failed on other subjects. If I tested it and it went wrong, the knowledge would have been lost. I am sorry son, I had no idea they would be so ruthless."

We sat in silence for a moment and drank our coffees. The truth was falling into place, and I didn't know what to say.

Dad broke the silence.

"I was aware of the two types of vampires, I didn't know that is what they called themselves or the history behind the two different types," he said, "but I have met a werewolf before, from my research in Leeds."

"Was the werewolf imprisoned like Thorn?" I asked.

"No, he was a willing participant. He would come in at night when his powers were strongest, especially at a full moon," he replied.

The night time work suddenly made sense.

"So you have the truth. I guess the question is, who is behind the scenes manipulating all these events? Can we find out?" I asked.

"It sounds like the Hunters are involved. I guess that means one of my bosses is part of the conspiracy. From putting the pieces together, Gabriel Fenwick is the first person to look at," he said.

"Cool, can I use your computer to do some research on him?" I asked.

"Yes, but I have a better idea. At work, I could try to access the main files. Gabriel's office isn't far away. I could break in and access his computer."

"Wouldn't it be dangerous?"

"Possibly, but that doesn't matter. I won't let them use you as a weapon in their war. You come first."

I beamed to hear him say that. In the past, work always came first. I spent all those nights alone in the house while he did his research. We never went on holidays either, as he couldn't bear to leave his work. Finally, all that had changed.

"Thanks, Dad," I said.

"Don't thank me yet. I will need a diversion. Something to get the security looking elsewhere, so I have free access to the corridors and his computer."

"Okay, I will think of something, but I will need a couple of days to get the materials I need," I said.

No more training. This time, it would be for real. I would get to find out how much I learnt through Thorn's training and how much I had changed. My war had started. Time for vengeance.

Chapter Fifteen

I spent the night researching and planning our mission to steal Gabriel's files. The next day, Dad went to work as usual, and Scarlett and I went shopping again, but a different type of shopping this time. I needed supplies to create a distraction.

We went to the DIY superstore first and picked up some tools and materials. Onto the garden centre next to get more materials and finally to an electrical component shop. I paid all in cash to avoid detection, as I knew purchases of such quantities would trigger an alert. On the way back, we stopped at the supermarket and filled up the back seats with food to cover the next few days.

We came home unpacked the materials, food and had some lunch. Next, I started on my plan. Scarlett helped by following my instructions, stripping back wires and sorting out the materials into assembled piles. We carried on for a few hours, getting it all ready until I reached a point when my concentration flagged. I decided to take a break to avoid accidents.

My Dad had brought all my stuff back from London, and my room looked as if I had never left. I found my Star Wars films and put one on for us both to watch. Almost like old times.

All-day, I fought with my feelings for Scarlett, using the preparation as a distraction by immersing myself in my work. I sat apart from her on the sofa watching the film, but it seemed wrong. We'd watched this film together so many times and always snuggled up. I felt odd not holding her as we watched it, and my desire and love for her exploded.

I glanced around at her, and she smiled back, her eyes dilating and face flushed. She shuffled slowly across the sofa, and I put my arm up on the top of the sofa, clearing her path. She slid in next to me and rested against my chest. I let my arm slide off the top of the sofa and wrapped it around her. She put her hand on my leg and sighed as we continued to watch the film together. With Scarlett in my arms again, I felt out of control, my heart pounding and body hot.

"This is nice," she said.

"Yeah."

"You are so warm. I don't remember you being this hot before," she said.

I couldn't tell if this was a subtle hint or the fact I really did generate more heat. Possibly part of the Dragan remnants, as Thorn's body generated a high heat as well.

We watched the rest of the film, and as it reached the end, she playfully rubbed her hand down the inside of my leg. It increased my heart rate, and my heat rose further. As the credits rolled, Scarlett turned around, gazing up into my eyes and smiled. I smiled back into her large black pupils. She moved all the way around and then stroked her hands along my arms and down the back of my neck. My skin tingled upon her touch.

Suddenly, she lunged forwards kissing me fiercely on the lips. Her leg flipped across as she straddled my lap. Her other hand grabbed behind my back, pinning me to the sofa. I didn't fight it. My love and passion seduced me into returning the kiss. My hands grasped around her back, pulling her in tight.

Then my thoughts cleared, *Thorn.* I pushed Scarlett onto the sofa and bolted out of my seat. My lips were wet and red from her kiss.

"Stop," I shouted.

"Why? It's what we both want," she said and jumped off the sofa and flung herself at me.

I held her back and pushed her away.

"I can't. You know I can't," I answered.

"You can. You are just choosing not to. Let me convince you," she said, and stripped off her t-shirt, undid her jeans, dropped them to the floor and stepped out of them.

Underneath, she wore the cream and pink laced coloured lingerie she showed me in the shop.

"I am wearing the nice lingerie, or would you prefer the naughty?" she said and winked.

I desperately wanted her. I had never seen her like this before, as our relationship hadn't developed that far. When we dated, I would have given anything to have seen her dressed like this. Her throwing herself at me would have been a dream come true. But now it felt wrong.

"Scarlett, calm down. This isn't like you," I said, backing away, but I wish it had been like her.

"Don't be shy. I want to know what a part vampire man can do. What powers can you show me?" she asked seductively and smiled. Her eyes widen to black saucers; her skin flushed and body pert.

It would have been so easy to give in and take her. But her last comment clicked into place. Powers. Of course, my Dragan power, the one I used on Amber. Thorn had told me if I desired a woman, hormones would be released, triggering the reaction that Scarlett was exhibiting. With Scarlett, the reaction was severe, as my passion for her was strong, and there was already an underlying emotional attachment between us. I had to get away from her quickly and calm myself down. I had to stop her and release her from my unconscious seductive powers.

"Scarlett, sorry. It's my fault. It's the powers," I said, and ran out the room, bounded upstairs to the shower room and locked the door.

I turned the shower on and rotated the dial to cold. She knocked on the door.

"Room for two," she said.

I stripped and jumped under the freezing stream of water and shuddered. The cold water dampened my ardour, and I hoped it would stop my powers. After a few minutes, I stopped, got out, dried off and changed back into my clothes. I tentatively opened the door. She pulled the door back and pushed me back inside, up against the glass shower door. I twisted her around, dumped her into the shower, and hit it onto cold. The water sprayed down, drenching her, and she screamed as I shut the shower door and held it tight. After a couple of minutes of her yelling and banging on the glass door, I let go, walked out of the shower room, and went downstairs.

About half an hour later, she reappeared, fully clothed, wet bedraggled hair and face bright red embarrassed. I sat in the kitchen, drinking a cup of coffee as she walked in. She wrapped her arms around her waist and looked at the floor. "I'm sorry. I don't understand what came over me."

"Sit down. I will explain," I replied and motioned her to the seat.

She scraped the wooden chair back across the white tiled floor and sat down.

"I have powers, as you know. The Dragans have the power to seduce. It's a weapon to lure in their prey. Unfortunately, because of our past and my inability to control myself, I think this power is pouring out from me and aiming at you."

"Really, but I do fancy you. It's not all the power," she replied.

"I know. Something has to exist for it to work. A base desire for it to work on. With our past, it's an increased reaction from me, and it is exaggerating your desires."

"So you tricked me into coming here with you? Tricked me into making a fool of myself?"

"No. I didn't do it on purpose. I thought you wanted to come?"

She glared at me. "I don't know. I had promised my mum and myself that I wouldn't get involved again if you returned. You're trouble, that is for certain. Yet, I was happy to see you. I wanted to know what had happened, but I told myself, I would leave straight afterwards."

She glared again and then looked away before carrying on. "But as soon as I was alone with you in that car, I felt different. I just wanted you. I couldn't let you go again. I had to stay with you no matter the cost… It was this seductive power of yours. You used it on me."

"Sorry, I didn't realise. It just sort of happens. I don't seem to have control over it yet."

"How can I ever be sure what I feel for you is real and not just a trick of my hormones?"

"Because it's how you feel when I am not about," I said.

"And what do you think about me?"

"I still fancy you and I still love you, but things have happened. I made a choice," I said.

"A choice! She used these powers on you. She seduced you and tricked you into it. How can you be sure how you feel? You owe her nothing," Scarlett said.

I knew what Scarlett said rang true to an extent, but I knew what Thorn's powers had done to me when we met. Yet I didn't care. Plus, when I rescued her, my altered Dragan state meant her powers were ineffective. I chose of my own free will to release her from her cell, but somewhere between breaking in and entering the cell, my powers and immunity to her seduction had worn off. I went to the research centre that night with only one intention, and that was to be with her.

"Yes, she used her powers on me. I knew that and I let her do it as well. Remember, I had lost everything. I had been mugged and then bullied, but worst of all, I thought you had betrayed me. Thorn saved me, as I saved her. I can't walk out on her now, as she needs me more than ever. The war is coming, and I have to choose a side. I have to stand with her or against her."

"I never betrayed you," Scarlett yelled, her face red.

"I know that now, but she rescued me."

"Do you love her?"

I couldn't lie and I knew the reaction my response would get. I breathed in deep to answer.

"Yes."

Scarlett's face drained. "Then why ask me here?"

"I love you as well. I am sorry, it's a rubbish answer. I love you both. You are both totally different. There are no comparisons between you."

"You need to decide, Jon. You can't have us both."

"Could we try it?" I asked, and half smiling, trying to be funny.

"NO," she said, and stormed off to the front room, and her chair clattered to the floor.

I followed her and she sat back on the sofa, arms crossed and face fuming. I perched on the sofa armrest at the other end.

"Sorry. I know it can't go on," I said to break the silence.

"You're scared of her."

"Of course, she's a killer, but it's not what is stopping me. War is coming. Thorn and I will be at the centre of the storm. I can't avoid her. I have no choice but to work with her. If I drag you into this war, you could get hurt or killed. It's not your fight."

"I can make my own choices, Jon. No one said you have to fight this war. Leave it to Thorn and her friends. You never chose this life. It was thrust upon you."

"Nice try, but I chose the night I went to the park and killed the gang. It's too late for me now. The Hunters want my body to uncover the secrets of the formula. They won't stop hunting me down. I have no choice but to fight back and that means working with Thorn," I replied.

Scarlett opened her arms from around her waist and sat upright. "Just think about it. Maybe there is another way. If you want us to be together, then we have to go into hiding and make our own plans. Perhaps you can then coordinate with Thorn, but you don't have to sleep with her. There is always a choice."

I nodded in agreement. There is always a choice, but they weren't always the easy ones. When I looked at Scarlett, my desires grew again, but with it the re-occurring dream of draining her blood. I wondered what her blood tasted like? To save her, I had to leave her alone. I shouldn't have got her involved again.

Chapter Sixteen

Over the next few days, we continued to prepare, and I tried to keep my desires for Scarlett under control, but I found it a struggle. A few times, I had to walk into the garden to calm myself down. I sensed from Scarlett's body language and psychic flashes that she struggled as well. I couldn't deny it anymore. I still loved her, but I loved Thorn as well.

The night before our mission, the tension between Scarlett and I had been rising again, so I took in some cold fresh air in the small grassy garden to focus my thoughts and cool my body down. I wore no coat, preferring the cold air to wash over me instead. My Dad came out wrapped up in a warm winter coat and deerstalker hat pulled down over his ears.

"You hiding in the garden again?" he asked.

I had told him everything that had happened the other day between Scarlett and me.

"Cooling down and gathering my thoughts," I said.

He stood in front of me, shook his head, and sighed. "Son, why not be with Scarlett? She is a wonderful girl, and she loves you. You love her as well. So what's the problem?"

"I am with Thorn."

Dad shook his head again and sighed. "She's a vampire. She isn't a real person. She's just using you."

"Dad, she's a Dragan for a start off. Secondly, she's a real person, just a different species to us, that is all."

"They are all vampires at the end of the day and you're not."

"You've run the tests on my blood and DNA. You know the truth, I am not 100% human anymore either," I replied.

"I know you have changed, but you were born human and your majority human still, and that is what counts."

"But the war and the Hunters. They will never leave me alone. My only chance is to fight back."

"There is more than one way to fight back. It doesn't have to be at Thorn's side. I know you never mentioned it, but it is obvious you and Thorn are more than friends. She is a hot blooded vampire. I am no fool," he said, and I blushed. "I am sure she is fantastic, but maybe you should think about what sort of life you would have with her. Maybe you should find out what a human female is like."

"I already know," I answered.

"Oh, I assumed you hadn't been with a woman before."

"I hadn't. It happened in Vegas while Thorn was away talking to Cassius. It was Thorn's idea for me to practice my seduction powers and get experience."

"Strange idea. Who was she?"

"Her name was Amber. When I left Thorn, it was her house I stopped at until I sorted out my flights."

"So more than just the once? More than just practice?"

I heard the accusation in his voice and felt guilty.

"Yeah, a few times, but I had to. She was letting me stay at her apartment."

He shook his head. "Don't lie. You had all that money. You could have easily just rented a hotel room for a few nights in Vegas. The truth is you wanted to, maybe because she was human."

I rubbed my eyes. "Maybe... I don't know anymore. I just reacted in the heat of the moment. Maybe I should have never left Thorn. I should never have cheated on her," I said, as the reality of my reactions hit home.

"I have no love for Thorn. She is a vampire after all, but if she cares for you and is genuine, then she deserves better," he said, and I grunted in acknowledgement. "However, it is done now and if you are going to make a clean break from Thorn, then I don't see what is wrong with you rekindling your relationship with Scarlett. After all, she was your first love."

He made sense.

"You would have me run away with Scarlett and hide."

"Yes, if it means staying safe and alive."

I controlled a small smile, pleased at his concern. "I am not running anymore. This is who I am now. I have changed. I've seen too much and done too much."

"Just think about it. How do you plan on getting back together with Thorn, and what happens to Scarlett after our mission is finished? You just going to drop her off at her mum's house and walk away forever?"

"I hadn't honestly thought about it too much," I said and stared up at the sky, looking for inspiration.

"Jon, you don't know what Thorn is. You told me that there were only ten Dragans left in the world, and there were no more Dragan pregnancies."

"And?"

"Your young ears don't hear the truth. Thorn must have tried to have a baby with every surviving Dragan male for her to say that. If your species were near extinction, you would have sex with every member of the opposite sex you could find to help reproduce your race."

I stared at him. I couldn't believe that yet again the truth had rushed past me without me realising it.

"Cassius and Cyrus," I said.

"Yes, most definitely."

"She said that they had fallen out. I am so stupid."

"Since you abandoned her and cheated on her, do you think she will stay faithful as well? When a Dragan male is her only company?"

"No!" I shouted, "No," and held my head in shock. This couldn't be happening. Surely, she wouldn't cheat on me.

"You should think about starting a new life by reclaiming your old life with Scarlett."

Tears welled up in my eyes and anger boiled away at the thought of her with Cassius.

"I don't know. It's just too confusing. My heart and my head say two different things. I love them both."

"You must choose. Once tomorrow night is done, you need to talk to Scarlett properly. You can't keep leading her on like this, especially with your powers. You are driving her crazy, and it's unfair to subject her to that torment," he said, and placed a hand on my shoulder and looked me straight in the eye.

"Yes, Dad, I will," I said, and he went back inside.

The thoughts about Thorn shocked me, and I couldn't help but think where and what she might be doing. I assumed she would be at the biotech centre in Seattle getting the answers to the questions on the formula with Cassius. But was she with Cassius as a friend or a lover? However, she could be just around the corner, getting ready to break into the house and take her revenge on me, or to re-ignite our love. I had no idea what her reaction would be the next time we met.

The night of our mission had arrived, and Dad had gone to work. He still needed to work occasionally at nights and generally preferred it, as he hated being in the house at night by himself. The army base was in the countryside next to a small village. Opposite the army base was a public woodland used by dog owners, walkers and mountain bikers.

The time approached one a.m., and we had already been in the area since darkness had fallen. I knew the army base well after living there for three months back in the summer of last year. I knew the guard's patterns, security weaknesses, and potential targets to pick.

When I had lived there, I feared the O'Keefe's would break in and find me. To help settle my nerves, the base commander had ordered a captain to give me a guided tour of the base, showing me all the defences. He also told me all the areas to stay out of as well, like the ammunition dump, weapons storage and training areas. I had drawn a map out when I first moved in. I didn't want to wander accidentally into unsafe areas and get blown up or shot. Plus, I wanted to be aware of the safe parts of the base in case I needed to get help or run from the O'Keefe's. They never attacked the army base to find me. Not sure if they knew I lived there or not, but I doubted they would have attacked. Back then, I spent my life as a paranoid and confused wreck.

I had already slipped under the fence a few hours ago, creeping around the base and preparing my distractions. I knew of a place where the soldiers slipped in and out to avoid the guards. They had created a dip under the fence and covered it up with bushes and wooden boards. You wouldn't spot it unless you knew it was there. I'd seen some soldiers slip through it one night when watching out of my bedroom window.

Scarlett and I staggered along the road approaching the gates, holding each other upright. We rambled on at each other incoherently, pretending to be drunk. When I lived there, I remembered hearing many drunks shouting at each other as they stumbled past the base, so it wasn't unusual. To give our act authenticity, we'd been to a pub just a half a mile down the road and had a drink, so we had alcohol on our breaths and it gave us some courage. Scarlett had been a bag of nerves and needed a couple of shots of vodka to calm down. I felt nervous as well but hid it from her so that I didn't encourage any fears.

I had dressed in casual jeans, black boots, black retro biker's jacket and a grey t-shirt. Scarlett dressed to attract attention in a clingy red dress matching her flame red hair cascading down her neck. She had added false lashes, glittery eye makeup, and bright red nails. The outfit finished off with knee length black leather boots falling short of the hem of the red dress. I had never seen her dressed up for a big night out before. I looked at her in shock when she emerged from her room, ready to go. My lust stirred inside, and I quickly focused my mind, controlling my seduction powers; scared I would trigger another episode, and this time, I would give into temptation.

We staggered onwards into the opening of the road towards the gates and along the wire fences enclosing the base. At the side of the gates, the guard sat in a hut looking at us and watching the CCTV cameras at his side. Nothing he hadn't seen before. I pretended to slip over.

"What you drop me for, you silly cow," I slurred at her.

"Stand up, you lightweight. I bet those guys could keep up with me," she said, pointing over at the guard and smiling.

"Get lost," I shouted.

I held my hand out for her to help me up. She turned her nose up, walked over to the guard hut instead and tapped on the window. The guard wearily slid the window to one side. Scarlett leant in and breathed alcoholic fumes all over him.

"Bet you could handle a girl like me," she said and winked at him.

He recoiled from the fumes, grinned and shook his head.

"Best be on your way, young lady," he answered.

I got back to my feet and shuffled over, grabbed Scarlett's arm and yanked her away from the hut.

"You are with me, remember?" I shouted.

She turned around and slapped my face, not holding back. The impact of skin on skin rang out, stinging my face. She had wanted to do that for some time. I stumbled back onto the floor, nursing a redraw cheek. The Dragan inside me fuelled my muscles with power. I wanted to lash out and fight back. I jumped up to face her. She positioned herself with her back to the guard blocking his sight. I threw a fake punch and Scarlett crashed back into the hut, shaking the windows, and then slumping to the floor. The guard jumped from his seat, opened the door and rushed around.

"Get back," he shouted at me and crouched down by Scarlett, who pulled a knife from her bag and held it at his throat.

"Don't move," she said, and I ran over and pushed him to the floor, then strapped his hands together with a black zip tie. Next, I shoved an old cloth in his mouth and tied a strap around his head to gag him.

I smiled at Scarlett, my ears still ringing and face red from the slap.

She grinned. "Face okay?"

I nodded. "You enjoyed that!" She smiled in response. "Get the car and wait for me at the rendezvous point," I said.

She scrambled to her feet and ran back down the street as fast as her black boots and clingy red dress allowed her. I dragged the soldier back through the gate into the hut and bundled him into the corner. I found the alarm button, pressed it and the gates locked back into place and red lights wailed. The phone rang. I picked it up.

"What's happened?" a voice said.

"Intruders on the base, Sir," I shouted, dropped the phone to the floor and ran off. I pulled out my mobile phone and sent three text messages. In seconds, a string of devices exploded around the base. Over at the research centre, smoke grenades went off and a small fire started. I hoped my Dad received the message and had hit the fire alarm. With a fire in the research centre, they would have to open all the doors and exit the building, leaving an unguarded route into Gabriel's office and access to his computer.

Next, an explosion erupted near the ammunition and weapons store across the other side of the base. With the explosions and an attack at the gate, I hoped the main forces would be diverted across the base and away from the research centre, giving my Dad time to access the files and to meet me at the dip under the fence.

I darted into the base and headed along the fence, clinging to the dark. I ran away from the explosions and towards the research centre, residential and office buildings, which were in the opposite direction.

My vision, especially at night, had improved, allowing me to see in the dark to the research centre as the staff began streaming out. Over the other side of the base, Army fire engines raced around, and armed soldiers ran to the gates and over to the weapons and ammunition stores. They had no reason to come over this side, the residential part, as nothing was happening.

I climbed into the back garden of one of the empty army houses and sneaked inside to watch out the window. The smoke billowed into the sky and jeeps hurtled down the road with re-enforcements. I worried they would catch my Dad. I stared at my phone, willing it to beep.

The research centre staff stood around in the car park, waiting for the fire crew to arrive and check it over. As per the plan, the fire crew focused on the diversions I had created. Finally, after thirty minutes, my phone beeped.

"X" the message read. The agreed response to say everything had gone well and to meet at the fence. I watched out the window and saw him striding across the base towards the fence. We had decided best for him to leave straight away and never return. They would work out who did it, eventually.

I made my way back outside, climbed over the wall of the house and whistled my Dad over as he walked past.

He juddered and spun around, and I ran over and put my hand on his shoulder.

"It's just me. Did it go okay?" I asked.

He padded his pocket and looked at the smoke filling the sky, and then at the mayhem across the rest of the base.

"You did all this?"

"Yeah, it looks worse than it is. Mostly just smoke and fear. No one should get hurt."

I grabbed his arm and guided him through the dark into the tree lined area up to the fence. I pulled back the boards with the bushes attached and guided Dad through on his front. He crawled through to the other side, and I followed on, pulling the boards back again. Just then, a car pulled up a few metres away, the door opened, and a black boot and a red dress climbed out.

I stood back up and helped my Dad to his feet and then weaved us through the dense trees and bushes into the light. Scarlett waited for us with the car door open, and we jumped in the back. Scarlett got back into the driver's seat. The car, a grey Mercedes I had stolen earlier, wheel span away from the base.

"You get it," she shouted.

My Dad's shaking hand reached into his pocket and pulled out a USB stick.

"It should all be here. I downloaded everything on Gabriel's computer I could. I have password locked it just in case, your first pet's name." Good old Jaws, the goldfish.

My heart raced with excitement from the mission and the thought of finally getting some proper answers. Dad shook all over as well.

"You did well," I said.

He nodded in thanks, putting the USB stick back into his pocket. I couldn't believe the plan had worked so well. I smiled to myself. Thorn would be proud of me. All her training had worked.

Scarlett sped away from the base, and I had to tell her to slow down else we wouldn't get away in one piece. We sat in silence on the journey as Scarlett drove us to the multi-storey car park about ten miles away in the city centre. There I had left Thorn's BMW packed with all our clothes and money ready to drive south to a cottage in Cornwall we had rented out. We would rest up at the cottage while I examined the files and prepared our next move. Then I could work out friend from foe, and who spoke the truth and who could be trusted?

Scarlett drove the Mercedes into the multi-storey car park, and up and around the circular ramps to the 3rd floor. She cruised along, cutting across the empty spaces and towards the lonely BMW. The car's engine echoed off the concrete walls of the nearly empty building. A few dodgy figures lingered further down. Nothing I couldn't handle, especially with a boot full of weapons. We parked and changed cars, and I got in the driver's seat, Dad in the back and Scarlett sitting next to me. She smiled and placed her hand on my arm.

"We did it," she said. I leant across, and we kissed for a couple of seconds.

A heat of the moment reaction. I withdrew and looked at her. She returned my gaze with a smile, like the first time we had kissed. My heart was hammering and body heating up. I leant towards her, caressing my hands around her neck and encouraging her towards me. She reciprocated, resting her hands on my neck and leaning in. We kissed, savouring our victory.

"Ummm uh," a sound came from the back of the car.

We stopped and looked around. Dad frowned.

"I am glad you two have finally put the past behind you. But I suggest this waits for later," he said.

Scarlett's face reddened, and my own face heated up, mirroring her embarrassment.

"Sorry, Dad," I said, and looked over at Scarlett and smiled. She giggled back, her eyes glinting, and then sat up and clicked in the seat belt.

The suspicious characters in the dark had started walking over to us, hoods up and looking around for other people. Best to leave now rather than cause a scene. We didn't want to draw any attention. I strapped in, started the car up, and navigated across the car park towards the circular exit ramps.

Out of the up ramp, three vehicles hurtled towards us. A black car rammed into the side of the BMW. Our car skidded across the car park and crunched into a concrete pillar. We jolted around in our seats as airbags burst open. The car alarm wailed out and metal crashed to the floor. The airbag saved me from the worst of the impact into my door and my head spun for a few seconds.

The Dragan instincts to survive took control, and I focused and snapped back to reality. I glanced over at Scarlett and Dad, who looked dazed but seemed okay, nothing damaged. I tried to get the car moving, but the engine wouldn't start. A white van pulled across the front, blocking my exit and another black car span around, blocking us from behind as well.

I shoulder barged the door open and clambered out through the air bags, pulling my pistol out from my jacket. The doors on the back of the white van opened and out jumped five dead, decaying vampires, snarling and growling. From the other two cars stepped three men from each vehicle, the drivers remaining inside. Scarlett shuffled across the seats; her door blocked by the pillar. She climbed out, putting her shaking hands on my waist.

"Jon!" she said in a dazed voice.

"It will be okay. Just do as I say."

Dad got out of the car as well, looking around at the assembled attackers. A man from the cars limped forward and pulled up the sleeve of his shirt.

"Jon, do you remember me from Vegas?" he said. He was one of the two Hunters that cornered me in the alleyway.

"You shot my foot and killed my friend. Not going to give you a choice this time, it's going to be the hard way," he said, and stared at Scarlet before pulling out a needle and injecting himself in the arm.

To the side of us, the Turned fanned out, blocking every exit. In front and behind, the Hunters all followed suit, spreading out, then pulled up their shirtsleeves and stabbed in a needle.

They all frowned and groaned, momentarily staggering on their feet and rocking backwards, or dropping to one knee before standing back up. I looked at the leader, the Hunter from Vegas. He opened his eyes to reveal dead pools of blackness. Thin claws cut through his fingers, and his skin turned pale and fractured. The injections had transformed him into one of the Turned. The other Hunters changed moments later.

"Not as good as your formula I know, but it will suffice," he said and growled, and the encircling Turned and transformed Turned all joined in.

The roars echoed around the car park, and the suspicious figures that had headed towards us ran for the exit. I had a sword and more guns in the boot, but the bullets would only slow them down. The silver coated sword and UV light offered my only chance.

One of the Turned leapt forward, and I fired a bullet straight into its forehead, and it dropped to the floor. I fired the bullets as each one of the Turned vampires came snarling forward.

"Move around to the boot. I have weapons!" I yelled at Scarlett.

She moved around the side of the car and flipped opened the boot, frantically searching through the bags. The vampires walked menacingly towards us, trying not to be the first, wanting to avoid my bullets. I fired conservatively, aiming at their heads and hearts, hoping damage to those vital organs would slow them down. I hit a couple, and they fell to the floor, but others dodged the bullets as they approached. I ran out of ammunition, and a Turned charged forwards, claws slashing in the air.

"Catch," Scarlett shouted.

I ducked as a sword skidded across the roof and over the top of me. I grabbed the trailing hilt and stabbed it into the vampire's dead heart. It shrieked and slid off the sword, crashing down, coating the floor in ash.

A UV light flashed across the faces of the approaching Turned. They ducked and weaved out of the way, pulling up hoods and zipping them over their chins and noses. It delayed them for a moment, but the UV worked on the Turned Hunters. When I had taken the formula and transformed into a Dragan, the UV and Silver didn't work. These transformed Hunters had all the weaknesses of the Turned. It gave me some hope of beating them and escaping.

Dad kept swinging the UV light about, occasionally catching their eyes, making them glance away. The next one attacked. I swiped my sword forward and he dodged backwards. Another jumped across the car bonnet, and I rolled forward to avoid his claws. As I rolled, I slashed my sword through a leg of a retreating Turned, cutting off his leg and toppling it to the floor. They circled around, grabbing at me with their thin claws. I slashed with the sword, pushing them back from every side. A battle would be hopeless.

"Scarlett, run," I shouted.

I looked behind as she swung the bag into a vampire and knocked him over and then ran for the exit. The vampire regained its feet and scrambled after her.

The attacking vampires' dead black eyes bore into me, and their yellow claws slashed and fangs snapped. Behind, Dad battled with a Turned by desperately trying to flash the UV into its eyes. Finally, he resorted to hitting it with the torch. I slashed back and forth wildly, trying to gain space so I could stand. I got up, swiped around backwards, and charged at one of the Turned blocking the way to my Dad. The vampire leapt back.

I slashed across, severing the top half of his head and jumped over its disintegrating body. Next, I stabbed through the heart of the vampire that had pinned my Dad's head backwards to reveal his neck. The vampire shrieked and exploded into ash over the sword.

"Run," I shouted.

Dad sprinted after Scarlett and the Turned that still chased her. I reached inside the boot, grabbed a silver knife and threw it arching around my Dad as he ran for the exit. It hit the back of the Turned just as it grabbed Scarlett. The vampire shrieked and disintegrated to ash. Scarlett screamed, shaking off the dusty hand as she sprinted through the car park exit and down the stairs. Dad chased after her, running through the shower of ash as a shot rang out. Dad stumbled to the floor. The transformed Hunter's gun smoked as he put it away into his jacket.

"Sometimes, the old ways are the best," he said, sneered and waved the others forward. They ran at me and I slashed at them in a rage, beating them back. I could see blood on the floor coming from my Dad. I had to rescue him.

Out of nowhere, a red car sped up the ramp, left the ground for a moment and smashed into the black car blocking us in. The Turned spun around to face the new threat. Two figures blurred out of the car and slammed into the vampires, cutting them to pieces. Another person, a man, tattooed, long hair, tall and muscular, stepped out of the car. Max the werewolf. It could only mean one thing, and I caught sight of Thorn's red violent eyes as she fought her way through. On the other side, Cassius attacked. Then the gun fired again and pain seared through my leg. I collapsed to the floor.

"We are leaving," the Hunter screamed, and two Turned grabbed either side of me and jumped us up over the BMW and through the open doors at the back of the white van. The other Turned continued to battle against Thorn and Cassius, holding them off from reaching us. I glimpsed Thorn claw through another Turned and Max punching one to the floor.

"My Dad," I shouted, and Thorn's face snapped over to his fallen body.

The lead Hunter jumped into the back of the van, and then slammed the doors and thumped the sides.

"Go," he shouted.

The van jolted forwards as its engine kicked in and it hurtled down the circular exit ramps.

'I will find you.' Thorn's voice sounded in my head.

In the back of the van, the Hunter's leader knelt down.

"Welcome to hell, Mummy's boy," he said and punched me in the face. My head snapped back and smacked into the metal frame. I went blank.

Chapter Seventeen

I slowly drifted back into reality, the harshness of life gaining its control over me again. I felt cold and wet. Leather straps clasped my wrists and metal chains suspended them from the ceiling. I found myself sat in a chair; my shot leg raised and encased in bandages. No noises filled the cell except the chinking of the metal chains holding my arms up. A tiny ray of light filtered in from a small window at the top of the cell with bars across it. The light seemed to come from a streetlight on the outside wall. All I could see through the window was just another brown brick wall. I could be anywhere.

Filth and blood daubed the walls, and in front, a grey metal door sealed off the small, dank and dirty prison cell. I tried to pull myself up and just about raised myself off the chair when I heard voices outside, and the hatch on the door slid. I played dead and slumped back down.

"This is him. The one Bramel wanted?" an older man asked.

"Yeah, Jonathan Harper," a rasping female voice replied.

"He doesn't look much."

"He killed the Hunter in Vegas and dispatched three of my vampires when we captured him. He did it all as a human. We couldn't find any formula in him."

"Really. How did he do it?"

"She's been training him. Plus, he seems stronger than he should be for just a human," the rough voice replied. She sniffed the air. "I can sense Dragan in him."

"How?"

"I don't know; you're the scientist. You tell us," the rough voice snapped back.

"I will run some tests," he answered.

"So will we. Bramel will want answers. This isn't what we expected, and we still don't have the formula and Thorn back. Are you sure we need them all?"

"Yes, his changes need investigating. I will need all the elements to work it out and to replicate it," the older man, the scientist, replied.

The hatch shut and they walked off.

Bramel. Thorn and Cassius had mentioned him when I asked them about the Turned. Bramel was the leader of the Turned, their King. He had led the way and was one of the first to revolt against his Dragan masters. It looked like I might get my answers after all. But at what cost? My mind flashed back to the car park attack, watching Scarlett running off and my Dad falling to the floor from the gunshot. Tears rolled down my face. I didn't know if he was dead or alive. Thorn could have saved him. Maybe Thorn captured Scarlett and had killed her. I couldn't be sure of what she would do.

A few minutes later, the door opened and in walked two Hunters with another man in a white coat. The lead Hunter from the car park led the way. The Hunter that had tried to capture me in Vegas. The one that had shot my Dad. He yanked my head up. I looked him in the eyes.

"Finally awake. Keep still. The doctor needs to take a look," he said.

The doctor wore a white coat over his normal clothes. He opened a box and the layered shelves rolled out, and he grabbed an empty needle. He approached with the needle in hand and the Hunters held my arms still as he took a blood sample. I thrashed about and kicked him in the leg. He yelled and hobbled back, and in retaliation, the lead Hunter stepped in, punched me in the face and twice in the ribs. I took the beating, unable to do anything else, as the doctor packed away and left.

They came back and forth over the next few days giving me medicine while checking my leg wound and taking more samples of blood, skin and hair. They untied me and put in a small bed and brought me three meals a day. As time wore on, I walked about the cell, regaining my strength. They gave me access to a shower and a change of clothes. An old orange boiler suit like the one's prisoners wear, but it felt good to be out of my blood and sweat soaked clothes.

After a week, I had recovered reasonably well. The doctor remarked on my quick healing, and I had been fortunate the bullet had only inflicted a flesh wound.

Beyond the visits from the doctor and guards, no one else came to see me. I tried to engage them in conversation, asking where I was, but I got no answer. Since the first time I woke up, I hadn't seen the Hunter from Vegas. I asked to see someone in charge and asked if my Dad had survived, but no answers were forthcoming. My questions hit a wall of silence.

During the day, I tried to look out the small window but could only see the opposite wall and the occasional feet going past. The daylight gave me a chance to look around the cell more, and I noticed former prisoners had written on the cell wall, in either blood, filth or scratched a mark with a stone. I noted a few names, but one caught my attention, 'Giles'. I hadn't thought of that name for some time, and I wondered what had happened to my friend Giles since his failed suicide attempt. I knew he had been committed to a psychiatric hospital but had no news since. I lived in hoped that my revenge on the O'Keefe's would offer him some comfort on his road to recovery.

One morning, a knock on the door came, as usual, to wake me up. I sat up hungry for breakfast when the door opened, revealing the lead Hunter and behind him the prison guard and two other Hunters. The Hunters wore beige martial art jackets and trousers.

"Time to play," the lead Hunter said and pulled out a gun.

I put my hands in the air, and the other two Hunters came into the cell, clicked my hands into cuffs, and dragged me out of the cell. They marched me along a dark corridor with other prison cells and then stuck a bag over my head before we stepped through a door. I couldn't see anything as they walked me through a maze of corridors, then stopped. They whipped the bag off my head and kicked the back of my leg, forcing me to the floor.

I rested on my knees in a large gym area with a huge square marked floor in the middle. On the square floor, rows of men dressed in beige martial arts jackets and trousers followed the moves of one man in front: a punch, a sidekick and then feet together. As they kicked, they shouted out their aggression in an explosion of synchronous yells and movements. They copied yet more movements from the man in front. A series of punches, a low kick and a high kick before returning to a standing position, fists at their sides. The man at the front bowed, and they returned the bow before running to the sides of the room.

The windows at the top of the room were covered in blackout curtains, and strip lights shone from the rafters. I winced and blinked, adjusting to the light. At either end of the room, two cameras were being set up and checked over. The lead Hunter unlocked the cuffs. I pulled my hands around and rubbed my wrists, pushing the blood back in.

Three more people walked in behind me and walked towards three empty chairs at the side and directly to the centre of the square arena. An older man, his hair grey but smartly groomed, wearing a black suit and white shirt unbuttoned at the top. The other person was a Turned vampire, her skin grey and decaying, eyes jet black and hair greasy. She wore black leggings and high heeled knee boots with a black t-shirt and a cropped white leather jacket.

Between them, another Turned vampire, a man that loomed over the other two. He had black hair tied into a long ponytail. He dressed like a Goth; all in black with huge leather boots with leather and silver buckles across them. He wore black jeans, a long coat over a black and white ripped t-shirt. His ears and nose were pierced, and huge metal rings covered each finger. His skin looked almost normal, almost human, not grey and decaying like the female vampire, but I could tell he wasn't human. Behind me, a Hunter whispered to a friend. "Bramel." So this was the 'King of the Turned.'

They sat in the three chairs and nodded over at the man leading the men in the training moves.

Three new men in black tracksuits and white t-shirts were escorted in by a Hunter and positioned in the middle of the floor.

"New recruits, sir," the escort said to the man at the front, then turned to the three new men, "Gentlemen, please tell us your previous units."

The first man stood at six foot four, brown hair in a ponytail and muscles pulling on his white t-shirt.

"Corporal Smith, 1st Parachute Regiment."

Next, an average sized man with shaven hair and stubble face, but wiry and strong. His frame was lean and muscles were well defined.

"Lieutenant Harkness, sir, SAS."

Finally, an Asian man, much shorter than the others, but with a huge barrel chest.

"Commander Rai, Ghurkhas, sir."

The man commanding the training looked at them and bowed. He stood six foot, with a clean, shiny head and a scar running from his left eye to his jawline.

"Good, but nothing will prepare you for what you are going to learn here. We are the best of the best because we have to fight more than just other men. We have to fight the darkness. Prepare to defend yourselves," he said and stepped forward.

The three men attacked, but the trainer moved quickly, counter-attacking when he could. The SAS man went down first from an uppercut into the jaw and crunching knee strike in the ribs. Next, Smith fell to a deftly timed spinning back fist. The Gurkha had seen enough and stopped.

"I yield," he said and knelt, but the trainer launched into a flying knee into his face, slamming the man into a bloody mess onto the floor.

"Dragans won't let you yield," the trainer said. The fight was over.

Other beige dressed Hunters walked on to the floor and carried off the defeated men. The trainer went to the middle of the floor and bowed to Bramel.

Bramel clapped his hands in applause, followed by the rest of the people in attendance. He then cast his gaze over to me and nodded.

The trainer smiled and stood back in the middle of the ring. Behind me, the two Hunters stood me up and pushed me forward into the combat area.

The one I had met in Vegas shouted out to the rest of the gym, "This boy is Jonathan Harper." The men looked around at each other in surprise. "He and his Dragan girlfriend are responsible for the deaths of your colleagues. They killed six fellow Hunters when escaping the London lab. They killed another two on their trail at a London nightclub. They killed my friend only recently in Vegas. Some of you will carry the scars of your combat with them. I know you all want revenge. Today is your chance."

A roar rose from the Hunters lined against the walls as they released their aggression. A few pounded their fists and stamped their feet. Others signalled a slit throat with their fingers across their necks. I wasn't popular.

"Number 1," he shouted, and the trainer clenched his fists, ready to fight.

I looked around the arena trying to find a way out but could see none as the man marched across the floor.

"Remember me, boy, you gave me this bloody scar when you came and rescued your whore of a girlfriend? You killed my friends," he shouted, face red and scowling, his words spitting out as he approached.

He pulled his fists up, charged and screamed at me, and I dropped into a fighting stance and prepared to defend. I parried a punch, danced around and then blocked a kick. I couldn't fight this man. He had dispatched three well trained men with ease. I moved around the gym, trying to avoid contact while I thought of a way out.

He stood back and then launched a left and a right punch, which I quickly blocked. I could sense his attacks and could react in time. Maybe I had been lucky. He attacked again, and I moved and blocked with ease. On the next attack, I took a chance, covered the second punch across his other arm and fired in a fist onto his nose. His head jolted backward and blood poured out. I stepped in and roundhouse kicked him in the knee, upending him onto the floor. His leg twisted in the wrong direction. He screamed and clutched his leg as he rolled about.

"Two," the lead Hunter behind shouted, and two men stepped forward and charged at me. The first beaten man, the trainer, crawled to the side of the arena. I couldn't believe I had taken him out.

I circled around, trying to make each of the men fight past one another to get to me. The first came forward, and I fired in a push kick, knocking him backwards into the second man. I followed up with a flying downward elbow strike to the top of the head, and he collapsed to the floor. The second man went to stand up, but I powered in a spinning kick to the head. He crashed out unconscious.

"Three," the Hunter shouted, and another three men stepped forward and attacked. I fought back, blocking, striking, moving backwards and trying to confuse them. I kept them moving around, never letting them encircle me.

Other men dragged the unconscious bodies off the floor and carried them outside. I had to take a couple of blows to get in close, but slipped down low and sprung up into an uppercut under the jaw. I followed immediately into a roundhouse across the ribs of another. Two of the attackers crashed to the floor. The last one-eyed his fallen colleagues and moved about quickly. He became the hunted.

The man with the hurt ribs pulled himself upright, and they both tried to attack again. I grabbed the man with the hurt ribs and spun him around as the other kicked at me, but only to hit his fellow attacker in the ribs again. He screamed, and I shoved him staggering forward, stumbling into the chest of the other man. He brushed him aside to the floor, but I had followed up with a flying punch to the face, knocking the man sailing into the air and smashing to the floor.

"Four."

This wasn't going to stop. I looked about the room and guessed at fifty men dressed in the beige martial arts gear ready for combat. They would get me eventually, as the numbers would be too much. My best hope was to survive and to take out as many as possible before the numbers overwhelmed me, or I grew careless.

I took on the next four and won.

"Five."

I started hurting, as I took too many blows to get in close and it slowed me down.

I carried on fighting group after group, slowly getting tired, bruised and battered. My eye blackened, I could hardly see out. My ribs were bruised, and forearms and shins were numb with pain from blocking the punches and kicks. The skin on my fists was raw and coated with the blood of the attackers. My own blood stained my face and clothes.

"Eight," he shouted, and then Bramel stood up and held out his hand to stop the eight moving forwards.

He strode towards me. His eyes narrowed and fists clenched. He fired in a punch. I parried the best I could, but the blow knocked me staggering backwards. He marched on and fired in more punches. I skipped back the best I could to put some ground between us.

Suddenly, he bolted forward past my defences and hit me in the face. His ring wielding fist impacted into my already bruised and tender face. The pain exploded in my head, and I crashed back to the floor. He walked on, but I scrambled back to my feet to face him.

Again, he bolted forward, and I threw a punch. He swerved to the side and hit the side of my head. I rocked back, stunned by the blow. He wrenched me towards him and twisted a knee into my spine. As my legs went under me, I yelled. I dropped to the floor, clutching my back, writhing in pain. I gritted my teeth, trying not to give him the satisfaction of my screams.

"Finish him," Bramel ordered and stared down at me before returning to his seat.

The eight walked forward, and each took turns punching and kicking me on the floor. The lead Hunter from Vegas joined in last.

"This is for my friend, Mummy's boy," he said, and spat in my face and then kicked me in the head.

With cameras recording, it had to be the test they talked about. Yet again, my life dissolved to just an experiment. Yet again, people had beaten and kicked me and filmed it for amusement. Just like before with Barry and his gang. Eventually, I passed out cold.

Chapter Eighteen

I could hear only words and couldn't open my eyes or move my body.
"It is done," a thick rough voice said.
A faint noise replied, and then the man spoke again.
"He fought well. Yes, I filmed it as you requested…Yes, he is still alive."
Silence again, followed by a faint voice.
"We will continue the tests, and I will leave Carmella and Gabriel Fenwick in charge, as I have other business to attend to."
A pause again.
A phone clicked shut, and I heard the chinking of footsteps. I opened my eyes a slither and saw the thick buckled boots of Bramel walking out of the cell door and shutting it behind him. I slumped again into darkness and sleep took me once more.
Slowly, my functions returned after another long period of unconsciousness. I had been stripped down to my pants. The chains pulled on my wrists again, and my legs sagged on the floor. I hauled on the chains, lifting myself up and put my feet down to stand upright. I swayed back and forth, using the chains to control my balance. My muscles were bruised and fatigued, and it took all my effort to keep up straight.
I had been returned to an empty cell as before. I heard voices outside when the door creaked open and in walked the older man and the vampire woman.
"Good show you put on back there. How did you do it?" the older man said with no hesitation.
I swayed on the chains, deciding what to say.
"You must be Gabriel Fenwick," I answered.
He smiled and waved a hand at the vampire woman. She stepped in and punched me in the stomach.
"Answer the question," she said.
I groaned and tried to think of a reply.
"You must be Carmella."
She stared. "Thorn told you about me?"
I smiled as I'd guessed her name from overhearing Bramel's conversation on the phone. "No, she never mentioned you."
She huffed. "Back to the questions, boy. How did you do it?" Carmella asked.

"What do you mean, do it?" I asked in pretend ignorance, trying to buy time.

They meant how I could defeat so many of their men. It had been a surprise to me as well, a full realisation of my hybrid powers.

"They were Hunters, most of them ex-military or highly trained in the martial arts. You are stronger and faster than you should be for a human," Carmella said, sneering.

"If you know the answers, then why ask?"

"How are you part Dragan?" Gabriel asked.

I looked at him in disbelief. They must know the answer unless they were trying to trick me. I looked at the floor and spat out some blood.

"You know how. What is it with the stupid questions?"

The vampire grabbed my head and held it up for Gabriel to look me in the eyes.

"The formula we have assumed, but our formula that transforms the Hunters into the Turned doesn't alter them afterwards as well. They go back to normal. How does your formula change you?"

I shrugged my shoulders. I didn't have to pretend; I didn't know.

"Maybe if you hadn't shot my Dad, then he could tell you. I do not know how this works or why you want it."

Gabriel answered. "Unfortunate about Clarence; he chose his side. We always knew you would return. I had some GPS trackers put into his items. After your raid, it was easy to follow you back to that car park. I didn't believe you presented that much of an issue to capture, but your skills surprised me. The Hunter you met in Vegas, Patrick, told us you were tricky, but I didn't believe him. Then Thorn arrived with company. That was an even bigger surprise. I guess she was tracking you. Her car I would have imagined."

Her car, of course, that is how she did it. I didn't think about it but should have known. We used the GPS, so she could always find a way back to me when she went out hunting. Sometimes I would park up and wait in the car while she used herself as bait to lure in her food. On her phone, she had an app that told her the car's location and could race back to me. I would have a similar tracker on her in case she needed a quick getaway.

"So, the formula gives you the powers of a Dragan, and afterwards, some of it remains. Where is the formula? Bramel wants it," Carmella asked.

"With Thorn. She has all of them."

"Why don't you have it? Why didn't you use it?"

I remained silent and received another two punches into the stomach and one to the face. I spat out more blood.

"Why?" she shouted again and kneed me in the groin.

I screamed, my guts rolling over and a sickness rising. My legs crumpled away, dropping my entire weight onto the metal chains. My arms jolted and strained as I pulled myself back upright again.

I didn't want to tell them the answer that I dare not use it after it killed Barry. They thought the formula could answer all of their questions, but if they knew about Barry's death, it would only open up more questions.

"Patrick. Continue interrogating him. I want to know everything that has happened to him. I want to know why he isn't using the formula. Why he ran away from Thorn," Gabriel said, and they turned to walk out.

"She will come for me. She will make you bleed," I said.

Carmella turned back around and laughed.

"Thorn, come back for you! Don't be stupid. The Queen of the Dragans hasn't lasted this long on sentiment and friendship. She is a ruthless killer," she said.

Thorn, Queen of the Dragans!

"Your face. You didn't know. Yes, Jon, she is the Queen of the Dragans. The first Dragan born to those who created themselves from the dark magic. The first four went mad with the two spirits sharing one body. They conspired against one another, eventually leading to civil war, killing hundreds and spawning us, the Turned, as their slaves.

"Thorn was the first natural-born Dragan. She didn't suffer from the infliction of a split persona. She eventually became the Queen, the only rightful heir, the first born, and she is the source of all true Dragan power. When you met her, I bet you thought she was just a vampire stuck in a cell. She was our prize catch. Her blood and the formula created from it could hold the power for my kind to become like her so that we can take our revenge. Thorn is the Queen of the Night. She is the power in the dark. Her blood still teems with magic. She will not come back for some misguided young boy who thinks she loves him. You are all alone."

My legs gave way again, and I slumped back down to the floor. My heart emptied.

"She loves me," I shouted.

Carmella walked forward and crouched down, head to head with me. Her black pupils like death and scarred clumps of skin peeled as its rotten stench assaulted my senses.

"Thorn loves power. She doesn't need you anymore when she has the formula. Why would she risk it all to come back for you?"

I dropped my head towards the floor. Thorn had a reason to come back for me if she loved me or not. The formula only worked on me. She had said I was the key.

"As I thought," Carmella said at my silence and walked out.

Both Carmella and Gabriel left the room, and Patrick limped in from the doorway. He wrenched my head back by the hair and glared at me; his face mere inches from mine

"We are going to ask some questions and you will answer," he said, some drool dripping from his mouth onto my face.

Behind him, another man pushed in a shopping cart, with an assortment of tools on top: jump leads and an electrical generator.

I looked away, preparing myself for the torture. I had to keep the secret about what Thorn said, that I was the key. If they knew, I feared I would never escape, or worse, they would cut me open to discover my secrets.

The first crocodile clip snapped onto my skin and then the other. I gritted my teeth through the pain, not wanting to show any emotion.

"You will scream!" he said, and fired down the lever and sent me into a convulsing electric fit. My muscles jerked and jolted. My arms seized and teeth gritted together. The muscles in my head tensed in agony.

I couldn't help but scream in pain from the electric shock. It ended and I panted, gasping for breath. My muscles relaxed, and I breathed in deep.

"Where is the formula?"

"Thorn has it," I replied.

The electric shock ripped through me again, and my body convulsed until the lever returned.

"Where is Thorn?" Patrick asked.

"I don't know," I said, which was the truth.

Again, the lever slammed down, and the electricity ripped through me.

"Why don't you have the formula?"

I searched for a plausible answer while my body recovered. "Thorn keeps them all."

I convulsed and screamed in pain once more.

"Why did you leave her?"

The truth was I didn't trust her anymore, and I wanted the truth about Scarlett and Dad.

"I came back to find my Dad," I said, trying to regain my strength between shocks. The lever went down again. "I am telling the truth," I shouted after the last shock finished and my body heaved in recovery.

He laughed. "I don't care, Mummy's boy. This one is for Gareth and Greg; she killed them at the nightclub." He slammed the lever down again. I screamed, and my body shook uncontrollably, then stopped as he released.

The release from the pain rebounded with adrenaline filling my body and fuelling my rage. "I'm going to rip your throat out," I shouted and felt the Dragan in me fighting to get out. My eyes burned and the muscles in my arm tensed. My finger ends stung, small cuts had appeared and the edges of claws were poking through my fingers.

I ran my tongue across my teeth to find the beginnings of two fangs. I focused my anger by trying to roar through the pit of my stomach, but my finger ends remained the same and the two baby fangs didn't grow either.

Patrick stood back, watching me force out a change. When nothing happened, he stepped forward and punched me in the face. My head spun around and blood ran from my nose.

"You aren't getting out of here alive, Mummy's boy," he replied, wiping the blood from his fist on a white towel.

My head spun in a daze.

"This one is for Luke," he said, and the voltage burnt through me again.

I kept telling myself it would stop. It was just a matter of time, but this time it carried on and on and on. My muscles spasmed, and I strained and arched as the electric shock burnt through my body. I screamed until my head swam in the darkness. The pain engulfed me, and I passed out.

Darkness surrounded me, pitch black all around. A flash of a body caught my eye, spinning me around.

"Who's there?" I shouted into the dark.

The flash again at my side, a woman with dark pony-tailed hair.

"Thorn, is that you?"

Then, to the other side, another flash, a man.

"Who's there?" I shouted again and spun around looking for the shapes.

I turned quickly and bumped straight into a body. I stepped back to see the grinning face of Patrick. "Welcome, Mummy's boy, no Thorn to protect you this time," he said.

I turned and ran, but the flash of the woman blocked my path and flung me backwards, my body skidding along the floor to the feet of Patrick.

"Thorn, help me," I begged, and the female figure rushed forward to stand over me with fangs bared and claws prepared. Her black eyes inset in her rotten flesh, Carmella.

"Wrong vampire," she said and laughed.

I lashed out a kick and jumped to my feet. An arm wrapped around my neck and pulled me back further into the darkness.

"You're ours now," Bramel said.

Carmella strutted towards me and over her shoulder, Thorn stood with arms crossed, looking sternly at me.

"Thorn," I gasped and reached a hand out towards her. She shook her head disapprovingly, turned and walked away.

"Shut it," Carmella said and slashed her claws across my face.

I woke with a jolt, chains rattling, and then I slumped down again. In front, light streamed through the opened door and around a dark figure. The figure reached out and claws brushed lightly across my face. *Thorn.*

"You are awake. Good."

Not the voice I expected. My eyes adjusted to view Carmella dressed in loose fitting black combat gear that hung off her skinny frame. The claws on her hands extended and her black eyes bore into me. My moment of hope had vanished.

"You seem disappointed. Expecting someone else? I have told you she won't come for you."

I said nothing and stared at the floor. Why hadn't she come for me?

"You want to be rescued?" she asked, circling me.

"Of course."

"Do you think Thorn is the only vampire that could rescue you?"

She walked around in front again. I shrugged my shoulders. I assumed she referred to Cassius, but didn't want to mention any names.

She smiled, and her putrefying skin cracked and yellow teeth showed through her dried up lips.

"I could rescue you. I could be your vampire mistress. Would you like that, to be free of these chains and these tortures?"

I nodded automatically, then cursed myself for showing emotion.

"Everything you have with Thorn, you could have with me. Do you like making love to a vampire?"

The thought of making love to her decomposing body revolted me, and I grimaced.

"I am not as pretty. I understand. Let me show you something," she said, then rushed forward, pushed my head aside and clamped her jaws around my neck.

She sucked hard, holding me firm with her hand around my back. I had no strength to struggle, and it would have been pointless, so I stayed limp in her icy embrace. She had her fill of blood and stepped back.

She wiped the blood from her mouth over her face. As she smiled, the festering lumps of flesh softened and absorbed into her skin, and then her face glowed pink. Her flesh plumped up across her body, filling out the loose black combat clothes until they were skin tight, showing off her soft, curvy body. Her whole body had transformed into what looked like a normal human. She stood before me, a dark curly-haired woman with olive skin and enormous almond eyes. She looked beautiful.

"And now?" she said and licked her soft, big, red lips.

I stared transfixed for a few moments, realising it was best not to answer. She spoke for us both.

"I must say, your blood is delicious. It must be the Dragan in you. I never felt this good before," she said, and licked her lips and ran her hands over her hips.

I looked away. She lifted my head up with her hand under my chin so our eyes met.

"I can last like this for half a night. On your blood, it could even be a full night."

"Maybe, but I am with Thorn."

"Really. I heard you were with Scarlett. Where is she, by the way?"

I didn't know. We had all organised our own plan B's and kept them secret in case. I just hoped she found somewhere safe.

"Jon, we are looking for her. When we find her, we will bring her here. Maybe you will be more talkative then?"

"Leave her alone. She has done nothing wrong," I shouted back.

"Oh, so you do still have feelings for her. Good. I would happily leave her alone. Plus, I could end these tortures. Pledge yourself to me instead of Thorn. I will teach you and train you. I will give you nights of pleasure. In return, I just require some of your blood to keep me young and to help unlock the formula's secrets."

I shook my head out of her hand. "Never."

"Never? Where is Thorn, your Queen? She isn't here to rescue you. She has only ever lied to you and used you for her own means. I give you honesty. An honest relationship based on simple transactions.

You think we are evil and disgusting? But we just want to be like our makers, the Dragans. What is wrong with that? What is wrong with trying to better ourselves? Can you imagine what it is like to be a Turned vampire? Living in this decaying, cold body?" she asked, running her hands across her chest. "The lust for blood and changes it brings is constant torture. Once a night I can turn through the blood, but even then, I can't use my powers without reverting to my rancid body. We often need to change back because, in our human likeness, we suffer from the weaknesses of both human and vampire, with none of our normal strengths."

"What about Bramel? He looks almost human. He stayed that way when fighting as well."

"Bramel is a first generation Turned. He is close enough to the source to change his vampire features in and out as needed. Second generation vampires don't have enough power to manage this feat. So we need the extra boost of the blood to make us look human. Third generation vampires need blood as well, but can only maintain their human looks for a couple of hours. Just enough time to get a feed."

I listened on, interested in the revelation of how the Turned lived, but I tried to pretend I wasn't.

Carmella continued. "A long time ago, I was just an ordinary woman. I had a life and a future. I lived on the coast and my family were fishermen. I was in love with a young man, Pedro, from the village. Our parents both approved of the relationship. A fantastic wedding had been arranged, and we had agreed on four children. The families were going to build us a house, and Pedro would come and work for my family after the honeymoon. Life would have been great. Then I was turned by the orders of a Dragan trying to build their army for their stupid civil war. I became a slave to my Dragan masters. Someone to provide them with entertainment at night while in my beautiful human form. Or to act as another soldier in their army. Whatever mood took them at the time, but Bramel set us free. We can be our own people now. We deserve better. Why shouldn't we have the same power as our creators? Instead of being locked inside these dead bodies."

I couldn't think of a suitable answer. I had only thought of them as a disease spreading across humanity and draining its blood. Too many Turned had been created, and they threatened the balance. However, I could sympathise as my life had been turned upside down as well. I had a future and a relationship that had been torn away from me.

She lifted my head up again and stared into my eyes.

"But the Hunters, what are they after?" I asked.

"They want the secrets for their own reasons. Any new world order will need a balance - Human and Vampire - the formula will let them create that balance and seize power. Just think of all the medical advantages the formula could bring humanity. It is selfish of the Dragans to withhold their power considering the good it could bring."

"But it could be misused to bring terror and pain."

"The same as the Dragans?"

"No, not like the Dragans. They are only a few. An army of transformed humans would be a terrible thing," I replied.

"But it is okay for us Turned to suffer, because of the Dragans. Why should we suffer so?"

I had no answer and shut my eyes.

She stood upright to leave, releasing me from her grip.

"I will leave you to think about it. I am going to enjoy my limited time with blood inside me. Tomorrow, Patrick will return with new tortures for you. Remember, I can stop it," she said and leant in and kissed me gently on the lips. She tasted sweet.

"Just scream out my name," she said, walking out the door, pulling it shut and plunging the room back into darkness.

I considered her offer as I hung in the cell. Had I been abandoned? Carmella might protect me, and I only had to give a little blood in return. But before I could think about it any longer, tiredness caught up with me, and I slipped back to sleep. I didn't dream, too tired to dream. My mind just retreated from the pain instead.

I woke with a shock, freezing cold water dripping off my blood-stained body. In front, Patrick stood holding an empty bucket that he threw to the floor.

"Time for more questions. I love this part. Hold him down," he said, turning to the two men behind him.

They moved past him and grabbed my legs and held my feet in place. Patrick reached behind to the trolley.

"Where is Thorn?" he asked, but I knew the answer didn't matter.

"Screw you, dickhead," I shouted, and he turned around to show a hammer in his hand.

He shook his head.

"Wrong answer," he replied and knelt in front of my secured foot.

He raised the hammer and smashed it down onto my big toe. I yelled in agony, pulling on my chains to lift myself away, but they held me firm. Tears of pain rolled down my cheeks, and the sweat poured down my back.

"Where is the formula?" he asked.

"I don't know," I cried in anguish and desperation, my toe smashed and bleeding. I didn't know how much of this I could take.

The hammer smashed down again onto my next toe. My head screamed in torment once again. Patrick put the hammer to the side, went back to the trolley and returned with pliers in his hand.

"Those toenails are broken," he said, "best remove them."

"No, no, please don't," I shouted.

"Why did you leave Thorn?" he asked.

"I told you, to come home and find out the truth about my Dad and Scarlett," I said.

"Scarlett, I am looking forward to meeting her," he said and knelt by my toes.

The cold of the pliers rammed against my skin, and I braced myself as he shoved them around my nail and yanked it off. I jerked back as the nail wrenched from the toe, tearing a gash in my skin. I tried every time not to scream, but the pain shot through me in an unbearable wave and the sound screeched from my mouth, high pitched and frantic.

"Why didn't you take the formula with you?" he asked.

"Because Thorn kept it all for safety," I replied through gasped breaths and sobs.

The pliers moved to the next toe and he removed the next nail. Again, I screamed as the toenail ripped away from my flesh, tearing open the raw skin. The sobs came as I tried to catch my breath, but the oxygen eluded me. I cried and howled, which only seemed to goad him. I slumped from constant pain, overloading my nerve endings. He returned to the trolley and came back with a small tub and knelt again down at my feet.

He smiled innocently. "You ever heard the saying to rub salt into the wound?"

I nodded my head and gritted my teeth. He pulled off the lid and slapped a hand full of salt onto my toes and rubbed it in vigorously. I screamed, shouted and then roared in pain. Tears rolled down my face and my muscles spasmed. I snapped my head up and down, moving from side to side as much as my bindings would allow. The salt was burning mercilessly into the bare and broken flesh of my toes. He stopped rubbing it in, but the pain of the salt and hammer remained.

My eyes cleared from the tears and pain, just in time to see the hammer raised.

"Next foot, where is Thorn?" he asked, and I sobbed in despair. My body shook with anticipation. I could see no end in sight. He continued with his tortures until I lost consciousness again and the darkness of my mind provided a way out.

I awoke curled up in a ball in the corner of the wet, damp cell. The chains had been lowered. The shutter across the door pulled back for a moment, then the door opened. I blinked my eyes to take in the light and in walked Carmella. She wore a long purple skirt and purple jacket with ruffles around the neck and along the edges to the waist. Underneath, she wore a plain black shirt and on her feet shiny purple ankle boots. Despite the pain that wracked my body, I forced myself up the wall to stand in front of her as she walked in. Her long black hair lay limp down the sides. As usual, her skin was scarred and dead, and eyes black.

"Another day with Patrick. Anything you wish to ask of me?" she said.

I shook my head. She wanted me to beg for mercy.

"I could end the pain for you, Jon. I could be your protector. You need friends. Thorn is never coming."

"She will," I said.

"She won't."

I looked to the floor. I couldn't look at her.

"Jon, there is no need to suffer. Thorn wouldn't expect you to endure this torture. She would understand your need for salvation."

"Never."

"Silly boy. When we tortured Thorn, with UV and lack of blood, how long do you think she lasted?"

I stood silently. It had never occurred to me they had tortured her. My muddled brain couldn't work out if it was true or false. I couldn't make sense of anything right now.

"She lasted just one week. A shame really, I so enjoyed watching her burn," Carmella said, answering her own question.

I stared at the floor, waiting for her to leave and her lies to follow.

"Just one week. She is the Queen of the Dragans, but after one week, she was our little pet. She did as I commanded. We took our samples, ran our tests, and she did as she was told."

I stared at the floor, trying not to listen and sang a tune inside my head as interference.

"You not talking to me tonight? You will. The tortures will continue until you tell them what they want to hear, or you die. No need to sacrifice your life for her. She isn't coming. You are just a pawn in her games. Give yourself to me and I will make you happy. I will look after you. In return, I just want answers and a little blood. Then, who knows? Maybe we could both become Dragans together. We could be the start of something new and powerful," she said, smiled, and then rested her hands on my arms and bent down to look into my averted gaze.

I stayed silent, not daring to respond in case I gave way to her offer. I avoided her eyes. My eyes seemed to be the only part of me I controlled. The silence continued between us; her hoping I would break, but I stared at the floor, daring not to utter a single word else the dam would open. She finally got bored, stood back up and crossed her arms.

"Well. I must go. I have plans for tonight. But first I will take an advance on the blood you will give me," she said and shot forward.

I moved my head to one side. Her fangs tore into my flesh and blood drained out of my body. She sucked hard, gulping it down, her hand gripping my shoulder and forcing me against the wall. My knees weakened and body slipped from her grasp.

Her face and body transformed again. The blood rushed around her body, filling out her decaying flesh and smoothing it back to a normal human appearance. Her black eyes rolled away to reveal her enormous almond eyes and beautiful olive skin. Her hair revitalised and lifted off her head as it became full of thick curls. I couldn't deny her beauty. Part of me wanted to scream her name straight away and enjoy what she had to offer if I hadn't been so broken. She smiled, stood back and pulled out a red lipstick from her pocket, and applied it across her pouted lips.

"Last chance, Jon, or another day with Patrick," she said and winked.

A tear ran down my cheek as I imagined another day with that bastard Patrick. I looked away again before her promises made me forget my loyalty to Thorn. She stepped in and kissed me passionately on the lips, staining them with red lipstick. The kiss tasted of cherries, and I accepted her warm lips without a fight and missed them when they left.

She spun around then strode out of the room, her purple jacket flapping at her curvy hips and skirt flapping about her legs. The door slammed shut, sending the room back into darkness. I slumped back into the corner, but with the taste of her cherry lipstick still glistening on my lips.

Each day, Patrick tortured me with more electric shocks and occasionally a straight forward beating. Then, two days after my feet, he repeated the exercise with my hands, two fingers on each. Each time after the torture, a doctor took measurements and samples of blood. This was more than just torture; they were experimenting on me.

Every night, Carmella would return and make her offer.

"Leave Thorn and accept me as your new mistress. I will protect you. I will make this pain stop."

"No, I can't," I would reply. Each night, she took some blood and left me with a kiss. With every visit, my resolve would weaken. The last night

I returned her kiss, and she passionately kissed back. Suddenly, I found my strength and jerked my head away, leaving her breathless.

She smiled with wet red lips. "You know it's the right thing to do. I will look after you and protect you. I am attracted to you too. Another of your remnant Dragan powers, probably. I can feel its pull on me. Remember, just scream my name."

Between tortures, I thought about Thorn and Scarlett again. I had been right about what I told Scarlett. The Hunters and the Turned would always chase me. I had only endangered her by bringing her back to Leeds to seek the truth. Thankfully, they hadn't captured her at the car park. Otherwise, they may have tortured her as well. Patrick and Carmella had hinted as much, and I couldn't bear the thought of them torturing Scarlett to get to me. To keep Scarlett safe, I had to stay away from her.

When I thought about the attraction incident in the house, I realised I could never be sure if she loved me, or the seductive powers just kept her keen. Leaving her alone would be the only way I could keep her safe from those that hunted me and from my own Dragan powers and desires.

My re-occurring nightmare of attacking Scarlett and draining her blood still haunted my memories. I had been selfish in asking her for help and bringing her into this dangerous world I now inhabited. I had made my bed and had to lie in it. I belonged with Thorn, and I knew it to be my destiny.

I had no power over Thorn, but we understood one another and protected one another. And in truth, I loved Thorn, even without her being here and inflicting her seductive powers on me. I loved her crazed personality. I loved the excitement and thrill of our nights together, and I longed to see her bright blue eyes, her tousled raven hair and silk white flawless features. I wished she could be here right now, even if in a rage at my abandoning her. Her Dragan features transforming her body into a killing machine and ripping apart those that inflicted these gruesome tortures on me.

She wasn't, but in my dazed state, I could almost see her as I did on that first night at the research centre. Her raven tousled hair blowing in a supernatural wind. Her cheeks and lips a passionate red. Her body warm, glistening and inviting. Her words echoing in my ears.

"Revenge, revenge."

I felt connected to her again and then heard something else.

"We will make them bleed. Remember, let your emotions fuel you," the image of Thorn said.

I woke from my trance and looked about the empty dank and dark prison cell. I still hung in my cell all alone. It felt too real to be a dream or a hallucination. It happened the same way as when we first met, when she had called me with her psychic powers. However, I looked around and I remained alone. Thorn hadn't come for me. Why would she? I had abandoned her in America, stolen her money and ran away. But she had been there at the car park trying to rescue me, or to take her revenge?

Either way, I couldn't take the pain much longer. Each night, Carmella visited me with a bite and kiss, and her offer of freedom. Every night, my strength to her offer had weakened. Carmella hadn't chosen to be transformed into a Turned. She only wanted a way out of her rotten vampire body, to be like her creators. I wanted the same. I wanted to be a Dragan like Thorn, too. Carmella was easy on the eye when transformed. I could live with her company. *Would it be so bad?*

During the daylight hours, Gabriel returned with Carmella to watch the progress and view the results. They would ask the same questions every day.

"Where is Thorn? Where are the vampire formula needles? Why didn't you take an injection?"

I told them what I said to Patrick when he tortured me.

"I don't know where Thorn is. She has the needles," I tried to make up excuses for not having the needles, "Thorn keeps them all," but they didn't seem to believe, or care if the answers were right or wrong.

Each time at the end of their visit, I always said, "She will come for me. She will make you bleed."

However, over time, I believed it less and less. *Where is my Queen?*

Another day of torture began. Patrick had wheeled in the trolley, and the two Hunters secured my feet to the ground again.

"You still have undamaged toes. It looks all out of balance." Patrick grinned.

"No," I screamed.

"Where is Thorn?" he asked.

"What does it matter? You don't want answers, you just want revenge. You're enjoying this."

"Well done. You are beginning to understand."

"Even if I had gone with you that day in Vegas. Someone would have still tortured me. Probably you. It looks as if you have done this many times before."

"And? It took you this long to work it out?"

"Then it was right he died. Self-defence."

"Screw self-defence, you're scum of the night. He was a good man with a life you snatched away," he shouted and whipped the hammer down.

"You will die," I roared as the hammer smashed down again.

I screamed as the hammer decimated the bones in my toe. Acid burnt up my throat and a shock wave of agony electrocuted my limbs and head. I accepted the rivers of tears down my cheeks. I couldn't take it anymore. The torture would never end unless I admitted defeat.

"Next toe," he said, and raised the hammer.

I had one last chance and I breathed in deep. She could still save me. I yelled with all my strength, my lungs heaving with the effort. "Thorn!"

Patrick stopped. The other Hunters looked around, their faces draining and eyes darting to the doorway. Time passed; everyone stayed silent, listening out for any indication of someone approaching. Nothing happened.

Patrick looked back at me, a nervous laugh erupting from his mouth.

"You had me worried for a moment. Let's get back to the matter at hand," he said, grinning and raised the hammer once again.

I still had breath left in me and tried again shouting with all my remaining energy.

"Carmella."

Patrick's eyes sprung wide open and a triumphant laugh escaped from his gaping mouth. The other Hunters laughed, releasing their hands from my feet. I swung my leg back and kicked one in the face with my shin. He dropped to the floor, clutching his nose.

"Are you joking?" Patrick asked and signalled to the Hunter to grab my feet again.

They re-secured my feet, and Patrick re-raised the hammer.

"Third time unlucky," he said and whipped it down.

I closed my eyes, tensed my muscles and readied myself for the sickening pain. Nothing happened. I opened my eyes, and Patrick knelt in front of me empty handed. Behind, a figure stood with the hammer in her clawed hand. She wore her black combat suit. Her dark hair tied back and fangs bared.

"You called me," she said and smiled.

I nodded in reply.

"Once more, please. Tell me what you want."

I breathed in deep, tears bursting from my eyes and rolling down my face. I shouted a tearful cry to her.

"Carmella, save me."

"With pleasure," she replied, her skin cracking in a smile.

Chapter Nineteen

I lay in my new warm bed and rubbed the sleep from my eyes. The pain in my toes and fingers returned, and I rolled over to the other side to grab a glass of water. I pushed open the blister pack of painkillers with my bandaged hands, then clumsily gripped the glass and downed the tablets with a gulp of water.

I had lost track of time since Carmella rescued me and took me to their hospital. A couple of nurses had fed and bathed me. Then bandaged up my feet and hands around the missing nails and then treated my bruised and broken bones. They put me to bed in an isolated room.

The room was nothing special; four walls painted battleship grey, clean sheets, and a comfy bed. However, after the prison cell, I felt like I had arrived in heaven. The door was locked, but it didn't matter as I had neither the strength nor the will to escape. I slept for nearly two days straight, only occasionally waking to use the en-suite toilet, and then climbing straight back to bed to disappear to sleep.

Carmella had visited a few times to check on my recovery, but the drugs made it seem like a dream. She stroked my hair and promised me everything would be okay. I barely woke to her soothing sounds and drifted away each time.

I had come off the morphine once the sleep depriving agony retreated. For the pain, I took a steady stream of co-codamol. I thought it was day three or four. I couldn't be sure, but it wouldn't be long before my rescue would need to be repaid.

I flicked on the table light and pushed myself up the bed to sit up straight. I pulled the book off the side to carry on reading to pass the time. They had supplied me with a few books and magazines. I had asked for a TV or computer to fill the hours, but I wasn't allowed anything electronic, as they were too scared I could use them to escape. Nor was I allowed any paper or pens to write. I got three books: two vampire books and one sci-fi classic. I was sick of vampires and read the science fiction book, *I Robot*, instead.

I read for a couple of hours, but soon my eyes tired again, so I slid down the sheets and read lying down. After a few minutes, my eyes inevitably grew heavy, and as the pages blurred, my head sank into the pillow.

I slept again but I couldn't tell for how long, as I had no watch or means to measure the passing of time. No natural light came into the room to show day or night. The meals did not indicate the time of day either. They came in at regular intervals, usually a piece of meat, some vegetables and mashed potatoes or chips. The last meal had been chicken and chips with peas. The meals wouldn't win any prizes, but at least I had food, which had been limited in the prison cell.

I woke and knocked the open book off the bed. The pain in my body returned, and I awkwardly popped the pills into my mouth and wash them down with a glass of water.

I stared up at the ceiling and tried to gather my thoughts. I wondered what had happened to everyone while the Hunters had tortured me, and Carmella had brought me under her protection.

I wondered if my Dad was alive? Had Scarlett escaped okay? Would Thorn be trying to rescue me? Or had Thorn left with Cassius to seek other Dragans and continue her war without me? I tried to picture Thorn's face in the hope I could make contact, but I struggled even to focus. Everything that had happened in the prison cell seemed to have affected my memory. When I closed my eyes, I could only see Patrick's grinning face as he punched me, bled me and smashed my bones. All I could seem to remember was the torture, as if the intensity of it had overwritten anything good in my life.

I heard voices at the door, someone requesting from the guards to enter. The door opened and in walked Carmella, my new protector, clothed in a little red dress and shoes. I weakly smiled.

"Awake my little pet," she said and rested herself on the edge of the bed beside me.

She had already fed as her skin was flushed with blood, giving her little red dress sexy curves to contain. Her enormous almond eyes looked into mine, and she placed her hand on my forehead to check my temperature. I looked back into her eyes and her olive-skinned face, framed with dark curly locks.

"You seem better. You should be well enough soon. Then if you can prove your loyalty, you can come and share my bed chambers. I can keep a close eye on you there and fulfil my offer completely."

I nodded in agreement. If I could get close to her, I could escape, or I wouldn't want to. Either way, I couldn't stay here forever. If I didn't do her bidding, I would be back in the prison cell at the torturous hands of Patrick. Admiring her beauty, I thought it wouldn't be too bad. I could get used to her in her transformed state. She was just a victim of the Dragan wars, like me. I needed to learn to accept it and adapt to my circumstances.

"I look forward to us being together," I replied, putting my hand on top of hers.

She smiled and kissed me with her cherry red lips.

"Good. First, you need to answer some questions. Prove to me you are on my side."

"Okay."

"Where is Thorn?"

My face and heart sank. I didn't know where she had gone. Thorn could be a few miles or hundreds of miles away.

"I really don't know where she is. Last time I saw her was in the car park. She could be anywhere by now."

"Okay, where could she be?"

"She has a house in London. She might be there. Or gone back to Seattle or searching for other Dragans."

"Good, you can give me the addresses in London and Seattle," she said and pulled out a piece of paper and pen from her red handbag and put them in front of me.

I scribbled down both the addresses. I didn't mention Max's Diner. It was a possibility, but I didn't want to get others involved. Thorn could take care of herself.

Carmella looked at the addresses.

"Why would she be at a research centre in Seattle?"

"That's where we were heading to from Vegas."

She pulled a puzzled frown. "I think you need to tell me the entire story. I want to know why you don't have the needles on you. Why were you going to a research centre? What are Thorn's plans?"

I had no choice but to explain. However, I could limit the truth and keep out certain people from the explanation, like Max and Amber.

"We went to Vegas to meet Cassius at the Vampire convention. When we met at his trailer, a group of Turned vampires attacked us, but we escaped and drove north."

"Yes, I know this, as we had tracked you all down to Vegas. Gabriel's hunters had attended the event in the small hope a Dragan would appear using it as cover. Typical of Thorn to flash her true identity in such a place. She has always loved Vegas."

Thorn hadn't been as clever as she thought. They knew her well.

"On the drive, Cassius explained the difference between the two types of vampires, Dragan and Turned and my part in the war."

Carmella let out a surprised gasp.

"They only just told you?"

"Yes."

"The Dragans are such liars and deceivers. I hope you can see that now? I have only been honest with you, whether you liked it or not. Please continue your story," she said and gave my hand a reassuring stroke as she held it.

Thorn's depth of deceit even surprised Carmella. At least she seemed more honest, even if it was a cruel and brutal honesty. But I could understand Carmella. Our lives had taken similar paths, as both of us had the vampire world forced upon us. We were just trying to make the best of it and adapt to our situations. We couldn't get our old human lives back, so we both wanted to become full Dragans instead and fulfil our potential.

I took a deep breath. "They were taking me to the research centre in Seattle to analyse the formula. They were going to take samples to work out what effect the formula has on me."

"Why do your powers remain?"

I nodded in response and decided not to mention my lack of weakness to UV and silver. Just enough truth to get me through this and win her trust.

"On the way, I realised Thorn had lied to me. She told me she would make me a vampire one day. But that would mean making me a Turned, not a Dragan. Dragans could only be born. I knew she would never make me a Turned."

"You are right. You would be a 1st Generation Turned derived from the blood of the Queen. You would be strong, especially with your existing hybrid state. You would be her natural enemy and devastating new power for the Turned. You could create a stronger second generation Turned than before."

I imagined the power I could hold as a Turned. I could be their new King.

"So I escaped and fled back to England before we reached Seattle," I said.

"But you didn't take the needles?"

"No, she keeps them with her at all times, plus I wasn't sure they were safe."

"Not safe. Why?"

I had to tell her all of it for the story to make sense.

"Before we left England, I fought and killed someone, a gang leader, who the Hunters used to bully and mug me."

Carmella nodded along, apparently familiar with the story.

I continued. "The leader got a vampire formula needle as he lay dying and injected himself. It didn't turn him into a Dragan, but a hideous monster. Eventually, he died from both the transformation and our attacks. I wasn't bothered about having the needles, as I feared they would kill me as well."

"Yes, we found Barry's remains as alerted by a police report. The formula would have never worked on him. It only seems to work on you."

I frowned. "You know all this already? That it only works on me?"

"Of course. Why else do you think we went to so much trouble to get you to test it?"

I scratched my head.

"Why not just make a new batch with someone else's DNA?"

"Why not? Good question. We tried the original on others, but they died like Barry. You were chosen to test it next. The order came from Bramel. I guess it was the quickest way once we realised about the DNA encoding."

"Why me? Why not my father? Why not make a new one with a different DNA code?"

"I don't know all the secrets, Jon. There are secrets even I am not allowed access to. I understand this way was quickest, or you are special. When you two burnt down the centre, they lost all the research. The existing formula and your blood is the only way of getting our answers now."

I looked down at the bed. I had told her everything, which I had resisted during the torture, but at least I felt better telling Carmella than Patrick.

"Is that it?"

"No, I came back to find Scarlett and my Dad, and find out if they had been involved in the setup to trick me into taking the formula."

"If it's any comfort, then no, they didn't," she answered, and it was some help, but I still wished I had never returned. My Dad was probably dead, Scarlett was running in fear, and I had betrayed Thorn and been tortured.

"Are you and Scarlett back as an item?" she asked.

"No, we had one kiss, but that was it."

"I don't believe you."

Not another jealous vampire.

"It's true," I said, looking into her eyes.

"Well, it concerns me little if you did or not. Is that everything?"

"Yes," I replied.

She stared and pursed her lips together.

"I knew most of this already, my little pet."

I worried I had outlived my usefulness and tried to think of other things to tell; something that would prove my worth. But Carmella spoke first.

"Don't worry, I keep my promises, not like those deceiving Dragans. You can still be my consort. You have proved your loyalty for now by telling the truth. In the meantime, you have a more immediate use," Carmella said, rubbing my hand again to provide reassurance.

"What is your command?" I said, feeling it to be the appropriate answer in my new position.

"Bait."

"Bait?"

"Yes, I mean to capture myself a Queen."

Chapter Twenty

I sat in the back of the van trundling down a bumpy road. A sack covered my head so that I couldn't work out the Hunter's and Turned's base. They had cuffed my hands together, and a Hunter sat either side holding my arms. We were on our way to meet Thorn, and I was the bait.

Carmella had told me the rest of the plan the same night I gave her my answers.

"I need you present else Thorn won't come anywhere near the meeting point. She needs to sense you to be lured in. Then I will capture her as before. Our Turned formula we use on the Hunters will be our secret weapon, plus another trick I have hidden."

"She's been in contact then?" I had said, realising what it meant.

"Yes, we agreed on a trade. You for the formula, but I mean to have all of it. Thorn and the formula, and I am not giving up my new little pet," she said and stroked my face.

Thorn hadn't forgotten me; I had betrayed her again. Carmella had seduced me, and who knows what ill intent she may have in store for me? I appeared to be nothing more than a plaything to her. I thought she actually had become attracted to me, but I believe it was the other way around. She had her own type of natural seduction powers; I tried to focus my seduction powers on her, to see if I could win her over.

She stared at me for a moment, licked her lips and kissed me once again, leaving the taste of her cherry lipstick behind.

"Nice try, but it won't work on me. I am made from Dragan's blood. I don't have your powers, but I am immune to them," she said, and I sighed and stopped the powers radiating out. "Tomorrow night we make the trade and once I have the formula, I will let you take it to heal your wounds."

"And test and observe me?"

"Yes, you are beginning to understand your place now. That is good. It will make life easier for you. Always remember you belong to me. You do as I command."

"I understand," I replied, and my shoulders slumped in defeat.

"Don't fret, my little pet. I will make sure you have a good life with me."

That had been the end of our conversation. Carmella left and later on, someone brought in clean clothes, jeans, trainers and a black t-shirt, and told me I had half an hour to get ready before we left to meet Thorn.

As I sat in the back of the van bumping along the roads, I sniffed at the air. I could smell both Turned and Humans riding along with me. They all remained quiet in the back, but I sensed apprehension and fear from the humans and nothing from the Turned. As Carmella said, they were immune to my powers.

I cleared my mind and tried to listen out for Thorn's thoughts, but nothing came. I tried next to reach out and see if I could send her a psychic message. Again, nothing happened. The journey continued, and I tried to picture Thorn's face, ready to see her at the exchange. Surely, she knew it was a trap. I hoped she had a plan, and we could be together again properly, and then I would be free of Carmella, the Turned and the Hunters. If they captured Thorn, who knows what they would have in store for us? At least we would be together again. Together, we might escape.

After about twenty minutes, we moved back to local roads until we finally slowed down and parked up. They dragged me out of the van, with my toes stinging in pain from the lack of toenails, and my bruises bashing against the sides of the van. We walked on for a few moments and then crashed through a set of doors.

In front, the Hunters and Turned walked in silence, then stopped. Everything went quiet. Lights flashed in my eyes as the bag got swiped off my head. I screwed up my eyes lids to shield them and blinked to adjust to the light.

Either side a Hunter stood holding my arms and then one of them unlocked me from my handcuffs. To the sides about thirty Hunters and Turned stood, with Gabriel and Carmella stood at the front. The Hunters wore combat greens, and the Turned an assortment of black clothes. Gabriel wore a navy blue pin-striped suit with a white shirt unbuttoned at the top. Carmella had dressed in red combat trousers and a white vest top. Her appearance was almost human like, with her thick dark curls tied back.

Everyone stared down the gloomy lit deserted warehouse to the other end. I followed their eyes, and then figures appeared in between the gaps of light from the overhead bulbs. The figures walked with intent marked by their long, purposeful strides until they stopped about twenty metres away.

Thorn had dressed in a skin tight black combat suit, and her raven hair pulled pack into a ponytail ready for action. She carried the UV light gun and had twin swords strapped to her back in an x shape.

Towering over her, Cassius stood with a sword across his back and black jeans, a red t-shirt and a dark jacket. A couple of steps behind them,

Max walked into the light. His long blond hair tied back and white sleeves rolled up, showing off his tattoos and wearing thick heavy jeans and boots.

He stood on the other side of Thorn, with her in the middle of those two giant men. She looked over at me, closed her eyes for a few seconds and then stared over at Gabriel and Carmella. Thorn's face showed no emotion. I spoke in my mind, hoping she would send me a psychic message, but nothing happened. She looked angry. I spoke in my head over and over.

'Thorn, I am sorry. You have to go, it's a trap.'

I heard nothing back and stared at her, hoping to prompt the smallest response. Anything that would show me she had a plan. Anything to show me she still cared. She must, while else would she have come?

Thorn stared ahead at Carmella instead. "Hello, Carmella. It's been a long time."

"When I last captured you," Carmella replied, "but I am surprised you contacted us, Thorn. We didn't think you would return for this boy."

"Well, you'd be surprised how much he grows on you. I want him back. We have unfinished business."

"He has certain qualities; I grant you. But he is my little pet. I am his new mistress. I would be sorry to let him go," Carmella said.

Thorn's stare narrowed further at Carmella.

"He belongs to me. Hand him over. Then you can have your formula."

"He's mine now. He surrendered to me."

"You hurt him, that is all. Now hand him over."

"Why? What is so important about him that you would risk it all and come here tonight? We know the formula only works on him. We know about his remnant powers. We have tested him and taken samples. It's just a matter of time before we work it all out. But to risk yourself and the formula doesn't make sense."

Thorn smiled but still kept her eyes firmly fixed ahead with no recognition of my presence.

"We have a deal, V and me," she said.

"V?" Carmella asked.

"Vengeance is his Dragan name," Thorn said. "Vengeance is what he will get."

"On who? You have been the one lying to him," Carmella said.

I couldn't wait any longer for their games to finish and shouted out. "My Dad and Scarlett, are they safe?"

Thorn kept staring at Carmella, but Cassius looked over.

"Scarlett is safe, we think. She just kept running, but we don't know where she ended up. Your Dad is dead. We couldn't help him as the wounds were too severe. I am sorry, little one."

It was my fault he was dead. I had asked him to get the information. Otherwise, he would still be alive. Tears burst out of my blackened eyes. My stomach twisted into knots and knees went weak. I dropped to the floor, but the Hunters on either side hoisted me back to my feet. I looked over at Thorn for the slightest acknowledgement of sympathy but nothing.

"Let's get back to the deal," Thorn said, her eyes fixed on Carmella.

"Yes, why are you here for him? We can sense he is part Dragan. He fights well, and his skills and abilities are impressive," Carmella asked again.

"You know why. Let's not play this game," Thorn replied.

Carmella huffed. "You need the formula and him back to unlock the secrets, just as we do. We have done our tests. Now the formula should be enough to complete the research and allow us to become Dragans," Carmella said.

"No, that is not everything. They made the formula from my blood. It has created a special bond between us, something no one expected. Plus, I told you we have a deal, and he has my money," Thorn said, and frowned.

"Whatever. You must think I am stupid to believe you two are in love. Dragan and Human, don't make me laugh. Just hand over the formula." Carmella snapped back.

"V first."

"No, the formula first. You have no choice; We outnumber you, even for your skills. We have silver swords and UV guns. Plus…" she said and raised a hand to signal.

The Hunters pulled out their needles and injected it into their forearms. They screamed and snarled as the formula flooded their bodies, and their DNA reassembled them into Turned Vampires. Their skin turned grey and flaky, and eyes transformed into black, dead, bloodshot pools as the transformation took place. Thorn, Cassius and Max stared at the changing humans. Carmella smiled.

"Yes, we have our own formula. Not as good as the Dragan formula but good enough. We will take the Dragan formula, you and Jon. Count yourself lucky we need you alive. After tonight, the roles will have reversed, and you will call me mistress."

Thorn scanned the transforming enemy. "We should have never created the Turned. Our actions were wrong, but you need to come off this path of destruction."

"You did this to us. We have no choice. We want what is rightfully ours!" Carmella shouted.

"It wasn't us that turned you anyway. Where is Bramel, by the way?" Thorn asked.

"It was on your orders he turned me. Tonight he has other business hunting other Dragans. He trusts me to take care of you."

Thorn half laughed. "Really! You're still in love with him?"

"He loves me, as well."

"Are you sure?"

Carmella scowled and pulled out her sword.

Thorn grinned and winked. "I am right then. He couldn't face me. Just like he couldn't before when you captured me. Only one woman will ever be good enough for him."

It was all becoming clear. This wasn't just Dragan against Turned, with Carmella and Thorn it was personal. Thorn must have turned Bramel. It would explain why he had the power to claim the title of King. Carmella's attention on me, another form of revenge on the woman her King wanted.

Carmella pointed her sword at Thorn. "Let's focus on the present. You are trapped, give up and I will make it easy on you. Easier than you were with me."

Thorn smiled and bared her fangs for a second and then reverted to normal.

"You know I can't let you have it all. The formula, me and V."

"What choice do you have, Thorn? You are outnumbered?"

From the back of the warehouse, other figures began closing in around Thorn, Cassius and Max. More Turned vampires.

Thorn looked behind and nodded to Max, who pulled off his shirt and growled, making his muscles enlarge and teeth break out into a row of canines.

"Even with a wolf, you are no match for us," Carmella coolly responded and waved a hand in the air.

Out of a dark corner, another man stepped forward. He stood at average height. His hair was wildly curly, and he had large bushy eyebrows connected across the top of his eyes. He ripped off his black t-shirt, revealing his black hairy chest and he growled back at Max.

"Come quietly or die," Carmella said.

Thorn pulled up the UV gun and aimed at Gabriel.

He took one step back, then steadied himself. The other Turned raised their guns in reply and aimed at Thorn.

"That gun won't work on me. I am human and the UV liquid won't harm me," he said as he scuttled backwards behind a Turned.

"The impact of the bullet casings alone would be enough to kill you," Thorn said.

He took another step back, looking for cover.

Thorn continued. "I can't let you have it all. It would only be a matter of time before you unlocked the secrets," Thorn said, scanning around the encircling Turned.

Her eyes bled out red tears. She gulped as a tear ran into her mouth, revealing the sad, lonely woman I rescued from the prison. She scanned about, looking around her as the net of Turned vampires closed in. Cassius pulled his sword out, ready for combat, and Max turned up the wolf power. She looked beaten.

Thorn looked back at Carmella and snuffled as the blood ran into her nose.

Carmella spoke. "You really do love him so much you would allow yourself to be trapped and die. Who would have thought the great and powerful Thorn, Queen of the Dragans, brought to her knees by a young human male? I thought I had seen everything. Bramel will find this highly amusing."

Thorn wiped away a tear but smeared the blood across her face instead.

"There is nothing wrong with being in love. It provides us with strength. Our emotions fuel us and feed us. I will not deny my emotions and the strengths they bring me. You would understand this if still alive and not rotting in that body," Thorn replied.

"You love him."

"Yes."

I smiled to myself. I knew she would come and rescue me. She would always be my Queen, and I loved her more than I realised. Thorn would make them bleed, and I would get to watch.

"You will sacrifice yourself for him. Sacrifice the Dragan race for your love," Carmella said.

Thorn shook her head from side to side and took a deep breath. Was that a no?

"In any war, there have to be sacrifices for the greater good. I can't let you have all the keys. I can't let you have him," Thorn said, with a face full of sorrow, red tears streaming down her cheeks. She took another deep breath, her hands shaking and the gun wobbling in her grip. She closed her eyes and briefly dropped her head down.

"V, remember that I love you," she said, her forehead frowning as she stared at the crowd, and then shouted, "and… I am sorry, but you should have never betrayed me. You took my money, ran off with another woman and gave away our secrets. The house in London and the Seattle research centre have been destroyed. I have no choice."

She aimed the gun at me. I jerked back reeling from the shock. Carmella, the Turned and the Hunters, spun around and looked at me equally surprised, briefly lowering their defences.

Out of Thorn's UV gun, the bullets blasted through a gap in the crowd, smashing into my chest and hammering me backwards. The two Hunters on either side dived for cover. Another bullet whizzed through the air, impacting onto my stomach. It forced me back, and I collided into the wall behind, slumping down to the floor.

The last bullet seemed to cut through the air in slow motion before it exploded into the side of my rib cage, breaking my bones, rupturing my skin, driving into my flesh and organs. Blood poured out of the gaping wounds while pain and confusion burnt through my head.

Everyone's faces were in utter shock until Thorn roared into a full battle cry. Her swords hurtled towards the first of the Turned and slashed through its head. Cassius followed into battle, his huge board sword hacking down two at a time, dispatching them to ash. Behind them, Max's body continued to change, his flesh bursting at the seams as the wolf in him broke out. His jaw extended out and teeth continued to erupt. His muscles pushed out and hair grew across his body.

Carmella bared her fangs. Her eyes turned black, and skin shrivelled back to her natural decaying grey. The rest of the Turned refocused and defended themselves from the onslaught.

The other man turned into a wolf, both of them staring at each other across the battleground. The Turned fired in UV bullets at Thorn and Cassius, who dodged and used other Turned as shields. The Turned disintegrated as the UV liquid seeped into their blood stream and vaporised their bodies to ash.

Thorn's sword slashed through the Turned as they counter attacked. Max, in full werewolf mode, bounded forward, smashing his way through the vampires, ripping their heads off with his giant jaws and spitting them across the floor. The Turned behind them screamed and charged forward into the fray, swords out and bullets flying. Thorn and Cassius dodged the bullets until one hit her and smashed to pieces against her combat suit. The liquid harmlessly splashed on the outside of the suit. *Armoured.*

I fingered at the blood pouring out of my stomach. My life ebbed away.

I felt light-headed, my legs numb and vision failing. I could only see blurred figures fighting in front of me as the other wolf bounded across the floor and charged into Max. They fought with tooth and claw tearing at each other's flesh.

The trauma hazed my thoughts, and it took time to realise that Thorn had shot me. My love had shot me. I'd become a sacrifice of war, a pawn in a game of chess. She would rather have me dead than risk the Turned winning. Moments before, I thought she would give everything up for me when she admitted her love. I had felt happy for the first time since my capture, but I must have misunderstood.

I had been a fool to think the Queen of the Dragans would sacrifice everything for me. Carmella had been right. I had been a misguided, stupid young boy. Thorn is a Queen, and I am nothing to her. I cried; I had ruined everything.

I placed my fingers in the wound and pulled them back to study the damage. On my fingers, part of the bullet casings sat on drops of blood. The casings contained nothing else, no UV liquid. I tried to think of why the bullets were empty, but the darkness enclosed and with it, the familiar feeling of death rode over me. I prepared for its release. At last, this misery would end. I had nothing to live for anyway.

In my darkness, a small tunnel of light appeared. Out of the light, a hand reached out and a warm voice accompanied it.

Come to me.

I grabbed the hand, and a face emerged from out of the light. It appeared to be the same face I had seen when I died before. Their features came into focus, soft fair curly hair and large blue eyes, and her face smooth and welcoming. It looked like my mum. I held her hand, and she guided me towards the light. My arm slipped out of its flesh and then the other arm. Next, the rest of my soul drifted away from my body. I looked back down as I floated, my body crumpled against the wall. My stomach was an exposed mess of red flesh. At the end of the tunnel, a figure waited, a man, my Dad. We would be a family all together at last. I would be free of the pain and suffering.

Suddenly, my spirit stuck and wouldn't move forwards anymore. I looked back to the mortal plane, as my legs were stretching back towards my body. Beneath me, Cassius hacked through two Turned and Thorn weaved away from the three slashing blades of Turned attackers. My body started shaking with energy pulsating through it. The hand released me, and my mum blew me a kiss as she sailed back into the light, and my Dad waved goodbye. I reached out to her, but it was no good. I had lost her again; at least I would be with her again one day.

The light had gone and the darkness returned. My heart started pumping harder and senses were igniting to every movement and thought in the warehouse. My eyes opened back into the real world. I looked up and saw the red glow of heat blazing from Thorn and Cassius, and the Turned showed no heat or energy. My eyesight focused on the battle with greater clarity. I saw the dead flesh on the Turned and could predict their moves as they swung their swords and fists.

My muscles shook violently and strength returned to them with renewed vigour. The flesh on my torso began knitting itself together. My toes were repairing, with the bones re-growing. The nails grew back over the top of my raw flesh, and the pain felt as gut-wrenching as when Patrick had ripped them out. I gritted my teeth and dug in the re-grown nails into my hand.

My return to the mortal plane and healing body could mean only one thing. Then it dawned on me why the bullets seemed to be empty. The liquid inside was red and had mixed in with my blood to make it indistinguishable from one another. Thorn had shot me with the formula.

Thorn caught my eye and stopped attacking. She stepped backwards, and Cassius and Max stepped back with her, allowing herself to be surrounded. The Turned advanced, letting my change go unnoticed. My strength returned. I stood up and approached the Turned army from the rear, my body repairing as I closed in.

Thorn had always taught me to use my anger, letting it run through me to ignite my powers. This time, I didn't need to think back into the past. The memories were raw. The pain of the hammer smashing my toes, the electric volt convulsing through my body, and my Dad dying on the floor of the car park. It wouldn't take any thought. The memories already boiled away, ready to enrage my body.

"Surrendering, Thorn. I thought you would fight to the death. How disappointing. However, Bramel will be pleased to keep you alive," Carmella said.

"Not surrendering. Distracting."

Carmella frowned and looked about at the other vampires surrounding Thorn, Cassius and Max.

"From what?" she asked.

Thorn smirked, and I heard her voice in my head.

Welcome back, V.

"From Vengeance," she replied, pointing her sword through the crowd.

Everyone's head turned around. The red mist of rage descended from the death of my Dad and my gruesome torture. My last memory of him collapsed on the car park floor, blood running from his body. Although my physical self had repaired, a phantom pain from the torture still rattled around in my head, the memories not so easily fixed - the hammer slamming into my toes and the grinning of Patrick accompanying it. The pain of my repairing body and the undiluted rage sparked around my body. The muscles shaking with energy as adrenaline soaked every fibre of my being. Vengeance is my name.

My muscles reacted fiercely to the power, harder than ever before. My fangs sliced through my top gums, matched by fangs from my bottom gums bursting through. My eyes burnt blood red like always with the transformation, and then seem to ignite, tinting the surroundings in a fiery dragon rage. The claws on my hands ripped through my flesh, bigger and stronger, and transformed my whole finger-ends into clawed talons.

My muscles tensed and flexed, as a wave of dragon scales transformed my arms and hands, and went up my neck and down my chest. I roared, straining my head upwards, and the air hazed in a pure white heat. I looked back at the watching group. Thorn beamed a broad smile, and her eyes glinted happily. The rest, including Cassius, rocked on their feet as uncontrollable fear washed through them. The total rage had pushed the formula further, igniting the very depths of the dragon power residing within.

Thorn wasted no time as they froze to the spot, by unleashing an attack into the crowded group of Turned vampires. Her swords slashed through, destroying a couple of vampires at a time. Cassius replied to me with his own battle rage, pivoted the broadsword high and wide, and hurtled back into battle, smashing through the vampires. Max followed on biting the head off a vampire and swiping his claws through another.

"Kill him," Carmella shouted, but a group of vampires sprinted for the door instead.

The others engaged against Thorn and Cassius, defending themselves, while Gabriel ran for the door. The transformed Hunters attacked me to defend him. They fired the UV guns, but the bullets exploded against my scales. The UV liquid dripped to the floor, glowing in blue puddles. I scooped up a sword, and my blade clashed with that of a vampire's sword. I swung and parried with such strength that it knocked the sword from his hand. I slashed back, slicing its body in half, turning it to ash as it cut.

On to the next with the same results, I smashed their defences away with ease, swiping and cutting them down one after another. A vampire sneaked around the rear and threw a silver knife into my back. It stuck in with no effect. I ripped it out and threw it back into its face, right between the eyes, destroying it with a shriek and a burst of ash.

"Silver and UV don't work!" one of the Turned yelled, spreading further panic, and they scrambled for the exits.

Carmella remained locked in a sword battle with Thorn, blades sparking as they moved back and forth, blocking and countering. Other vampires attacked Thorn from the sides. She instantly altered her attack pattern to cut past their defences.

More attacked. She twisted around and ran up the wall back-flipping over two attacking Turned and decapitating them in mid-air. She landed in a crouch, ducking a blow from Carmella and then pouncing up to counter attack. The sword battle continued one on one, with the other Turned vampires fleeing.

Their swords continued to clash until Thorn's dual blades locked Carmella's in place. Thorn cart-wheeled to the side, ripping the sword out of Carmella's grip and slinging it across the warehouse into the back of an escaping vampire, which exploded.

Thorn placed her blade at her opponent's neck.

"What is he?" Carmella asked, looking over at me.

"He is mine," Thorn replied, and swung the blade back and beheaded her.

For a split second, regret of her death flitted across my thoughts. But it was an act at the prison. Patrick was Mr Nasty, and she was Miss Nice. She meant none of it. She wasn't my saviour. It was brainwashing and seduction.

Patrick disengaged from fighting as Cassius dispatched the two vampires in front of him. He headed for the door, but I blocked the way and threw my sword to the floor. I had him trapped, no way out except to fight me. He charged, thrusting with the blade. I swayed out of the way, dodging and ducking the sword. Thorn and Cassius cut through the last of the other vampires, and the other werewolf retreated and bounded away from the superior numbers gathered against him.

Behind Patrick, two other vampires watched and tried to get in on the action, unaware they were the last ones left. Patrick thrust in with the sword again. I blocked and parried with my talons, knocking him backwards. I roared at him again, hazing the air between us and forcing their faces away.

He attacked again in blind panic and fear. I stepped to the side and moved in, wrapping my arm around his sword arm, and locked it in place against my body. I yanked my arm up, snapped his arm in two, and his sword clattered to the floor. I leant my head back and head butted him in the face. His nose smashed and black eyes filled with blood as his head flopped back, exposing his throat. I opened my double fanged jaws around his neck and tore out his throat. I told him I would.

With the fleshy lump of his throat in my fangs, I tilted my head back and squashed it inside my mouth. I squeezed out the blood, and drunk it down with relish. Then I released his arm, and his lifeless body crashed to the floor. I spat the drained lump of flesh onto his dead body, and then it all exploded to ash. Victory had never tasted as good. Vengeance for my Dad. Vengeance for my torture.

The two vampires screamed, and Thorn stabbed through their hearts from behind with her twin blades. Their ash scattered to the wind. We had won.

Thorn yelled in delight, threw her blades to the floor, and jumped into my arms, wrapping her legs around me and kissing my face. My fangs and claws retreated, and I kissed her back vigorously. Cassius laughed and walked out of the warehouse, with Max transforming back to his human form, and then changing into the spare clothes he'd left at the doorway. We finished trading kisses, and I put her back on her feet. She smiled and the red tear stains marking her face melted away into her skin.

"Let's go, I have lots to tell you," she said, grabbing my hand and leading the way out of the warehouse through piles of vampire ash scattering in the post battle breeze.

Chapter Twenty-One

We darted out of the warehouse, sprinting down dark roads before they could return with reinforcements. A couple of miles away, we reached our transport, a black Range Rover with tinted windows. Cassius drove with Max in the front, and Thorn and I got in the back, with her straddling me and smothering me in kisses.

"Can you two wait?" Cassius shouted.

"No," Thorn shouted, her eyes blazing red with passion.

We arrived back at their base, a rented three bedroom house on a local estate, and Thorn led me straight to the bedroom in the basement. She threw me onto the bed and jumped on top, tearing at my clothes, just like old times.

"The best thing about arguing," she said, through panting breath.

"The making up," I replied, ripping at her clothes.

We didn't come out of the room that night and slept off the night's exertions during the day. Night came around again, and I lay in bed next to Thorn. She woke up as the sun went down and rolled over to face me. She brushed back her tousled raven hair and smiled with her sky blue eyes gleaming with pleasure.

"You are still Dragan?" she asked.

"Yes, the formula is lasting longer each time," I replied.

"The professor told us it would."

"You got the results?" I asked.

Thorn nodded.

"We need to talk. I will tell you what we have been up to if you promise to tell me the whole truth as well," she said. "No need to fear your answers. I shall be calm."

We needed to trust each other, and as I continued to develop my Dragan form, I would be safer from her rage.

She took a deep breath.

"After you fled like a spoilt child," she said and smirked. I guessed it was a fair comment and nodded in agreement. "We carried onto the research lab and met Professor Hickling. He ran the tests on the formula and the samples you sent.

"While waiting, I received an alert from my alarm system on the house. When you entered the house, the alarm sent me a message. We got flights over and then tracked you down on the GPS on the car. We found you at the car park, slightly too late," she said.

"The results?" I asked.

"The formula is genetically encoded to work on your DNA. That is why it failed on Barry. It is, as you can see, perfectly safe for you to use," she replied.

"So you shot me with it!" I said, fangs protruding for a moment.

"Don't be a baby. It worked."

I was the one getting ill-tempered and irritable. It must be the Dragan blood.

"Yeah, but the gunshot killed me first."

"Well, let's call it revenge and rescuing all in one," she replied. "Anyway, the professor told us, the permanent changes to Dragan powers appear to be a side effect of the formula. Over time, continued use will ultimately change you forever. The needles we have left should be enough for the complete transformation. You can become like me, and we can spend our lives together. If that's what you want?"

"The formula doesn't affect the Hunters the same way. They still have all the normal vampire weaknesses," I replied.

"You're different. Your formula is encoded to your DNA. I guess that is why it happens."

"Thank you for telling me the truth. What you said agrees with what my Dad said. He said he designed the formula but had encoded it to his genetics so that it couldn't be misused. As his son, I have a similar enough genetic code."

"You were testing me," she said, sitting up.

"Yes," I replied. Now I smirked.

"Your turn," she said.

I shook my head; she still hadn't told me everything.

"There's more. Tell me everything about you, Bramel and Carmella."

She pursed her lips together. "Become close, did you? She called you her little pet."

"Just tell me the truth. I heard what she said to you at the warehouse. Is this just a personal vendetta?"

"For her, maybe. You probably worked it out from our conversation. After another Dragan house had killed my family, Cassius and I raised our own Turned army. I had turned Bramel. He in turn created me an army and we sought our vengeance."

"In the course of this war, Carmella was turned by Bramel?"

"Yes, and she fell in love with him, but I had turned Bramel, and he was bound to my will. Bramel hates me and loves me. I would never return his affection and it drove him crazy. In turn, he refused Carmella. His creation was a necessity of war and so was Carmella's. We had no idea how this would turn out."

"They were people. They had lives. How could you?"

"It was war. I wanted revenge at any cost. I look back now and realise I was wrong, but it's too late. This is now a new war. The Turned have grown in numbers and are hungry for power. The numbers aren't sustainable without a shift in power between vampires and humans. Everyone, human and Dragan alike, is now under threat."

"Anything else you should tell me?"

She shrugged her shoulders. "Probably a hundred things. I have been alive for centuries and the war has raged for so long. When it comes to mind and is relevant, I will tell you. I can't recount several hundred years. Anyway, it's your turn to talk."

I waited in silence, hoping she would speak some more, but she just raised her eyebrows and nodded as a signal to talk.

I reluctantly broke the deadlock. "I left and went and stayed at Amber's until I got tickets back. I left her the money."

"I know. We found your phone in the car. She sent you a message, as she needs your help. She is in trouble. We will talk about that later," she said. Thorn took her turn to test me. "I guess you spent more time together?"

I knew it would be a potentially explosive point, but I had agreed to tell the truth, and I knew what she meant by spending time together.

"Yes. We did," I said and watched Thorn's reaction as she squeezed her lips together for a moment.

"Well, she has made you a better lover at least, but no more seduction training," she replied.

Not the answer I expected and suddenly wondered what I had done wrong before, but I decided to forget it and let Thorn have her dig at me without replying.

"I came back to England, to the house, took the car and found Scarlett. Who, by the way, isn't an agent but was a victim of Barry's and the Hunters as well. They drugged her that night."

Thorn raised her eyebrows but remained quiet.

"Anyway, she came north with me to help find my Dad and speak with him. He told us he been set up by Gabriel Fenwick. Gabriel dropped off the formula only moments before I arrived on that first night."

"That is true. Gabriel came down and told your Dad the formula was completed and to keep hold of it. I heard his thoughts about what the formula was for and what it did. When you came downstairs, it seemed like a perfect opportunity."

"I think you were played, Thorn. I think he knew you would be listening and purposely encouraged my Dad to invite me down," I said.

"Another ten needles had just arrived when you turned up again to rescue me."

"It's always been just the Hunters then, using us all to create an experiment. To find out if the formula worked as they realised it had to be tested against my Dad, or me, because of the way he had encoded the genetics. But they lost everything in the end."

"Not just the Hunters, the Turned are the ones behind it all," Thorn interrupted.

It reminded me of the Turned I had seen at the Hunter's base.

"Bramel was in my prison cell."

"Doesn't surprise me."

"I overheard him on the phone to someone. The filming of my fight against the Hunters and him was done for someone."

"Another mystery for us to solve."

I paused for breath and plucked up the courage to carry on.

"I am sorry for running off and leaving you, Thorn. I should have trusted you, but I wanted the truth from my Dad and Scarlett. I wanted a normal life again. In Vegas, I saw happy couples and people getting married. I realised I can never have that. Get married, have children and live a normal life."

She rubbed my arm, comforting me.

"We can have whatever we want, V. Who decides what normal is? It's all ours for the taking. Maybe children are impossible for us. Maybe the formula will unlock the secrets. We are Dragans. The rules of normal don't apply to us. We are the power in the night," she said and smiled.

I reflected her smile. She spoke the truth. We were Dragans.

"So, what happens next?" I asked.

"We prepare for war. We need to gather more allies. We are tracking down Cyrus. If we find him, it may lead to other Dragans. We can then seek out the 1st Generation Turned, including Bramel, and destroy them."

I still thought about Scarlett and memories of the kiss we shared before being attacked by the Turned.

"What about Scarlett?" I asked.

Thorn scowled. "What happened between you two, all alone together?"

I blushed.

"We kissed once and only for a few seconds, nothing more," I said, as I only counted the one in the car, as the other one I had withdrawn from.

Her fangs jutted out as her eyes turned red.

"You expect me to believe that? All that time together and you kissed just once," she said.

"It's true. I am sorry. I know, body not the heart. I can't just switch it off completely. I realise I can't have you both... Or could I?" I asked cheekily again.

"NO," she shouted and pinned me to the bed.

"Okay, sorry, just a little fantasy popped into my head. I know I must choose. I choose you. This is my life now. My old life is in the past and I must let it go, but don't expect me to forget her," I said.

She shoved me into the mattress and then let go, twisting around to face away from me. I placed my hand on her arm.

"Thorn, I can't abandon her. She is in danger from the Turned and Hunters. She helped me get the information from Gabriel's computer."

Thorn remained silent, her face furrowed in thought. "Okay. We will make sure she is somewhere safe. I have people I can pay to track her down and get her to safety."

"Thank you."

"Okay, but you are not to see her."

I went on the attack.

"Are you completely innocent with Cassius as well?" I asked, remembering what my Dad had said.

She spun back to face me and stared. "What?"

"Come on, I worked it out, only ten Dragans and no Dragan pregnancies. You must have all tried to reproduce the race together at some stage."

Her eyes widen. "Well, yes, but it was a long time ago, V. In fact, it was before you were born and before your parents as well. I won't deny it. It's in the past."

"You and Cassius, and Cyrus."

"Yes," she said, "every Dragan male that was still alive. I had to. I had to try and save my race."

"Every male Dragan I meet, you will have been lovers with."

Thorn shrugged her shoulders. "Lovers may be too strong a word for most of them. But yes, I have had sex with them all. Deal with it. I am with you now, and I have let you get away with a lot."

I understood, but it still hurt to know I might have to meet them all. It would be difficult to ever look at Cassius again without thinking of them together.

"V, we all have a past. What is done is done. I have forgiven you for running off with Amber and stealing my money. Then running into the arms of your ex-lover. I will make no apologies for trying to save my people. We have to move on, but for now, let me seethe in peace."

I left her lying in bed and staring at the wall. I got dressed and left the room.

In the kitchen, Max and Cassius were drinking coffee and sat on either side of a glass table in the centre of the room. On the table between them was a large pile of newspapers. At the edges of the kitchen, surrounding them, were cupboards and a cooker, with the sink in front of the windows giving a view of the dark garden.

They stopped their conversation as I walked in and Cassius grabbed another cup.

"That was impressive, little one. The fight last night. In the old legends, the first of the Dragan could transform into part Dragon. No Dragan has done that since. You are incredibly powerful. You herald a new era of Dragan power," Cassius said, and poured the coffee.

I hadn't thought about the severity of my transformation after the fight, as other more pressing demands filled my thoughts.

"More than Thorn? They told me she was the Queen of the Dragans," I said, trying not to think about Thorn and Cassius together.

"It is true. Thorn is the Queen of the Dragans. Your power is strong, but you don't have control over it yet."

I smiled at the recognition of my transformation. I dragged back a chair and joined them at the table.

"So what took you so long to find me?" I asked.

Cassius pushed the pile of newspaper towards me. "Read for yourself."

I looked down at the headlines from a few days before. *"Another Gang Busted."*

I flicked through the rest of the headlines over the last couple of weeks: *"Vigilante on the loose,"* , *"Criminals on the Run,"* , *"Police take the praise."*

"She ripped apart the supernatural and criminal underworld to find you. Often, the Turned vampires work for criminal gangs, providing extra muscle in return for easy blood," Cassius said.

"But surely she attracted too much attention to herself. It's not her way."

"You're right, but she did it anyway. The message got through and we were able to start the negotiations. We knew it would be a trap, but Thorn had a plan."

"Shoot me," I replied.

"Yeah. They didn't know about the formula's ability to revive you and your immunity to silver and UV, but Thorn did."

Her jealous rage had killed me once before, but the formula had saved my life. I drank back my coffee and noticed my Dad's USB stick on the table.

"Your Dad gave us the USB memory stick, but it's locked down," Max said.

"I know the password," I replied, and Cassius shouted out to Thorn.

Within a couple of minutes, Thorn walked through carrying a laptop bag and dressed in tracksuit bottoms and a white t-shirt.

"Coffee, please," she asked and unzipped the bag, pulling out the laptop and plugging in the USB stick, and then spun it around to face me without saying another word or directly looking at me. I guessed her seething was still ongoing despite the possible unravelling of the truth.

Cassius passed her a hot coffee. I accessed the stick and typed in the password. Time to find out what my Dad had died for. Behind, Max and Cassius scuttled their chairs around while Thorn watched over my shoulder. The file directory tree opened up into a list of folder names.

"01 Research, 02 Personnel, 03 Admin."

"Let's find out who's who," I said and clicked the personnel folder and a list of new folders with names of people scrolled down the screen. I scanned down the list to see all the names of the people involved. Most of the names I knew: Thorn, myself, my Dad, Scarlett, Barry, Subject V, Subject vii, subject x and Carmella, but then I noticed a name I didn't expect to see, Giles.

Giles had been my best friend at school, who the O'Keefe gang beat up, and he eventually tried to commit suicide. Strange that he should be mentioned, but I wanted to view my Dad's and Scarlett's folders first to confirm their innocence. I opened my Dad's first and it confirmed everything he told me about his research. The job offer in London and his questioning after the London research centre had burnt down. I would review it again later but wanted to move on. I opened Scarlett's folder and file.

"Name Scarlett. Aged 19, Jonathan's girlfriend in London. Her intervention with him at the college was unexpected. Their friendship posed a barrier to our plans. In the end, we tried to use it against Jonathan. We recruited a local gang to attack Jon and bully him. He didn't react immediately to the attack due to his relationship with Scarlett. She was comforting and protecting him. We pushed Barry, the gang leader, to increase the bullying and as luck happened, Scarlett presented the perfect opportunity at a party. Barry drugged Scarlett and posed several photos with her. These were used to humiliate Jon at college, and finally, he reacted and took the formula."

The document confirmed her innocence. I read further on to the last paragraph.

"After Jon unexpectedly freed Subject X [Thorn] and stole the last ten needles, we have been in contact with Scarlett as a means of contacting Jon and bringing him back. We will continue to monitor her. Jon may try to re-establish the relationship in the future, especially if the relationship with Thorn is broken."

I pushed away from the table and walked off into the kitchen. I took a deep breath. Scarlett had been innocent the whole time. After speaking with her, I knew it was true. I could have avoided this dark path after all. I looked at Thorn and bit my lip, not wanting to start an argument. Then Thorn surprised me.

"V, I am sorry about Scarlett. It seems she was innocent after all. It must be difficult. If it's any consolation, I don't think they would have stopped until you took the formula. They would have continued to escalate until they got what they wanted. These people don't take no for an answer."

"Thank you. I don't want to seem ungrateful for all you have done for me."

"I understand better than anyone what it is like to have your future snatched away from you. I could still have a husband and son if it wasn't for the Dragan wars."

She understood or at least was making an effort. Our relationship had changed for the better.

I heard the mouse clicking away at the computer and after a pause, the rest of the truth came out.

"They also mention other Dragans they have been hunting, Rip and the Twins. Doesn't look like they had any success. The other wolf was Subject V. The V is Roman numerals for 5, and I was Subject X, Subject10. Other Subjects vii, the Hunter to Turned formula."

"Okay," I replied, trying to make sense of the news.

"Something else, Jon. Subject V is being used to build an army of werewolves to kill the Dragans. Subject V has an apprentice using the werewolf formula," she said.

"Okay, we must stop them. Explain to them the errors of their alliance,"

I answered.

Thorn shook her head.

"It's not that simple. His apprentice is Giles, your best friend from school. The boy who tried to commit suicide," she said.

The shock silenced me. "You mean the best friend I betrayed?" I gulped.

"Yes."

Chapter Twenty-Two

Thorn, Cassius and I sat outside the biker's bar in the black van. Behind, waiting in their car were Max and Eleanor. It had been a few days since the events at the warehouse when Thorn had rescued me. The formula had taken nearly two days to wear off and had left me stronger and more powerful again.

Since then, Thorn had employed a couple of private detectives to find Scarlett and make sure she had reached safety. However, there was still no news if they had succeeded, so I had checked out any family she still had in Leeds and her home in London, but with no luck.

I also desperately wanted to attend my Dad's funeral, but due to the Hunters, I couldn't. I would have to say my goodbyes another time. From a safe distance, I watched my aunts and uncles attend with my cousins. I decided not to contact them. I didn't want to place them in any danger.

We had left England and returned to America for our team bonding, rescuing Amber. We were back in her town, Twin Falls, as she had left me a message asking for help. Thorn and Cassius had tracked her down to the biker bar and a group of bikers called 'Hell's Warriors.'

In front of the bar, a row of motorbikes had been parked and music blasted out of the windows. The biker's bar sat at the side of the road that headed out through a rough part of town and onto the main highway. No one nearby complained about the bar or its customers for fear of reprisals, which suited us.

Thorn opened her eyes and re-connected into the normal world.

"She's inside, I think. Lots of noise and drunken thoughts, so it's hard to tell."

I nodded and climbed out of the passenger seat side. She grabbed my arm, pulled me back inside and glared at me.

"Remember, I am only doing this to get my money back, and for you to get through the needles," she said, her voice on the edge of anger.

She had only agreed to it after much persuasion, but I knew she would never leave another woman in such a state of peril. She had even protected Scarlett outside the nightclub in Leeds from unwanted male attention.

"I know, Thorn. I appreciate it, but I couldn't leave her to suffer. I feel guilty about having given her the money. Would you really have left her to this fate?"

She snarled back. "Maybe not. You know me too well. When you have lived for as many centuries as I, and seen the things I have, then you would be the same."

"Thank you anyway."

"Just remember, we rescue her only. Max will look after her. This isn't a happy reunion."

"I know. I understand."

"Make sure you do. Now, let's go," she said and released my arm.

I climbed out, and Thorn and Cassius followed. We walked across the street, Thorn in the middle, with Cassius and I on either side. We dressed for the part in dark clothes; Thorn in her tight black combat suit with a black leather corset and knee high boots with huge black straps. The same outfit she wore at the vampire convention. She had decided to play the part tonight.

I had dressed in the same clothes from the vampire convention, with a long black coat, black jeans and a black t-shirt. Cassius had dressed in his black jeans, boots and a tight red t-shirt. We strode across the road and up the steps. Cassius and I pushed open the huge double doors for our Queen, Thorn, to walk through.

The Hell's Warriors were sprawled out on the chairs and tables and had taken over the whole place. The bar appeared to be an old church hall. The room was a long rectangle, with the bar against the wall by the entrance. Down the hall, big bench tables lined up against each wall. At the far end, a dance area and small stage decorated with a huge stars and stripes flag behind it.

Pictures of Hell's Warriors at gatherings hung on the walls, along with other pictures of low rider bikes and glossy posters of naked women thrusting their sexuality at the lens. Sometimes the naked women straddled the bikes, and sometimes the women were with the Hell's Warriors.

Loud heavy metal music pounded out of the speakers, and low lights made the bar even dingier and threatening. The Hell's Warriors poured out beer from huge jugs into glasses and drank them down. Some munched down on fat boy burgers and took fist full of fries, scoffing them into their mouths. The women sat on their laps while the men groped and kissed them. A few of the women danced in the open space at the back of the bar.

Even through the music and activities in the bar, our entrance had caused a stir. Some stopped and watched as Thorn strolled through as if she owned the place. Then they looked over at us, her two royal bodyguards. Thorn walked to the bar and leant her back against it, facing the bikers. We joined her, standing on either side against the bar.

One of the Hell's Warriors with a girl on his lap nudged another and pointed over. I stared at him and the girl. The girl had red hair, a bruised face and her eyes seemed gone out, Amber. The other biker stood up and thumped across to the bar. He stood six foot five at least; broad shoulders, shaven head and with a shaggy beard, and dressed in a combination of denim and leathers. His jacket carried the gang symbol on the back, as did all the members.

Cassius squared up to him, and Thorn played it easy and showed no emotion. The biker signalled to the barman, who turned the music down. The other twenty Hell's Warriors watched intently, not used to others in their domain.

He looked at us and sneered.

"I think you are lost. You'd best leave."

Thorn answered. "We take the girl and be on our way."

"Which girl?"

"Amber," I replied and pointed at her on the other man's lap.

The Hell's Warriors in front of us turned and laughed.

"George, they want your girl."

George dumped Amber on the floor, and she scuttled against the wall and curled into a ball. He laughed at her and strode across to us. He looked smaller than the other guy at only just over six foot tall. He'd dark grey hair and a scar across his right cheek, and he wore the same uniform as the rest, denim and leathers and gang patches. He stopped to the side of the first man.

"I don't think so, you dumb idiots. She is my walking bank account. My friends gave her to me," he said and pointed over to a group in the corner.

The bikers from the sports bar Amber worked in. They raised a glass to me. I should have known this was because of them. They would pay. I should have fought back at the sports bar after all. At least she would have been safe from then on. The fat one from the group stood up and waddled over to the other two Hell's Warriors.

"This is the rich boyfriend I was telling you about," he said.

"Really. Well, you can buy her back then," George said. "I hear you have lots of money."

"Yeah, he threatened me. Said he could buy people to protect him," the fat man said and laughed and looked at Thorn and Cassius.

George glared at us. "This it then rich kid, a woman and some freak. There are only three of you."

"I didn't pay for them. They are my friends. Now hand her over, or else," I said, impatient for the fun to start. I couldn't wait to take my belated revenge.

The three of them laughed, as did the rest of the bar.

"Do you know who we are? We take orders from no one. We are outlaws. We are Hell's Warriors, you dumb arse," George responded.

Thorn looked at him with contempt and gave her best dark stare. Her eyes narrowed, and her forehead contorted to show the precursors of her Dragan powers.

"You have no idea, pathetic human. Time you met the real Hell's Warriors," Thorn said and placed a hand on my arm. I pulled out a needle, stabbed it into my neck and forced the plunger in. The bikers glared at me.

I had so craved a normal life recently, but who wanted normal? Everyone spent their lives trying to avoid normal. This had become my life and at last I had accepted it. I would become a Dragan, and this needle was the first of many to make it permanent. In the meantime, I would practise for the war with the Turned. Tonight, a bar full of bikers would be my training.

The formula did its work and my heart pumped faster and faster, the muscles spasming as it altered my body. My head swam and forehead broke out in a cold sweat. But I wouldn't let the agony of the change show. Each needle had to almost kill me for the transformation to occur.

Thorn and Cassius stood upright at the bar as I became a Dragan. I waited with eyes closed, as not to give the game away. As my muscles burned with rage, I clenched my fists and gritted my teeth. I didn't want to ruin the surprise. I threw the needle away and opened my transformed blood red eyes and fangs snapped out of my mouth. Thorn and Cassius did the same, eyes burning blood red, fangs cutting the air and claws ripping through our finger ends.

The three men in front froze, colour draining away and feet stuck to the spot. Thorn leapt up at the tall man and punched him in the face. He sailed off his feet, crashing onto the floor and skidding down the bar, knocking over the women watching on the dance floor. Cassius punched George in the face, exposing bone and blood, and he crashed back into a table, knocking drinks and food flying. The other Hell's Warriors jumped to their feet.

I leapt high into the air and roundhouse kicked the fat man in the face. Even his size couldn't stop him from crashing to the floor. I jumped over him and attacked the others from the sports bar. I punched the first one in rapid succession and then kicked another out of the way. I ducked a blow, slashed with my claws across another, then head-butted the last one to the floor. I stood over him so that he could take a last glimpse before slamming my foot into his face and breaking his jaw. I had wanted to attack them back in the sports bar, but the time and the place were wrong. However, the timing and location were now perfect. I also got to do it as a Dragan with Thorn at my side. It couldn't get much better.

The other Hell's Warriors charged in, not understanding what they faced. They attacked with knives, fists, broken bottles and chairs, but we ripped through them. Then shots rang out, but I dodged the bullets and grabbed a biker as a human shield to reach the gunman. I piled the shield into the gunman, spilling the weapon from his hand, and then ripped his neck open and took a quick snack.

Cassius hammered his way through two Hell's Warriors at a time. Thorn slashed through her opponents in a blur, leaving a trail of blood-soaked bodies in her wake. The rest of the biker gang knew they were beaten, and they smashed open windows and the fire doors to escape.

Amber's eyes had re-focused back to reality, and she cowered in the corner away from the mayhem. I walked over to her with the blood soaking into my skin.

"Relax, it's me, V," I said psychically, sending out calming messages into her mind before I scooped her up into my arms.

She touched my Dragan, vampire features and stared eyes wide in wonder.

"You really are, V. You really are a vampire."

Thorn appeared at my side, leaning over Amber, with her face in Dragan mode.

"So am I, and he's mine," she shouted at her.

Amber's eyes widen, and she rocked back in my arms before passing out.

"Give her to me," Thorn said, reaching out.

"You promised not to hurt her," I said and held her tight.

"I won't, but you don't get to rescue her and act the hero. Remember what I said. I will take her to Max."

She pushed her arms underneath Amber, and I released my grip.

I had to trust her, and I agreed not to get involved with Amber in the rescue, but it was too tempting not to have even the smallest of a reunion. A chance to apologise and let her know the truth.

Thorn marched back outside towards Max waiting in his car. The bikes of the escaping Hell's Warriors roared down the road. Cassius picked up a remaining motorbike and sent it smashing it into the others, toppling them over like dominoes.

Max got out of the car and opened the passenger seat. Thorn placed Amber's unconscious body inside.

"I will take care of her for you. It looks like they kept her out of it on drugs and drained her of some of the money you gave her," Max said.

"I thought I was doing her a favour giving her that money. I hoped she would go back to college."

"You weren't to know. So what next for you two?" Max asked and looked at us.

As usual, Thorn hadn't told me of any plans, and I hadn't thought to ask beyond rescuing Amber, as wanted to stay on her good side. Thorn held my hand, squeezed it gently and smiled at me.

"We have unfinished business. I am taking him home."

Chapter Twenty-Three

Time raced on and I would be late. However, I wanted a dramatic entrance. She could wait for me. I rolled up my sleeve and flicked the cap off the needle containing the vampire formula. Or should I call it the Dragan Formula? I had to get changed first if this was going to work.

The needle pierced my skin, and I forced down the plunger to inject the formula into my arm and circulate it into my blood stream. The formula performed its magic, and the change ripped through me just as it did the first time in the park. My heart rate thundered, the blood redirected to the transformation and drained away from my skin leaving it sickly pale. My sight blurred, head span and a buzzing noise rattled through my ears. I clenched my fist as the world went dark around me for a few moments and my heart seized.

All went quiet. My heart returned to normal, the blood flushing my skin back to its normal colour. Finally, my hearing went quiet, and the room stopped spinning. It was getting easier.

Each time I injected, the process hurt a little less. I guess it had less to change as each injection took me further towards my goal of becoming a full Dragan. We had carried out some tests after the bikers' battle and confirmed I had become less human, more Dragan. Now all I had to do was finish the injections over a safe period of time. Thorn had been advised to leave it at least a week between doses in order to let any lasting transformation take hold. It had been just over a week since rescuing Amber, and Thorn couldn't wait any longer.

The last of the change from that night's formula settled down. I snapped out my fangs and claws to confirm it had completed and to break the seal of skin. I rolled the sleeve back down and stood up. I unhooked my suit-jacket off the hanger and swung it on. I took one last look in the mirror; brushed down the suit jacket, adjusted the collar on the white shirt and checked the pocket of the matching suit trousers for the required token. My hand gripped around the small box, and the enormity of what I was about to do suddenly became real. My hand around the box trembled. I steadied myself, as this was not the way a Dragan acted. I should be calm and cool. Finally, I groomed my gelled hair and walked to the door of my bedroom.

Thorn, Cassius and I had come from America to Thorn's home, her Gothic Mansion. The mansion nestled in thick woods in the south of

France. The room decorated in a suitable gothic style; a four poster bed with drapes tied up at the sides, deep red carpet and dark wooden furniture. The window arched and patterned in metal edging.

I shut the door and walked down the corridor to the grand staircase. The walls had half-height dark stained wooden panels and the rest painted bleach white. On the walls hung paintings of landscapes and dotted in between sat marble busts of ancient Greeks.

I meandered down the sweeping stairs, admiring the classic paintings on the walls. At the end of the staircase on the railing, I tapped the marble gargoyle on the head. I crossed the hallway that acted as the centre of the mansion for other corridors that went into the back. I followed the corridor to the right and passed several doors, as it curved around the building and reached a dead end with wooden double doors.

I took one last deep breath. No going back; I had made a choice. My insides fluttered and hands trembled on the door handles. I closed my eyes and focused my strength to calm my butterflies, but they fluttered on. I would just have to work through it. I depressed the handles and flung the doors open and strode through.

Inside, the room reflected the rest of the mansion with a dark red carpet, half-height wooden panels. On the white walls were more paintings but of people, not landscapes. They were other Dragans, her mother and father.

Cassius stood by the fireplace and small flames flickered within. He turned around and smiled. He had dressed up in a dark purple suit, white shirt and purple cravat. He looked over at Thorn stood by a window with a huge black shutter rolled back in order to view the night.

She stared out into the darkness, showing off her backless red dress that exposed the flesh until just before the first curves of her hips. Spike red heels accompanied the outfit, and her raven hair curled in ringlets flowed down the back of her neck and onto her shoulders.

"There are actually bats here. I never noticed before," she said and spun around with a big smile that touched her eyes.

I laughed. When first visiting her house in London, I was surprised at the normality of the place. She had joked about owning a Gothic mansion but didn't believe it had bats. It did have bats after all.

"Anyway, what took you so long?" she asked.

I pushed the doors closed behind me and walked towards her.

"I had to get changed," I said, flashing my blood red eyes and piercing fangs.

"Good, else it wouldn't be the same," she replied and walked to me.

We met in the middle of the room, kissed and held hands. When we first kissed, Thorn had been taller than me. Now we stood at the same height. The last injection had altered my body again and tomorrow I would evolve one more step to my destiny.

"Are you ready?" Cassius asked.

"Yes," we both answered at the same time.

I gently gripped her hand, and we walked hand in hand to stand in front of Cassius, who had turned his back to the fireplace.

There was no going back. My butterflies had multiplied, but I didn't mind or worry about it any longer. I just let them carry me away.

"At the birth of our race, four Dragans came forth. These Dragans invested the authority in any future Dragan to create formal unions between its own kind. Any of the two may join as long as a third agrees to that match. Today, I am acting as that third, and it is my privilege to agree to the match of Thorn and V," he looked at us both in turn, "do I have your permissions to continue?"

"Yes, I would be honoured," I responded.

"You have my permission," Thorn agreed.

"Good. It is a simple ceremony, but a solemn agreement that should not be undertaken lightly. Do you both have your tokens?"

"I do," I answered and reached into my pocket to retrieve the small box.

Thorn reached into her cleavage and pulled out an object she kept hidden in her hands.

"Good. Time to exchange tokens of your Union. Tokens of your love. Ladies first," Cassius said.

She opened her hand to reveal a gold ring, textured with a pattern of dragon scales.

"V, you are my rescuer, you are my Dragon and you will be my King," Thorn replied.

I put forward my wedding ring finger to receive it.

"No, V. This isn't a marriage and we aren't humans. There is no honour and obey in this relationship. This is a union, a partnership. We are Dragans. The other hand," she said, smiling as she spoke.

I put forward my other hand and she slid on the gold ring.

"Your turn," Cassius said to me.

I opened the box and removed the gold ring with a wreath of black metal thorns patterned around it.

I gazed into her eyes. "Thorn, you are my Queen and my love. I will always trust and protect you."

She put her right hand forward. I took her hand in mine, and I slid on the ring, keeping eye contact as much as possible.

"Good. The words have been said, but this Union is not yet complete. However, once complete, it can be broken at any time by either party. All it takes is to return your token, back to the giver, having bled onto it. Let us hope that day never comes. To finish the ritual, the two parties must consummate the Union in front of the third to prove it is real."

She smiled, and then a glint of red grew in her eyes and fangs snapped out. She launched into my neck and bit. I held steady for a second, holding back my instincts from the pain, then I returned the bite into her neck. As I sucked down her blood, I felt it rush through my body as my blood raced into her mouth.

I recalled my fangs and Thorn copied. We kissed, allowing each other's blood to flow into one another's mouths, mingling it all together. My arms wrapped around her back, my hands on her exposed skin. She placed her hands on my waist and pulled me closer. Her warm body pressed against mine, raising my temperature.

We kissed for some time, the blood on our mouths smearing and slipping across our lips. Eventually, we stopped and stood back with our hands held together. The blood on her mouth and chin soaked in, and she swallowed our joint blood. I swallowed the Union blood down as well, and my heart soared as my butterflies carried me away.

"The Union is complete. You are as one. You are King and Queen of the Dragans."

Thank you for reading

Did you enjoy it? Did you love it?
Reviews are the life blood of books. They are quick and easy. It's fangtastic to get them.
I would greatly appreciate a review to spread the word.

You only need to click your number of stars, write a sentence on why you liked it and add a quick couple of words for a title. It will only take you as long as sending a tweet or posting a quick message on facebook.

Other books by P.A.Ross on Amazon.

http://www.amazon/P.A.Ross

The adventure continues in:-
The Enemies of Vengeance – Vampire Formula #3

And concludes in:-
The War of Vengeance – Vampire Formula #4

Printed in Great Britain
by Amazon